4/19/96

A sardonic smile of intense satisfaction lit Luciano's strong features.

She had lost her head. She was breaking down. He would
find out what he needed to know.... And then? He finally
understood why no other woman had yet been able to
excite his interest. He still wanted *her*. Why? Had five years
shut away from a world that had moved on without him
left him trapped in time? In one sense, he acknowledged
the truth of that. But he also thought his own urges were
a lot more basic. Desire and revenge made an intoxicating
combination. He hated her, but he still burned to have
her...hear her cry out his name, learn the pleasure he
could give her...before he took it away again.

Lynne Graham comes from a Scots-Irish family and lives in Northern Ireland. When she was fifteen she tried to sell her first romance—without success! When she graduated from Edinburgh University in Scotland, her ambition was to be a criminal lawyer...until she discovered she couldn't afford to fund the extra year's tuition required.

Soon Lynne found happiness with husband Michael and gave birth to her eldest daughter. She started writing again, and this time sold to Harlequin Presents. Since then she has written nearly forty top-selling romances. She says she feels only half-alive when she's between books!

These days, Lynne and Michael live in the countryside and now have five children. The last four were adopted from overseas. Lynne writes mornings and in the evenings after her younger kids have gone to bed. Sometimes she's been known to work all night...!

Books linked to DARK ANGEL by Lynne Graham:

HARLEQUIN PRESENTS

SISTER BRIDES
2271—AN ARABIAN MARRIAGE
2277—THE DISOBEDIENT MISTRESS
2283—THE HEIRESS BRIDE

LYNNE GRAHAM
GRAHAM
DARK ANGEL

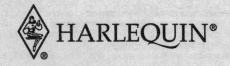

HARLEQUIN®

TORONTO • NEW YORK • LONDON
AMSTERDAM • PARIS • SYDNEY • HAMBURG
STOCKHOLM • ATHENS • TOKYO • MILAN • MADRID
PRAGUE • WARSAW • BUDAPEST • AUCKLAND

ISBN 0-373-83571-X

DARK ANGEL

First North American Publication 2003

Visit us at www.eHarlequin.com

Printed in U.S.A.

CHAPTER ONE

CRUSH barriers held back the baying media horde brandishing cameras and microphones outside the Royal Courts of Justice.

As Luciano da Valenza emerged, surrounded by his triumphant legal team, his new security men rushed to block those climbing the barriers in an effort to reach him. Standing six feet four tall with the lithe, powerful build of an athlete, Luciano dwarfed his companions. For a split-second he stilled, stunning golden eyes brilliant in his lean, bronzed face, the only outward sign of the strong emotions gripping him.

He was free: no handcuffs on his wrists, no guards by his side, no prison van waiting to return him to a cell eight feet wide by ten feet deep. For the first time in five hellish years, the right to liberty and dignity was his again. But the moment was soured by the reality that nothing could bring those years back, or alter the harsh fact that the English legal system might have set aside his conviction as unsafe but had stopped short of declaring him innocent.

'What will you do now?' an Italian journalist shouted above the general mêlée.

'I will fight on.' Responding by instinct to a fellow countryman, Luciano was none-the-less amazed at the naivety of that question, for it was unthinkable to him that he might rest before his name was cleared and his enemies had paid the price for what he had endured.

'Your immediate plans?' The same paparazzo was quick to press his advantage.

A dangerous smile slashed Luciano's lean, darkly handsome features. 'A glass of 1925 Brunello Riserva and a woman.'

That declaration was met by a burst of appreciative laughter from those who understood enough Italian to translate that audacious declaration of intent.

On the sidelines, Luciano's lawyer, Felix Carrington, wondered which of the many women who appeared to find his dynamic client irresistible would qualify for that ultimate accolade. Costanza, the sleek Italian brunette, who was surely the most devoted and discreet personal assistant in existence? Rochelle, the sexy blonde beauty, who had withdrawn her evidence on the grounds that she had been drunk and distraught when she had made her original statement? Or even Lesley Jennings, the fiercely intelligent and attractive solicitor in Felix's own legal firm, whose determination to win Luciano's release had become a crusade? More probably, Felix decided, a fresh face would capture the younger man's interest: one of the glossy media or society females who had taken up his cause with such vigour.

Yet five years earlier, when Luciano da Valenza had been tried, found guilty and imprisoned, only a few lines in a local newspaper had reported the event. A foreign troubleshooter headhunted from Rome by the Linwoods, he had been better known in Italy as the up-and-coming aggressive young business blood that he was. But by slow degrees, Luciano's plight had assumed a much more colourful guise.

In the aftermath of the original trial, Count Roberto Tessari, an Italian nobleman of enormous wealth and unblemished integrity, had come out of nowhere to engage Carrington and Carrington to supply a top-flight defence team on Luciano's behalf. The older man had also secured Luciano's assets against the fines imposed by his conviction by paying them out of his own pocket before pledging his bottomless bank account to the long, tough battle of appealing Luciano's conviction and gaining his release.

In spite of Tessari's painfully embarrassing efforts to keep his involvement a matter of total blanket confidentiality, someone somewhere had talked. When the rumours had begun, a prominent newspaper had printed a double-page spread on Luciano da Valenza. Their investigation of his background had helpfully delivered those elements beloved of the popular Press: secrecy, illegitimacy, suffering and poverty. At that timely moment, Luciano had then proved that he was indeed an unusual criminal. While recovering from a savage beating by fellow inmates, who resented the attention he was receiving, he had risked his own life to rescue an officer from a fire in the prison hospital. A television documentary questioning his guilt had followed and, if it had lingered a little too lovingly and often on the lady producer's clear admiration for Luciano's dark-angel good looks and heroic stature, certainly the programme had generated an amount of interest in his cause which had done him no harm.

When, eighteen months ago, Tessari had died after finally acknowledging Luciano as his son and in an apparent expiation of his guilty conscience had left him everything he possessed, Luciano had become a extremely rich man. Yet not once during the years of Luciano's imprisonment had the noble count visited his son or even attempted direct communication with him. In addition, Felix had been forced to utilise very persuasive

arguments to convince his proud and independent client
that he could not afford to refuse that golden inheritance
if he wanted his freedom.

'Thank you for all that you have done,' Luciano
breathed with quiet sincerity as he took his leave of Felix
Carrington with a firm handshake. 'I'll be in touch.'

A glass of wine and a woman? A meaningless sound-
bite. Who had he been trying to impress? Luciano asked
himself as he swung with lithe grace into the waiting
limousine. He no longer needed to play to the gallery to
secure support. A grim smile set his wide, sensual
mouth, the anger he concealed at what he had withstood
still as fierce as it had ever been. It seemed as though
all his life he had been fighting other people's low expectations of him.

'What's the point of you working so hard at school?
It won't get you any place... You're Stephanella da Valenza's bastard brat and nobody's *ever* going to let you
forget that! Don't draw attention to yourself, just be like
the other boys,' his late mother had urged him with
frowning anxiety, struggling to comprehend a twelve-
year-old hungry for so many things that she herself had
neither wanted nor valued.

Then, as now, Luciano had travelled his own path. To
act alone was not new to him. He knew that he would
not savour the Brunello Riserva, that superb vintage
wine from the Tuscan hills of his childhood, until he had
settled several outstanding scores to his own satisfaction.
Primarily, those scores centred on the Linwood family
and their supporting players. As the only outsider and
expendable, he had been set up as a fall guy. In return,
he would bring down the chain of wine stores on which
the Linwood fortunes had been built. In fact that process
had kicked off over a year earlier. Of the Linwood circle,

only Rochelle would escape unscathed. In recognition of Rochelle's belated efforts to redress the wrong she had done, he was prepared to stamp her account more or less paid.

Last but far from being least, however, came Rochelle's little stepsister, Kerry Linwood. At the thought of his former fiancée, a hard smile set Luciano's firm lips and his aggressive jawline clenched with formidable purpose. She had brought out his protective instincts and he had convinced himself that to offer her anything other than marriage would be an insult. Yet when the Linwoods had chosen him as the sacrifice to throw to the wolves, Kerry *must* have been in on that selection process.

Of course she had known he had been framed! Why else had she broken off their engagement without any adequate explanation only the day before his arrest? What he had believed he felt for her had been a rare flight of romantic fancy that had cost him dear, he acknowledged with brooding bitterness. *Not* a mistake he would ever make again with a woman. Kerry had betrayed him with quite outstanding completeness.

Revenge? No, it was simply payback time. Drama was not required. Luciano was prepared to allow that the volatile Italian and Sicilian genes that mingled in his family tree might dispose him more towards the darker forms of vengeful retribution. But at the same time, Luciano was very much a sophisticate. To secure the natural justice that he desired, every step he had already taken and would take in the near future had been and would continue to be both businesslike and ethical. His maternal grandfather might have fled Sicily when it became too hot to hold him but Luciano was better educated and infinitely cleverer. Even so, perhaps blood would out,

Luciano conceded thoughtfully. The primal pleasure
with which he looked forward to watching his victims
sweat and suffer was a sensation which his brutal Sicilian grandfather would have entirely understood and approved.

'You shouldn't be thinking of the Linwoods,' the
slim, svelte brunette seated beside him lamented in liquid Italian, her dark eyes as soft as only a precious few
could ever have seen them, for, much like himself, she
was not given to revealing her emotions. 'This is a very
special day...*live* it, Luciano!'

As Luciano surveyed Costanza, a slow, shimmering
smile illuminated his grave, dark features. He grasped
the expressive hand which she had lifted in a wholly
Latin gesture to accentuate her frustration. 'We will live
it together...I promise you,' he soothed in his rich, dark
drawl.

'Then let's go home to Italy,' Costanza urged. 'Right
now, before one more hour passes!'

'I'm not ready yet,' Luciano confided equably. 'Why
don't you allow me to treat you to a vacation instead?
After working tirelessly on my behalf for more years
than either of us care to count, you certainly deserve to
spoil yourself for a change.'

At that suggestion, Costanza compressed her
raspberry-tinted lips and said nothing. She recognised a
warning when she heard one, knew exactly how far she
could go with him and was always careful not to breach
that boundary.

Suppressing a soundless sigh, Luciano lounged back
in an elegant but deliberate sprawl in the corner of the
limo. That amount of space was a luxury he had learned
to live without. Piece by piece all that was soft and civ-
ilised in him had been stripped away by the prison re-

gime while he fought the system. That unyielding system, the unspoken, unwritten and oft-denied rule that nevertheless decreed that a man who continued to plead innocence of his crime could not be seriously considered for early release by the parole board or even for the reward of a transfer to a less regimented open prison. Luciano had served his time and all of it had been *hard* time. Often, in prison parlance, he had been 'banged up' in his cell for as long as twenty-two mind-numbing hours a day, a particularly cruel torment for a male who had never lost his deep appreciation for the wide open spaces of the countryside.

Leaving that thought behind, for Luciano deemed looking back with regret to what could not be changed a weakness, he experienced a sudden fierce yearning to once again smell the delicate lemony aroma of the flowering vines flourishing on the steep slopes of the Villa Contarini estate. He had lived there until he was eight years old. He had played in the oak woods, raced around pretending to hunt wild boars, had dug without the smallest success for truffles and had brought home fresh fungi as an offering for his overworked mother, only to see his gifts continually claimed by his bone-idle grandfather instead.

But now in Luciano's imagination, he saw himself standing high at the head of those lush green, close-planted rows of vines to look up at the bright blue cloudless sky and the endless hot sun and rejoice in what he had once taken entirely for granted. He left behind that vision with wry dark golden eyes and contemplated the astonishing fact that he now owned his childhood playground: the Villa Contarini, which stood high on the list of legendary Tuscan vineyards. Once too, he recalled without a shade of amusement, he had nourished a sentimental fantasy of bringing Kerry home as his bride to a very much smaller vineyard where he was paying a winemaker to live out what had once been the height of his own boyish dreams.

Fate gave with one hand and took with the other. Luciano had long accepted that unavoidable fact of life. To buy the vineyard and finance the hopeful creation of a wine to be reckoned with, he had had to concentrate his talents on forging a reputation in the business world and earning serious money. But nowhere was it written that he could not now rearrange his priorities. Ironically, the father whom he had despised from the instant of their first unforgettable meeting had finally forever ensured that he need never again earn his daily crust from humble toil.

'I kept on a skeleton staff here...I thought you might like to have someone cook for you and answer the phone when I'm not around,' Costanza told him as they vacated the limo outside a smart townhouse in one of London's most impressive residential squares.

Accepting the key she handed him, Luciano strove not to wince at the underwritten threat of the possessive brunette welding herself to him like a second skin. Above all else, Luciano had always revelled in his freedom of choice and the loss of that privilege for so many years had made that liberty all the more precious a commodity.

'Mr da Valenza...' In the spacious hall beyond the front door, a nervous older woman in a plain dark dress hurried to acknowledge his arrival. 'I'm Mrs Coulter, your housekeeper. You have some visitors waiting for you in the drawing room.'

An exasperated frownline divided Luciano's winged ebony brows. In a helpful gesture, Mrs Coulter opened a panelled door on the other side of the hall, for, never having even visited the house that had once belonged to Roberto Tessari, he could have had no idea where to find his uninvited guests. Entering the gracious room, he fell still at the sight of the three women seated together in silence and almost groaned out loud in frustration.

Rochelle Bailey, Harold Linwood's blonde, beautiful and bold stepdaughter by his second marriage, dressed to telegraph pure availability in a neckline low enough and a skirt short enough to bring on a heart attack in a sex-starved male.

Lesley Jennings, the very fanciable and clever lawyer from Carrington and Carrington, whose consultation visits to the prison and keen wit and humour had enlivened many a boring hour for him.

And, finally, Paola Massone, a distant cousin and daughter of the famous but currently struggling vintner, who had inherited Roberto Tessari's title but none of his money. Self-assured, dark-haired and undeniably gorgeous, she gave him an expectant look that demanded that he acknowledge what she clearly saw as her superior claim to his attention. The equivalent of an Italian 'It' girl, born from a long and illustrious if impoverished line of ancestors, Paola wanted to marry her class to his cash and make wine and…other things with him.

A mocking smile on her pink lips, Rochelle stood up. 'So, it's make or break time, girls. Which one of us do you want to stay, Luciano?' she demanded with typical bluntness.

Costanza entered the fray to widen scornful dark eyes. 'Doesn't it occur to you that Luciano may not be in the mood for guests?'

'Didn't you hear what your boss said outside the court? We watched it on the lunchtime news and although getting a translation out of Paola here was like yanking out her little pearly teeth one by one, we're *all* clued up now,' Rochelle declared, tossing back her rumpled blonde mane in unashamed challenge of the PA's contention. 'He wants a woman…and here we are.'

Lesley Jennings simply laughed out loud in reluctant appreciation.

It was beneath Paola's dignity to look anything other than supremely bored.

But not a single one of them showed any sign of making a move to leave and Luciano recognised that he had a problem…unhappily for his conscience-free libido, Rochelle, who had a seriously liberal attitude to loose living, was totally out of the question. Lesley? Not when he still had current dealings with her legal firm, for, even if she was willing to risk her reputation by consorting with a male still shadowed by criminal charges, he was not willing to help her to make that mistake. And Paola? As exquisite, perfect and downright practical a proposition as she was, it was far too soon for him to contemplate that level of commitment.

Every muscle straining at the effort required, Kerry heaved the log into the wheelbarrow.

When the barrow immediately tipped over beneath the weight and the log rolled out again, she could have sat down and howled like a baby. Snatching in a steadying breath, she blinked back tears of frustration, set the wheelbarrow straight and made herself start again. The spring days and nights were cold. She had two fires to keep going for her grandparents' benefit and only the largest, heaviest logs burned for any appreciable length of time in the massive hearths at Ballybawn Castle.

Unfortunately, her sleepless night had drained her of energy. Was it any wonder that she was still in shock about Luciano's successful appeal against his conviction? For hours she had tossed and turned while her mind ran round in tortured circles, continually throwing her back in time to Luciano's arrest on charges of false accounting and theft, *and* her own initial disbelief. But brick by brick the evidence against Luciano had mounted. When a single fingerprint had been identified as his on a damning document, she had accepted that he was guilty. Then she had also believed that fingerprinting was an exact science and irrefutable proof. How could she ever have foreseen that, five years on, respected forensic experts would enter a court of law on Luciano's behalf and discredit the reliability of the fingerprint which had played such a heavy part in the original prosecution case?

Yet that was what had happened only yesterday, Kerry acknowledged, shaking her head in lingering bewilderment as she finally got the log into the barrow and trudged back along the wooded lane to the castle. Luciano was free…and a tension headache was pounding behind her brow. Why could she think of nothing but Luciano? What did his freedom have to do with her? But *was* he innocent? That was what the newspapers were saying. Could she have misjudged him on that score at least?

Yet the male being deified by the Press was the same male whom she had loved more than she had ever dreamt she could love anyone and he had *hurt* her more than any soul alive. He had slept with Rochelle and in her heart of hearts had she really been surprised by that? After all, her stepsister was everything she herself was not: gorgeous, sexy and irresistible to men. Even her own father preferred Rochelle, Kerry reminded herself painfully. Possibly only a woman with the looks and personality of Helen of Troy could have kept Luciano faithful.

Just as she was comforting herself with that reflection, a car slowed up behind her, drew level and then stopped. It was Elphie Hewitt, whom Kerry had been friendly with since childhood. Now an artist, Elphie rented the Georgian wing of the castle as a *trompe l'oeil* showroom to display the decorative special paint effects at which she excelled.

'What are you doing with that wheelbarrow?' Elphie questioned with a frown. 'Didn't Dad offer to bring you over a load of logs?'

Although embarrassed by that reminder, Kerry was reluctant to accept a favour which she could not return and, even worse, the kind of favour that the older man might well have felt obliged to repeat. 'Your father has enough to do on the farm—'

'He would still be glad to help out. Only the other day he was saying how sorry he felt for you,' Elphie confided. 'You've such a battle to keep the estate going. And your grandparents…bless them, they're lovely people…but they're a big responsibility for a woman your age!'

Kerry was mortified when she pictured the Hewitts, both of whom were her grandfather's tenants, discussing her in such pitying terms. Not for nothing was Elphie renowned for her excessive lack of tact.

'How's business?' Kerry asked in the hope of changing the subject.

Elphie groaned. 'All right…*just*. The interior designers are hiring my services but I need to be working for clients direct to make a decent profit. Heck, is that the time? I've got an appointment!'

As soon as Elphie had driven off Kerry forgot that the

conversation had even taken place, for her own restive thoughts had zoomed straight back to centre on Luciano again. In fact, only twenty minutes later, having finally carted a fresh supply of firewood into her grandmother's sitting room, Kerry could no longer keep the lid on her own emotional turmoil.

'How do you feel about all this stuff about Luciano in the newspapers?' Kerry asked the older woman tautly. 'I don't know what to think or how I'm supposed to feel about it but I can't get it or him out of my mind.'

'I do so worry that you don't sew,' Viola O'Brien remarked in startling disregard of the subject which Kerry had opened, her gaze resting on her granddaughter with vague concern. 'A talent with a needle and thread is *so* essential these days. How else can you hope to repair the torn sheets in the linen cupboard and re-cover the dining-room chairs?'

'Grandma...' Kerry frowned and then said gently, 'Didn't you read the newspapers that I gave you this morning?'

'Yes, darling. Luciano has been set free. Of course he's innocent. I wasn't surprised to hear that news,' Viola O'Brien declared in the same even tone as if the events that had shattered Kerry over the previous twenty-four hours were no more worthy of surprise than a mild change in the weather.

As she received that discomfiting response, Kerry's slender figure tensed even more. It was not a moment to easily bear the reminder that her grandmother had refused to contemplate the possibility that Luciano might be guilty as charged five years earlier. If Kerry had not been impressed by that partisanship at the time, it had been because she was well aware that the older woman had always been reluctant to deal with anything unpleas-

ant in life. A burglar caught red-handed in the castle
would also have received the benefit of the doubt. In
much the same way, her grandmother preferred to ignore
the reality that those dining chairs which she had just
mentioned as requiring recovering had long since gone
to the saleroom.

'It would have been *very* romantic had you been waiting outside the court when Luciano emerged a free man,'
her grandmother contended in misty-eyed addition. 'I do
wish that you'd paid heed to my little hints. There are
times when it would be quite improper for a young
woman to be that forward but there are also special oc-
casions when *too* much reticence might even appear un-
gracious.'

At that assurance, Kerry just closed her eyes in despair, gritted her teeth and flopped down into the worn
armchair opposite. 'I expect there are but that wasn't one
of them.'

When she opened her eyes again, Viola O'Brien was
still sitting in perfect tranquillity, stitching at her embroidery. A slight woman of eighty years of age, she
wore her hair in the same plaited coronet she had fa-
voured since her girlhood and dressed in layers of fluttering draperies as though the clock had stopped ticking
at some grand dinner party in the 1930s and never
moved on again.

'Well, there has to be *some* reason why I heard Florrie
crying every night last week…Florrie usually only wails
when there's a wedding in the offing,' Viola reminded
her granddaughter of the O'Brien legend. 'One would
think that after four hundred and fifty years, Florrie
could learn to be more cheerful. Still, I suppose there's
no such thing as a happy ghost.'

'I wouldn't know....' Kerry sighed. 'I've never heard her.'

'I expect you tell yourself that the noise she makes is the wind in the trees.'

Breathing in deep and slow, Kerry parted her lips and said, 'Grandma...it's been five years since I decided *not* to marry Luciano.'

'Yes, darling, I do appreciate that. Do recall too that at the time I was rather concerned that we *didn't* hear Florrie when your wedding was only supposed to be a few weeks away.'

Kerry ground her teeth together so hard it hurt while also wishing that she had had the nerve to tell her grandparents the real reason why she had broken off her engagement instead of settling on the less humiliating pretext of a simple change of heart.

'But I can't believe that Luciano will hold your past misgivings against you. I expect he'll make a great deal of silly noise about it in the way that men do,' Viola opined in continuation. 'But you remain the woman who rejected him and he will know no true happiness until he regains your love and trust—'

'There is no question of *any* reconciliation between L-Luciano and me!' Kerry broke in to protest in frustration, her voice sharp and laced with the stammer which she had overcome in her teens but which still returned to haunt her in moments of stress.

Viola O'Brien raised her fine brows in mild reproach but her clear surprise at even that slightly raised voice having been directed at her sank her granddaughter into discomfiture and won her an immediate apology.

'I understand, darling,' Viola murmured in instant forgiveness. 'Having to wait for Luciano to make the first move is very tiresome and must be a considerable strain on your nerves. Unfortunately that is why putting in an appearance outside that court room yesterday would have been the easier path to follow.'

At that very trying repetition of an outrageous proposition, Kerry sprang in a restive motion out of her armchair again. She knew that the older woman could have no idea how much such fanciful suggestions and expectations could still wound and hurt. But then perhaps she herself was more at fault for being oversensitive, Kerry thought guiltily. She adored her grandparents for the unquestioning love which they had always given her. Her reluctant father, Harold Linwood, had never been prepared to offer his daughter a similiar level of affection.

'Eventually Luciano will wend his own way over to Ireland,' her grandmother forecast with an obvious wish to proffer that prospect as a comfort.

'That is *very* unlikely.'

'I think not, darling. After all, he does more or less own Ballybawn Castle,' Viola countered abstractedly while she rustled for fresh embroidery thread in her hopelessly messy work basket.

Kerry studied her grandmother in open-mouthed astonishment. 'Sorry…what did you say?' she queried, convinced that she must have misheard that staggering statement.

'Your grandfather will be annoyed with me…' Viola O' Brien's soft brown eyes revealed dismay before she returned with almost frantic purpose to her search for thread. 'He *did* ask me to keep that a secret.'

For several taut seconds Kerry hovered in sheer bewilderment, her mind refusing to handle that additional piece of supporting information.

'It's vulgar for a woman to discuss business,' her

grandmother declared in harassed and obvious retreat
from the threat of further questioning. 'I don't believe I
understood what your grandfather was trying to explain.'

In dismay and concern, Kerry noticed that Viola
O'Brien's thin hands were trembling and she paled at a
sight she had never seen before. 'I'm sure you didn't,'
she forced herself to say with artificial calm.

Her mind whirling, Kerry left the sitting room as soon
as she could. In the dim corridor, she sucked in a slow,
steadying breath. How could Luciano virtually *own* her
grandparents' ancestral home? Yet it was evident that
her grandmother believed that he did. That her grandfather should have broken the habit of a lifetime to discuss a business matter with his lady wife was a very
alarming factor that suggested that the impossible might
be more possible than Kerry wanted to believe.

After all, Kerry was already uneasily aware that on
the strength of their brief engagement five years earlier
Luciano had insisted on giving her cash-strapped grandparents a very large loan. Soon afterwards a proportion
of the roof had been mended though some of it remained
in disrepair. Kerry had concentrated her own energies on
cutting costs and striving to raise extra income on the
estate in an effort to ensure that the older couple could
at least live out their lives in their vast and dilapidated
home. However, her grandfather had never allowed her
to take charge of the accounts or, indeed, even examine
them but she had naturally assumed that the loan repayments were being kept up to date.

Perspiration dampened Kerry's short upper lip. The
very idea that Luciano might have some kind of claim
on Ballybawn Castle horrified her. *Could* her grandfather
have been struggling to handle major financial problems
which he had kept from her? Regardless of his grand-

daughter's degree in business and her strenuous efforts to make Ballybawn Castle a paying proposition, Hunt O'Brien still cherished the gallant if impractical outlook of a bygone age when it came to his womenfolk. He believed that even Kerry was a poor, vulnerable little woman who had to be protected at all costs from the frightening stress of monetary woes. Therefore, Kerry conceded worriedly, that the older man should even have considered mentioning such an issue to her grandmother suggested that a very serious situation had developed...

Running Hunt O'Brien to earth within his own home was rarely a challenge. In his younger days, eager to follow in his own father's footsteps, he had been a keen inventor of elaborate mechanical devices but, sadly for him, technology had repeatedly outstripped him in pace. Abandoning his workshop, her grandfather had turned to scholarship instead and, rain or shine, he was now to be found in the library happily surrounded by books. In fact, books were heaped on the bare floor, stacked on the threadbare chairs, and his enormous desk was so covered with them that her eighty-two-year-old grandparent preferred to squeeze himself into a corner of an old sofa and use a battered antique lap desk instead. There for the past half-century he had been weightily engaged in writing his definitive multi-volume work on the history of Ireland. Nobody at Ballybawn had ever been honoured with the opportunity to read a word of his life's work and Kerry rather doubted that any publisher would ever be permitted the privilege either.

'Is it time for lunch, my dear?' Having finally registered her presence, Hunt O'Brien peered at her over the top of his round-rimmed spectacles in enquiry.

Luciano, Kerry recalled with a sharp unwelcome pang, had once remarked that her grandfather must be very much in demand to play Santa Claus. Small and portly with the still-bright blue eyes that were the O'Brien inheritance, he was given a rather merry aspect by his shock of silver hair and his beard. And, in truth, he was an exceptionally kind man but possibly not very well matched to the challenges that had unexpectedly become his when he, rather than his elder brother, had inherited Ballybawn.

'No,' Kerry replied. 'I'll see to lunch soon.'

'What's happened to Bridget…is she ill?' Hunt enquired absently, his eyes already roaming back to the notebook he had been writing in seconds earlier.

It was well over a year since Bridget, the very last of the stalwart old-style retainers employed as indoor staff, had entered a retirement home at the age of seventy-eight. But her grandfather had never in his life had to live without a cook in the household and continually forgot that fact. Had he not been called to meals, he would have gone without food and indeed was as incapable of looking after himself as her grandmother was. Remorseless time had ground on outside the walls of Ballybawn Castle while the elderly owners within remained trapped in the habits of the previous century.

'Grandpa…' Kerry cleared her throat to regain the old man's attention. 'Grandma said that Luciano more or less owned the castle.'

At those words, Hunt O'Brien stopped writing and his silver head jerked up at rare speed as he directed an almost schoolboyish look of guilt at her. 'I was—er—I was p-p-p-p-planning,' he finally contrived to get the word out in the tense waiting silence, 'to tell you soon.'

Gooseflesh prickled at the nape of Kerry's neck and her knees developed a scary tendency to wobble. 'Yet

you discussed this with Grandma rather than with me?'
she prompted in near disbelief.

'*Had* to…no choice,' Hunt O'Brien confided tautly.
'I have to start preparing your grandmother for what lies
ahead. At our age, bad news is better broken little by
little and, as it seems that we shall all be forced to move
out of the castle now—'

'*Move out…?*' Kerry echoed in unconcealed horror.

'I'm afraid that I've f-f-failed you both.' The older
man removed his spectacles, rubbed his eyes and shook
his head in weary self-reproach. 'We've managed to live
from day to day but, in spite of all your many wonderfully enterprising ventures to keep the estate out of debt,
for the past four years and more there's been nothing
left over to cover that loan.'

Four years and more? Shattered by that admission,
Kerry removed a towering pile of books from an old
armchair and sat down in front of her grandfather. 'Try
to give me all the facts,' she urged as gently as she
could. 'Loans can be restructured. I might still be able
to sort this out for you.'

'It's far too late for that, my dear. I know I've been
foolish.' Replacing his spectacles, Hunt O'Brien loosed
a heavy sigh. 'I just stopped opening the letters that
came from the legal firm handling Luciano's affairs
while he was in prison. After that most unf-f-fortunate
business with my late brother's will, I simply couldn't
afford to make the loan repayments.'

'I wish you'd told me that long ago…' Kerry was
aghast that important letters had been ignored and, well
aware of the debacle that had followed her great-uncle
Ivor's death, she finally asked a question which she had
often longed to ask but never before dared to press.

'How much *did* you have to pay Ivor's ex-wife to drop her claim?'

Her grandfather grimaced and whispered an amount that left Kerry bereft of what remained of her breath. No longer did she need to wonder why it had become impossible for the older man to pay all dues and still make ends meet at Ballybawn.

'I didn't want to upset you or your grandmother by telling you what a complete mess I've made of things. If truth be told,' her grandfather continued unhappily, 'I only accepted that loan in the first place because I believed that you and Luciano were getting married.'

Kerry paled and lowered her discomfited eyes in acceptance of that latter point.

'I didn't worry too much then about how I would repay it because the castle would have passed down to you and your husband anyway on my death,' he pointed out ruefully. 'I saw that loan in terms of Luciano making an advance stake in your future together here. I also believe that he saw it in the same light *then*…but of course, only a few weeks later, you decided not to marry him and everything changed.'

'Yes…everything certainly changed,' Kerry conceded unsteadily, thinking back to the agonising aftermath of Luciano's conviction. She had resigned from her job working for her father's wine-store chain, packed her bags, moved out of the Linwood home and returned to Ireland to live with her grandparents again. But neither distance nor different surroundings had eased the terrible pain of having to walk away from the guy she loved, and making a fresh start had been an even bigger challenge when Luciano's infidelity had destroyed her self-esteem.

'At first, I hoped that matters would improve and that

I would be able to catch up with the loan arrears. When that didn't happen, I prayed that the bank would come to our rescue.' Rising to his feet, Hunt O'Brien went over to his desk and with some difficulty tugged out a bottom drawer. 'I'm afraid the bank turned my request down, and yesterday while I was walking in the demesne I was approached by a young man who asked me who I was and then virtually *stuffed* this document into my hand!'

From the cluttered desk top, the older man lifted a folded sheet. 'I'm facing a court order for repossession of the castle.'

In the act of looking into the drawer, which was packed to bursting point with unopened envelopes, Kerry straightened to stare in appalled silence at the legal notice that her grandfather had already been officially served with.

'I've spoken to the family solicitor,' the old man confided wearily. 'If I don't comply with a voluntary arrangement to settle my debts, I'll be declared bankrupt, which I believe would be worse.'

Homeless or bankrupt? What a choice! A surge of rage blistered through Kerry's slight, taut frame. How *dared* Luciano threaten to evict two harmless, helpless, elderly gentlefolk from their only home at this stage of their lives? How *dared* he subject her grandfather's weak heart to the stress of fear and intimidation? How *dared* he make her grandmother's hands tremble with nerves? What sort of a merciless bully had prison made out of Luciano da Valenza?

Hadn't he done enough harm yet? Wasn't it bad enough that he had wrecked her life? She lived like a nun sooner than risk that amount of pain and disillusionment again. She no longer trusted men. The guy she adored had gone behind her back and slept with a woman who hated her. At the age of twenty-six she was so much 'on the shelf', as her grandmother liked to call it, that she might as well have been nailed to it!

'I'll look into this, Grandpa,' Kerry murmured in a soothing undertone, eyes as bright as sparkling turquoises in her flushed and furious face.

'If it makes you feel better, go ahead,' he said wryly. 'But I assure you that nothing short of a miracle could help us now.'

'Just you go back to your book,' Kerry advised.

'I am hoping that we'll be quite comfortably off once I sell my books to a publishing firm,' Hunt O'Brien declared, startling his granddaughter with an ambition which he had never mentioned before. 'I've almost finished the eighth volume. It's my final one, you know.'

'Congratulations,' Kerry told him with as much enthusiastic and matching optimism as she could muster at that instant.

'Of course, the other seven volumes could probably do with a little tweaking.' He settled back onto his sofa and reached for his pen with a smile, the gravity of their plight clearly wiped from his mind again as he contemplated the comforting creative challenges that still lay ahead of him.

While the older man returned to his notebook, Kerry lifted out the entire drawer of unopened letters and carried it from the room. An hour later, after she had only got through about a third of what had been a one-sided effort at communication stretching back over more than four years, her heart was heavy. Interest and arrears had swollen the original debt to a colossal and terrifying size and her grandfather's total lack of response to those warning letters had put him very much in the wrong.

The loan had been secured against the castle, and the
castle was her grandfather's sole asset. There was no
way that she could raise the kind of money that was now
owed to Luciano. Nor were there any valuable family
heirlooms left to sell: Great-Uncle Ivor's grasping ex-
wife had seen to that.

In the midst of those increasingly panic-stricken
thoughts and in desperate need of fresh air to clear her
buzzing head and restore her concentration, Kerry went
outdoors and headed for the lake that lay below the castle. Her feet crunching on the lush green grass of late
spring, she finally came to a halt beneath the spreading
branches of the willow tree that overhung the water.

A low swirling mist was rising from the still surface
of the lake to lend an eerie, dream-like quality to the
reflection of the pale limestone battlemented walls and
turrets of Ballybawn. For five years she had worked
round the clock in an effort to make the great house pay
for its own upkeep and she had honestly believed that
she was on the brink of *finally* achieving that objective!
Had it all been for nothing?

But Ballybawn meant so much more to her than a
responsibility: it was the only real home she had ever
had. Her mother, Carrie, had walked out of her life when
she was only four years old. Prior to that, Kerry had dim
memories of frightening adult scenes in which her father's rage had made him seem, perhaps unfairly, a cruel
and threatening man. When the marriage had finally
ended, her mother had left England to return to Ireland
and her childhood home. Although it had been more than
ten years since Kerry's mother had even spoken to her
parents, the older couple had offered a warm welcome
to their wayward daughter and her child. It was at the
castle that Kerry had first learned what it was to be

happy and, even when Carrie later went away and failed to return, the O'Briens had continued to make their granddaughter feel secure and loved.

But Luciano da Valenza had never managed to make her feel secure or loved, *had* he? Kerry swallowed the bitter lump in her throat. Abandoning caution and common sense, she had fallen in love with the first slick and sophisticated, handsome male who looked her way. She had refused to think about the fact that she was not beautiful or even especially sexy like Rochelle or the other women in Luciano's past. She was five feet three inches tall and her build was what her acid-tongued stepmother had once described as 'almost asexual'. Men did not do a double take when they saw Kerry on the street. Her infuriating ringlets ran every colour between copper, russet and orange, depending on the light or indeed the observer's outlook on red hair.

Of course, Luciano had labelled that same colour 'Titian', which had been a surefire impressive winner with a girl who had gone through school tagged with less complimentary nicknames…a girl whose first boyfriend had been stolen by her stepsister, a girl who was a total dreamer for all her seeming practicality. At the age of twenty-one, however, Kerry had thought of herself as mature.

But, with hindsight, she knew that when she had first seen Luciano da Valenza springing out of his sleek sports-car her very lack of experience with men had been a handicap. Taking one stunned look at Luciano, she had been so mesmerised that she had walked backwards into a flowerbed and got soaked by the sprinkler system. He had thought that was very, very funny. She squeezed her burning eyes tight shut and told herself furiously to stop thinking about *him*.

Broken engagement, broken heart, broken dreams. Kerry shivered and lifted her hands to her tear-wet face in shame: she had always been too sensitive, too trusting and soft. Luciano's infidelity had devastated her. But then, that Luciano should *ever* have shown an interest in her had been surprising and her own father had told her that too, hadn't he?

'You were never da Valenza's type. I should've suspected that he had an ulterior motive. Now, if he'd gone after your stepsister, Rochelle, again, *well...*' Harold Linwood had stressed meaningfully. 'That would have been the normal thing to do.'

In frustration, Kerry breathed in deep and emptied her mind of the painful memories that still taunted her. The past was over and gone, she reminded herself squarely. Ballybawn was under threat again, but this time around the threat she had to overcome came from Luciano. Luciano, who had been outraged when she handed him back his ring and as incredulous as a predatory, prowling cat suddenly punched on the nose by a mouse. Luciano, who always played to win with ruthless, relentless purpose.

But exactly what would Luciano want with a cold, comfortless castle in the hilly wilds of Co Clare? The cosmopolitan delights of Dublin city were at a most inconvenient distance. And wasn't it truly fortunate that Luciano had come into the reputed squillions of cash left to him by his natural father? She was relieved by the idea that Luciano had become so wealthy that flogging a tumbledown Irish castle would not enrich him to any appreciable extent.

Unhappily, those small positive elements aside, Kerry also knew that she had only one immediate option: she would have to fly over to London and see Luciano in

person, for only he would have the power to stop that
repossession order progressing as far as the High Court.
But how could she face seeing him again? And on such
demeaning terms? Coming cap in hand like a beggar to
him?

Shivering at that degrading image, Kerry felt cold inside and out. Somehow she had to find the strength to
do what had to be done, for, like so many other tasks
around Ballybawn, there was nobody else but her available.

CHAPTER TWO

FOUR days later, pink in the face, out of breath and all too well aware that her delayed flight out of Shannon to London had made her almost fifteen minutes late for her two o'clock appointment with Luciano, Kerry sank down in the smart reception area on the top floor of his brand-new office building.

In an effort to get a grip on her own mounting stress level, Kerry made herself concentrate on the challenge ahead. She needed to tell Luciano why the loan was in arrears and ask for more time to make good on the payments. He was first, foremost and last a businessman. If she could convince him that he would make more money letting her grandparents stay on in the castle, surely she would have a chance of winning his agreement to a stay of execution on that repossession order? With an anxious hand she checked that the business plan she had drawn up was still safe in her bag.

Striving to steady herself, she then looked around herself, desperate for anything that would take her mind off the coming confrontation. Her opulent surroundings had that classic sharp-edge design flair that distinguished a successful business. It had been eighteen months since Roberto Tessari's death and, regardless of Luciano's imprisonment, his father's companies had continued trading. In those circumstances, it was hardly surprising that Luciano should have decided to set up a London base of operation for da Valenza Technology. But how it must have galled him to have to work through and rely on intermediaries rather than have access to and sole control of what was his.

Luciano had never, ever been a team player. Or, crept in the anxious thought, very hot on the forgiveness and understanding front, Kerry reflected miserably. That she had arrived late for their meeting would have struck another bad note. Luciano had an inner clock that never let him down and he equated poor timekeeping with a lack of respect.

Kerry breathed in deep, struggling to keep herself calm, but minute by minute her nerves were winding up like coiled springs. For four days solid, she had fought not to think about what it would be like to see Luciano again. But now, even before she saw him, she was finding out. It was terrifying. Her brain felt like mush and her palms were sweating.

'Luciano will see you now…you have fifteen minutes left!'

Startled by that snappy but familiar voice, Kerry rose hurriedly to her feet.

Costanza Guiseppi strolled forward. Clad in an enviable blue cropped jacket and shift dress, Luciano's PA looked like a million dollars. It took only one scathing glance from Costanza for Kerry to be aware that her own dated grey skirt suit was the poorest of shabby comparisons.

'How does it feel to be a leech?' Costanza turned her head to enquire with venom as Kerry accompanied her down the corridor.

'I don't know what you're talking about.' Kerry tilted

her chin, telling herself that she ought to have been prepared for that attack, for the brunette was very loyal to Luciano and very fond of him. Their friendship was a close one, for Costanza had, after all, first met Luciano at school. As ambitious as Luciano was to succeed in the world, she had gone to work for him as soon as she left college.

'I don't suppose it even occurred to you five years ago that Luciano could have done with that loan being returned. If he'd had more funds, he could've afforded top-flight legal counsel and he might never have gone to prison.' The Italian woman watched Kerry turn ashen pale in shock. 'You cost him and you're *still* costing him, and that makes you a leech on my terms!'

'If Luciano had asked for the money back then my grandfather could still have given it back,' Kerry protested sickly.

But Costanza wasn't listening. 'I'm so looking forward to viewing your Irish castle *without* you in it.' The other woman savoured that assurance. 'Your cheek in coming here today is your biggest mistake so far.'

As Costanza cast open the door ahead, Kerry walked in past her without even hearing that final taunt, for she was much too keyed-up about seeing Luciano again after so long.

'Thank you, Costanza,' Luciano murmured drily, knowing that the brunette's satisfied expression meant that she had exercised her sharp tongue with barracuda-like efficiency.

As Luciano strolled forward, Kerry found herself just staring and staring. She was helpless in the grip of that overwhelming compulsion to take her visual fill. Even though she had already seen a half-dozen newspaper photos of him, the sight of him in the flesh and poised only feet from her reduced her mind to a literal wasteland.

'Take a seat,' Luciano suggested, his dark, deep drawl achingly familiar to her.

Her mouth running dry, her heartbeat speeded up in the taut silence but still she was looking at him. His sleek, dark business suit had the smooth, perfect fit of expensive tailoring over his wide shoulders, narrow hips and long, powerful legs. But even in that first moment she immediately recognised the changes in him: the shorter, more aggressive cut of his black hair, the cleaner, tougher angle of his proud cheekbones, the bleak, uncompromising line of his beautiful sculpted mouth. He was still extravagantly gorgeous, she thought painfully, but there was a quality of indifference stamped to his lean, dark features that was new to her.

Unwarily, Kerry tilted her head back and finally collided with narrowed dark golden eyes that stilled her in her tracks. Beautiful, bold, brilliant eyes, framed by a dense black fringe of lashes. As a tiny sliver of snaking heat curled low in her belly, she went rigid and dragged her gaze from his. Indeed a whole array of secret sensations that she had almost managed to forget she could feel assailed her in punishing reminder: the sudden melting weakness deep down inside, the stirring swell of her breasts within her bra, the feel of her skin tightening over her bones in excitement. Embarrassed colour washed her face, stark shame engulfing her. One look was all that it had taken to strip away her defences and make her cringe at her own failure to remain untouched by his powerful magnetism.

'It's been a long time…' she mumbled, sitting down in haste and trying not to wince at the inanity of her own greeting.

A long time, a very long time, yet her own grief at losing what she had once felt they had still felt as fresh as yesterday to Kerry. She had been crazily, wildly happy with him and that was impossible to forget. She had believed that he was sincere and honourable and that had proved to be a cruelly empty illusion. The day after he had been sampling the gold satin sheets in her step-sister's bed, he had lied without hesitation about his movements. And he was one *very* smooth liar, she recalled painfully, for not once during that phone conversation had she sensed anything amiss. What a pathetic judge of character she had been!

Just then Luciano was recalling how long it had taken for him to stop lusting after her skinny, undersized little carcass. That same self-applied verbal-aversion therapy hastened to inform him that he could not be attracted in any way to a skinny, vertically challenged woman with child-sized feet and hands. Not even one with translucent skin as smooth as silk, eyes the clear, glorious colour of a mountain lake and a mouth as tempting and luscious as a ripe fruit. He watched her lower her head. Straying curls from the riot of Titian hair that swung clear of her slight shoulders glinted like fiery question marks against the pale, delicate curve of her cheek. He saw the faint purple shadows etched by too little sleep below her eyes. Without the smallest warning, the dark, bitter anger that he had believed he had under full control seethed up in him with formidable effect.

'I suggest that you start talking fast,' Luciano advised flatly.

Her brain a sea of conflicting promptings, Kerry went for what mattered most to her at that moment and broke straight into speech. 'Costanza said that if we'd offered to return the loan after you were arrested, you could've hired a better lawyer to defend yourself!'

His wide, sensual mouth took on a cynical slant. 'Untrue. Back then, I had touching faith in the British legal system. I didn't realise that I needed a hotshot defence team. I assumed that such outrageous charges could never be made to stick.'

His rebuttal of Costanza's contention only eased Kerry's sick sense of guilt a little. Her conscience had always been easily stirred but she was also uncomfortably aware that the first six months after his arrest were still just a blur of unimaginable pain in her own memory. It had been a very long time before she had regained the ability to think with any clarity.

'Even so,' Kerry said tautly, 'I wish that my grandfather or indeed I had thought of that angle for ourselves.'

Ironically, Luciano was inflamed by the apparent sincerity with which she expressed that regret. Why didn't it occur to her that that oversight had been the very *least* of her sins of omission? Even had her decision not to marry him had no relation to his subsequent arrest, what about the faith that she should have had in him and the support she could still have offered him? Instead she had turned her back on him as totally as if he had never existed.

'You're not here to catch up on my life,' Luciano derided with a roughened edge to his accented drawl. 'It *has* been five years since I last saw or heard from you. But then, I imagine you felt quite secure sitting over in Ireland and ripping me off—'

'It wasn't like that!' Kerry exclaimed in dismay.

'Wasn't it?' Luciano sent her a flaring golden look of disagreement that was like the lick of a whip scoring tender skin. 'I was in prison and too busy fighting for my freedom to spare the time to instigate court action over that loan. Nice one, Kerry. I get banged up for a theft I didn't commit while *you* virtually steal from *me*!'

At that condemnation, the last remnants of colour drained from Kerry's shaken face. 'That's not how it was…for a start, you agreed that loan with my grand-father, not with me,' she reminded him angrily, rising to her feet again in a driven movement. 'I've never had access to Grandpa's financial affairs either. Although I offered to help, he insisted on dealing with the accounts and the bills himself. In fact, it's only four days since I found out that he'd fallen behind with the loan and only then because he couldn't keep his difficulties a secret any longer!'

Luciano elevated a doubting winged ebony brow. 'You want to go back outside and come up with a more convincing story?'

'Whether you want to accept it or not, that's the truth!' Kerry squared her shoulders but she did not look directly at him, for every time she looked her concen-tration fell apart again.

'But why would I believe anything you said? Why would I trust you?' Luciano derided harshly.

Kerry shot him a helpless look of reproach and then hurriedly veiled her confused eyes in self-protection. For if she did not trust him, how could she expect him to trust her? When he had been convicted of stealing from the family firm, hadn't she started to believe that she owned the moral high ground and that her every worst suspicion of him had been proven true? In fact, hadn't it suited her to believe that? But where was it written that infidelity and financial dishonesty went hand in hand? With a mighty effort of will, Kerry closed her mind down on the torrent of dangerous thoughts rushing in on her one after another.

'Let's recap,' Luciano continued levelly. 'The loan repayments stopped dead after the first six months. That's over *four* years ago. Yet you're trying to convince me that you had no suspicion whatsoever of that reality? Sorry, I'm not impressed!'

Faced with that intimidating derision, Kerry stiffened with annoyance. With every word that Luciano spoke she was receiving a daunting insight into his attitude. It was obvious that he was in no mood to give her a fair hearing. 'You're not really listening, though, are you?'

'Are you getting that *déjà vu* feeling?'

'What do you mean?'

'This is how you treated me the day you told me that you'd changed your mind about marrying me. I didn't get an explanation either and you didn't listen to a word I said.'

At that unwelcome reminder of that nightmare day, Kerry's breath snarled up in her throat, her strained eyes darkening. She marvelled that he had the gall to refer to that occasion. 'I *thought* I was here to discuss Grandpa's loan—'

'Which he only got in the first place because I couldn't stand you worrying your little head off about how your grandparents were managing in their draughty castle. There's a personal dimension here that you seem determined to ignore.'

'What else can I do?' Kerry demanded, her temper flaring.

Did he think she was a caged animal to be prodded through the bars to provide him with better entertainment? First he tossed one spoiler, then another, and every angle he took caught her by surprise. After the way he had treated her, only the cruellest of males would even have referred to their short-lived engagement. Smarting pride and pain over that reference to a *personal* dimension only increased her resentment.

'Admit the truth. It's possible that that might win you five more minutes of my time,' Luciano delivered with crushing contempt.

'What truth? Are you actually asking me *why* I broke off our engagement? You still haven't worked that out for yourself?' Kerry could feel her heart thumping inside her chest too fast, her outrage rising out of her control. 'That amazes me but I'm still not going to lower myself to the level of telling you why now!'

'Is that your last word on the subject?'

Kerry pinned her soft lips together and jerked her chin in defiant affirmation.

'Then I don't have any more time to give you.' Striding past her, Luciano crossed the room, threw the door wide and dealt her a cold, hard look of expectancy.

Her eyes flew wide in disbelief and her stomach clenched. 'That's not fair…you can't do that!'

Chilling golden eyes assailed hers and his jawline squared. 'I can do anything I want to do in my own office.'

Kerry stared fixedly into space, willing back the shaken surge of tears stinging behind her eyes. So he got his kicks out of intimidation now, she told herself, hating him with every fibre of her being for forcing her into a humiliating position where she had no choice but to climb back down off her high horse. Had she really once admired that sheer ruthless force of will of his?

Luciano was still as a statue, untouched by the shock that was emanating from her slender figure in waves. He had waited what felt like half a lifetime for what he was determined to hear from her own pink lips and he would let nothing get in the way of the best opportunity he would ever have.

Kerry forced her attention back to him and clashed with challenging dark golden eyes that carried not a shade of remorse or discomfiture. Her slight shoulders rigid, she screened her gaze and with a wooden lack of expression said, 'All right…but first you let me explain about the loan and you listen *this* time.'

With a fluid shift of a lean brown hand, Luciano sent the door thudding shut again. The silence that fell throbbed. Her very muscles hurt with the strength of her tension. She sank back down in her chair, stiff as a coat hanger.

'I'm waiting…' Luciano lounged back against the

edge of his fancy glass desk with infuriating self-assurance and cool.

For an instant Kerry searched those lean, darkly handsome features, saw the strength written in the hard angles of his fantastic bone structure and, before she even knew what was happening to her, hunger leapt inside her. It was a wanton physical craving that had a life all of its own and it shook her up even more. Her concentration destroyed and furious with herself, she battled to regain it. But she was remembering the many nights she had woken up hot and ashamed of her feverish dreams of what it might have been like if he had ever made love to her…only to *always* be forced to recall, both during their engagement and after his imprisonment, that Rochelle had already had that pleasure ahead of her and that nothing would ever change that demeaning reality.

Without even thinking about what he was doing, reacting by male instinct to the flash of awareness he had seen in her eyes, his own male hormones already on red alert, Luciano was picturing her stripped on his office carpet, dominated by him, begging him for it. Only something in him recoiled from that crude image even as raw arousal flared through his powerful frame with a white-hot, burning ferocity that reminded him just how long it had been since he had had any woman in his bed. Five years and four months. Four months wasted on her, four months putting her needs way ahead of his own, four months waiting on a wedding night that had never happened. His lean, bronzed face paled with anger. He had to be sex-starved to still be excited by her and certifiably insane to be wondering if she could still be a virgin.

Kerry was sick at heart from what she had relived, unable to look at him and agonised that she could still be that vulnerable to his potent sexual aura. That was all it was, she told herself feverishly. He was just a very good-looking, very masculine guy and lots of women reacted the same way around him. It certainly didn't mean that she was carrying some stupid torch for him. It just meant that she was behaving like a total idiot and that it was time she got her act together.

'Are you still a virgin?' Luciano enquired, choosing to travel the certifiably insane route and doing so with a question that emerged smooth as silk.

Kerry's head tipped back on her shoulders and she stared at him with aghast blue eyes, so disconcerted that she started stammering, 'Wh-wh-wh-wh—?'

Luciano surveyed her with grim satisfaction. 'So that's a *yes*. No, don't bother arguing with me. If you'd loosened the lock on your mental chastity belt, you wouldn't still be blushing or embarrassed about it.'

In furious mortification, Kerry set her teeth together and snatched in sustaining oxygen but the silence lingered while she prepared herself to speak again without that revealing hesitation over every word. 'How many twenty-six-year-old virgins do you know?'

'You're in a class of your own. The loan,' Luciano prompted, content to let the previous issue drop while he let his attention be drawn by the restive way she crossed one slim knee over the other and then changed it back again.

Drawn up short by that reminder, Kerry swallowed hard and endeavoured to rise above her fury over that demeaning taunt and concentrate on her grandparents' plight. She had to get across certain facts in the hope that he would understand and accept that nobody had *ever* had the slightest intention of defrauding him in any way. 'Grandfather's elder brother, my great-uncle Ivor, died soon after you went into prison—'

She still had fantastic legs, Luciano conceded. Slowly his appraisal climbed, memory filling out what he could not see as she sat there: the slim but highly feminine curve of her hips, her tiny waist, the surprising fullness of her small breasts. At the speed of a bullet, sexual heat exploded in him, sentencing him to an exquisite aching discomfort that made his even white teeth clench in outraged denial.

'I don't remember you ever mentioning him before,' Luciano breathed curtly.

'I used to forget Ivor was around. He lived like a hermit in his own wing of the castle.' Aware of the terrible tension in the atmosphere and putting it down to his reluctance even to hear her explanation, Kerry talked even faster. 'Grandpa only inherited Ballybawn because his father disinherited Ivor for running up so many debts when he was a young man. In the 1970s, Ivor was badly hurt in an accident and he was never the same afterwards. He became antisocial and difficult, he couldn't hold down a job and his wife, who was a lot younger than he was, went off with another man. Then about twenty years ago Ivor finally came back to Ballybawn because he was broke and he had nowhere else to go, and Grandpa took him in—'

'Where is this long story leading?' Luciano cut in very drily.

'Grandpa felt very guilty that his brother had suffered

so much. He wanted Ivor to feel that he had as much right to live at Ballybawn as he himself had, *so*…' Kerry grimaced '…Grandpa signed over half of the castle to Ivor—'

'Why am I only hearing about this now?' Luciano growled in wrathful interruption.

'I didn't know either until it all blew up in Grandpa's face.' Finally, Kerry lifted her head to clash with shimmering dark golden eyes. Her mouth ran dry and her spinal cord notched up another inch in rigidity.

'But you *are* telling me that Hunt took a loan from me knowing that he didn't have full title to the estate?'

'At the time, Ivor made a will leaving his half to my grandparents and their descendants,' Kerry hurried to explain. 'Only unfortunately, after his death, that will turned out to be invalid because it hadn't been properly witnessed and his *old* will, the one drawn up while he was still married, left all his worldly goods to his ex-wife and…and she claimed half of Ballybawn.'

Wretchedly conscious of Luciano's brooding and incredulous scrutiny, Kerry muttered tautly, 'Grandpa settled out of court with her and everything that could be sold was sold but it meant that he could not maintain the loan repayments.'

'Even if I was to accept this highly improbable story,' Luciano drawled with sardonic bite, 'why didn't Hunt himself come forward with it long before now?'

'He couldn't handle it and so he tried to pretend it wasn't happening. He blamed himself terribly for what happened with Ivor's will and it knocked the heart out of him. I could show you an entire drawer full of letters from your accountant and your solicitor that Grandpa didn't even open...the minute they arrived, he must've put them in there. Luciano...I honestly *did* only find out about this a few days ago!' she told him in helpless appeal.

As the phone buzzed Luciano turned away to answer it and Kerry pleated her restive hands together, striving to gauge his reaction from his chiselled bronze profile. She studied the arrogant jut of his nose, the proud angle of his cheekbone, the unyielding edge to his wide, sensual mouth. He had been so very kind to her grandparents when they had come over to London to meet him. He had liked the older couple, had not seemed to find them as eccentric as other people did. Surely there was something of that tolerant compassion still left in him?

Replacing the phone, Luciano swung back to her, and as she dredged her troubled gaze from him her cheeks warmed with self-conscious colour.

'In business, it's important that you stick to the issue,' Luciano delivered with cool golden eyes, cold anger having checked his powerful libido. 'However, it seems that you need me to clarify what that issue is and what it *isn't*. It doesn't relate to your great-uncle Ivor or your grandfather's foolishness or even whether I believe in either claim. But by telling me that Hunt concealed the fact that he only owned part of the estate against which the loan was secured, you've done his cause no favours.'

Unnerved by that caustic speech, Kerry said vehemently, 'I thought that when things had reached such a serious climax, honesty was the best policy—'

'What are you? A little girl in Sunday school?' Luciano shook his proud, dark head in wonderment at her naivety, for she had just given him more ammunition for the repossession order. 'The bleeding-heart routine doesn't have a place here. So before I lose patience or we run out of time, I suggest you keep your end of the bargain and confess *why* you ditched me…and, more importantly, you have to tell me *who* told you to do it.'

Even as Kerry coloured at that crack about bleeding hearts, her brows pleated. 'Who *told* me to do it?' she repeated in bewilderment. 'What are you trying to suggest?'

Luciano settled shimmering golden eyes on her with incisive force. 'That it's cards-on-the-table time. I had only one reason for agreeing to see you today and it had nothing to do with how much money you owe me. That reason is that the Linwood half of your family tree set me up for five years in a prison cell!'

At that far-reaching condemnation, Kerry stared back at him with astonished incomprehension. 'How is it my family's fault that the police didn't investigate your case properly? And why should you believe that anyone set you up?'

'Right out of the blue you broke off our engagement and the next morning I was arrested. Now, only a fool would credit that those two events weren't closely connected,' Luciano continued in the same soft, sibilant undertone that from the outset of that disturbing speech had had the most terrifyingly chilling effect on her. 'To save you and your family from embarrassment, one of your Linwood relatives warned you to dump me and I want to know which one of them it was. Why? Because whoever did that was involved up to their throat in framing me!'

'I can't believe that you've been thinking like this

about my family and me all this time,' Kerry admitted shakily half under her breath, stark strain visible in the prominence of her fine facial bones. 'But I had good reason to tell you that day that I didn't want to marry you any more. I certainly didn't need anyone else to tell me to end our relationship. Your behaviour did that for me all on its own.'

'*My* behaviour? After what I've come through, I'm not prepared to swallow your insults.' As she spoke, scorching anger had flamed in Luciano's intent scrutiny and his lean, strong face was rigid. 'So stop right there and think very hard about what you're about to say to me. In fact I think you ought to sleep on it!'

Kerry gave him an even more perplexed look. '*Sleep*…on it?'

'Your time's up. I have a meeting to attend and I see no reason why other people should be kept waiting on your behalf,' Luciano asserted with acerbic bite. 'I'll see you tomorrow morning at eleven.'

'You can't expect me to come back here again tomorrow!' Kerry argued in disbelief.

'You should've been on time this afternoon.'

Kerry jumped to her feet. 'For goodness' sake, I have a flight booked home this evening!'

'Then you have a problem. And do think very carefully about what you plan to tell me tomorrow because you *won't* get a second chance to spill the beans.'

'What's that supposed to mean? Hasn't anything I've said today made the slightest impression on you?' Kerry pressed in dismay.

'Nothing,' Luciano admitted.

At that uncompromising confirmation, her heart sank.

Recognising that she had no choice whatsoever but to meet his demand that she return the next day, Kerry dug into her bag to remove the file and walked over to set it on his desk. 'Then at least look at my business plan for Ballybawn before I come back…that *is* sticking to the issue and practical and should be much more your style.'

'Kerry…one final word of advice.' Luciano shot her a grim look of incredulity. 'The very last thing I'm likely to be interested in is *your* business plan for a property that will soon be mine!'

A sense of desperation surged up so hard and fast in Kerry that it made her feel light-headed. She had got nowhere with him but then, she dimly recognised, she was not firing on all cylinders, was she?

'I can't quite believe that I'm here with you,' she muttered out loud, belatedly recognising her own maddening sense of dislocation throughout their meeting. 'It doesn't feel real.'

Smouldering golden eyes rested on her delicate features. Not a single reference had she made to his imprisonment for a crime he had not committed. Not a single word of even insincere regret had she proffered. A story-book princess in a fairy-tale tower could not have been more detached from the hard realities of *his* recent past.

'I can make it feel real,' Luciano murmured silkily, snapping his hands over hers and drawing her close before she could even guess his intention.

'What are you d-doing?' Every skin cell in Kerry's body leapt in shock as he used his strong hands to clamp her to his lean, muscular frame. Her heart felt as though it was about to burst right out of her chest.

'Making it feel real, *cara mia*.' A hard, slashing smile on his lean, dark face, Luciano looked down at her, the lush black screen of his lashes merely accentuating the fiery gold challenge of his gaze. 'When was I ever in your radius this long without touching you?'

With those words he set free a dozen evocative memories that she never, ever allowed herself to consciously think about. In the act of bracing her hands against his sleeves to break his hold on her, Kerry met his eyes and intimate images bombarded her without mercy: sunlight on her skin, Luciano in her arms, the potent allurement of him, the wildness of her own longing and the soaring belief that she was the luckiest woman in the world.

He took her soft pink mouth in a hard, deep kiss. Faster than the speed of light, her own body reacted to the surge of heat that flared in her pelvis. Her head swam, her knees shook. She could no more have halted the chain reaction of her own desire than she could have pulled back from him. More primitive reactions had taken over, making her push herself into contact with the hard muscularity of his lithe, powerful frame. A startled whimper of burning excitement broke in her throat as his tongue ravished the tender interior of her mouth.

Luciano set her back from him. Adrenalin on full charge, he was on a complete high. At that moment, it didn't matter that the fierce ache of his own sexual hunger was actual pain. He was getting too big a kick out of watching her stumble back from him like a blind woman to steady herself on the chair back and he was revelling in the shell-shocked look on her face. Had the entire range of his ancestors crowed in triumph with him

from the heavens he would not have been surprised, for
never had his Sicilian genes been more in the ascendant.

'I see you haven't lost your taste for me,' Luciano
murmured in husky provocation.

Kerry flinched as though he had doused her with a
bucket of cold water. Paper-pale from the aftermath of
her own degrading response to him, she hovered,
stricken blue eyes locked to him. Bitterly aware as she
was of the terrible pain that he had already caused her,
her temper exploded. She slapped him hard enough to
numb her hand and make her wrist ache.

'You bastard!' she condemned. 'I h-hate you!'

Luciano did not even wince and, as Kerry watched
the marks of her own fingers flare up red over his cheekbone, she went into deeper shock at her own behaviour.
Nothing he had said excused her violence and never before had she lost control to the extent that she had struck
someone else. Blinking in shaken turmoil, appalled that
she had let herself down to that extent, she muttered a
harried apology.

Luciano surveyed her with lethal golden eyes and an
unnerving degree of impassive cool, for he was simply
chalking up one more score to be settled. 'I'll see you
tomorrow…and don't be late this time.'

As the door closed on Kerry's hurried departure, a
sardonic smile of intense satisfaction lit Luciano's lean,
strong features. She had lost her head. She was breaking
up. He would find out what he needed to know tomorrow. And then? He finally understood why no other
woman had yet been able to excite his interest. He still
wanted *her*. Why? Had five years shut away from a
world that had moved on without him left him trapped

in time? In one sense, he acknowledged the truth of that. But he also thought his own urges were a lot more basic. Desire and revenge made an intoxicating combination. He hated her but he still burned to have her under him, to have those long, perfect legs wrapped round him, hear her cry out his name, learn the pleasure that he could give her...before he took it away again.

Outside the impressive building that housed da Valenza Technology, Kerry came to a sudden halt on the acknowledgement that she did not even know where she was going.

Stepping back from the milling crowds on the pavement, she attempted to still her jangling nerves. It did not help her to appreciate that she had made a complete hash of her meeting with Luciano. That kiss followed by that slap. Stupid...stupid...*stupid*, she told herself angrily as she noticed a café on the other side of the street and headed for the crossing.

He had accused her of trying to ignore the 'personal dimension' but what else could he have expected from her? Compassion? Forgiveness? Understanding? The anguish and self-blame that his infidelity had inflicted would live with her until the day she died. Just when she had been within reach of finally believing that she was someone of value, he had dashed her down lower than ever before.

The seeds of her difficult relationship with her stepsister, Rochelle, had been sown right back in childhood, Kerry acknowledged heavily. Within months of divorcing Carrie, her mother, her father had remarried. His second wife, Pamela Bailey, had been a widow with two

young children. However, Harold Linwood had made no
attempt to remove his four-year-old daughter from the
care of her Irish grandparents. In fact, it had been six
years before he thought better of that arrangement and
finally came to Ireland to take Kerry back to England
and into his own home.

By then, Rochelle had been twelve and the spoilt darling of the household. While her fifteen-year-old brother,
Miles, had accepted Kerry, neither his mother nor his
sister had been as tolerant. Rochelle had been outraged
by the belated revelation that the stepfather she adored
already had a daughter from a previous marriage. Yet
there had never been any risk of Kerry stealing Rochelle's place in the family. Kerry's father had been infinitely fonder of his pretty, playful stepdaughter than he
had ever been of his own child. Kerry had reminded him
far too much of the ex-wife he still hated and denigrated
for having humiliated him with her lovers. In addition,
her stepmother had truly resented having to raise her
irresponsible predecessor's child.

The following five years had been very unhappy ones
for Kerry. At home, she had endured regular taunts about
her mother's promiscuity and at school she had been
relentlessly bullied by Rochelle and her friends. Finally
reaching breaking point, Kerry had run away from home.
When her grandfather had phoned Harold Linwood to
inform him that Kerry had shown up safe and sound at
Ballybawn, her furious father had washed his hands of
his daughter altogether and left her there.

In spite of that, however, six years later, fresh from
university and with her business degree and, if anything,
even more desperate than she had once been to win ac-

ceptance from the older man, Kerry had still applied for
a job at Linwoods. She had hoped that as an adult she
might achieve the closer relationship with her father that
she had failed to establish while she was a child. Looking back, she could only wince at her own innocence,
for the older man had only employed her out of a grudging sense of duty. Blood bond or not, she had always
been an outsider in the Linwood family and growing up
hadn't changed that fact.

Nor, unfortunately, had it changed Rochelle. And
even more than five years after the event, Kerry still felt
sick when she recalled the day that she had learnt to her
horror that the man she loved, the man whose engagement ring she wore, had in fact slept with Rochelle long
before she herself had even met him. Eighteen months
earlier, her stepsister had enjoyed a weekend fling with
Luciano while she was modelling in Italy. It had been a
ghastly coincidence that nobody could have foreseen or
even guarded against. Naturally, Luciano had not asso-
ciated Rochelle Bailey with Linwoods, and when he had
been headhunted into the task of revitalising the flagging
fortunes of the Linwood wine chain Rochelle had been
living in New York.

'It was just a casual thing,' Luciano had explained
after Rochelle had walked into the office one day and
all hell had broken loose when the outspoken blonde
realised that Kerry was engaged to one of her own former lovers.

When, regardless of all Luciano's efforts to comfort
and calm her, Kerry had continued to be extremely distressed, he had finally studied her with frowning pertur-
bation. 'It was no big deal to either of us,' he had rea-

soned. 'I'm not proud of it but I'm not ashamed of it either. At times, I've been forced to work such long hours that it was impossible for me to sustain a longer relationship. Don't make so much of this. It's very unfortunate that Rochelle is your stepsister, but we're all adults and Rochelle and I parted as friends.'

Only Rochelle had wanted *more* than a friendly parting. And Luciano had either been unusually obtuse in refusing to concede that fact or far too clever to highlight it. That same afternoon all Kerry's happiness in their engagement had died, only to be replaced by a helpless sense of threat and insecurity. She had needed no crystal ball to foresee that Rochelle's competitive instincts would soon cause trouble.

Within forty-eight hours, Rochelle had drawn up the battle lines: her stepsister, whose loathing for daily employment was a standing joke, had signed up for a temporary office job at Linwoods and had sashayed into work in a clingy top and a very short skirt. Her stepsister had used every seductive weapon she possessed in her determination to tempt Luciano back into her bed. Kerry had stood on the sidelines like the spectre at the feast while Rochelle flirted shamelessly with Luciano, and when Kerry complained about that Luciano had groaned out loud and told her to stop being 'paranoid'. Within the space of ten days, he had been telling her that jealousy and possessiveness were very unattractive traits.

Inevitably, Rochelle had won, Kerry reflected painfully as she sat over her untouched coffee in the café where she had taken refuge. Each memory that forced its way through the cracks in her self-discipline was more painful than the previous one...

Just a few short weeks later Kerry had returned from a brief trip back to Ballybawn, and Rochelle, having picked a very distinctive gold designer cuff-link up off her bedroom carpet, handed it to Kerry with a taunting smile of triumph.

'Yes, Luciano slept with me last night. Why should I cover up for him?' her stepsister asked, her amused gaze pinned to Kerry's shattered face. 'But don't be too hard on him. He's a *very* passionate guy. How could you think that you could hang on to a rampant stud like Luciano with that pitiful I-wanna-be-a-virgin-on-my-wedding-night routine?'

'He told you...*that*?' Kerry was sick with humiliation that something so very private should have been shared and equally aware that only Luciano could have provided that same information.

'We had a laugh about it,' Rochelle mocked. 'You're a right little goody-two-shoes. However, if it's any consolation, the sex may have been tremendous but Luciano's not planning to ditch you and replace you with little old me—'

'Shut up!' Kerry shouted, distraught, but there was no silencing Rochelle.

'But then, I won't come endowed with the greater part of Daddy Linwood's chain of wine stores, *will* I?' her stepsister continued spitefully. 'Naturally Luciano has his eye on the main chance. How else do you think he clawed his way up out of the back streets to become what he is now? While you've got your wine-store dowry, you've got him. Maybe you should consider trading in your sensible underwear and unlocking the bedroom door to prevent him straying again...but then I doubt that a little prude like you could match his incredible stamina and inventiveness between the sheets!'

Choosing to conserve what little pride she had had left, Kerry had decided not to confront Luciano on the score of his infidelity and had simply returned his ring to him. Why had she done it that way? She had felt that while all three of them were still working together at Linwoods, *she* would suffer the greatest humiliation if Luciano's behaviour was to become open knowledge. Had she shared that story with the rest of the family, Rochelle, brazen to the last, would have used that as an excuse to ensure that all their friends and employees also found out why Kerry's engagement had been broken off. The next day, while she had still been steeling herself to go into work, Luciano had been arrested.

A tight, hard knot of pain over those recollections remained with Kerry as she sank back to the present and drank her cold coffee to ease her aching throat. She had loved him, she had loved him *so* much. She shook her head as though to clear it, angry that the past could still have such a powerful effect on her, and made herself concentrate on the practicalities of her position. Where, for instance, was she planning to spend the night? Of course, Miles would put her up. Relief travelling through her as she came up with that obvious solution, she took out her mobile phone and rang her stepbrother.

'Of course you can stay. You don't even have to ask. But what are you doing in London?' her stepbrother asked in surprise. 'And why didn't you mention that you were coming?'

'I had some business to take care of and I didn't realise that I'd have to stay over until tomorrow.' Comforted by the familiar warmth of Miles's welcome, Kerry had to resist the urge to tell him then and there about the repossession order hanging over Ballybawn. He was at the office and she could hear voices in the background and he would not be able to speak freely.

'I wish I'd known that you were going to be here because I've got a business dinner to attend with your father tonight,' Miles complained.

In disappointment at that news, Kerry pulled a face. 'So I'll keep you up late when you get back.'

On the way to the train station, she shopped for a few necessities for her overnight stay. At the same time, finding that she was no longer able to block out the demeaning memory of her own wanton response in Luciano's arms little more than an hour earlier, she cringed with shame. What on earth had come over her? He had taken her by surprise and she had been upset and on edge, she reasoned feverishly. But why had Luciano kissed her? He could only have done it out of sheer badness. It had been the mother of all put-downs, administered by a male who had raised the skill to the level of an art-form.

As Kerry boarded the train to Oxford she considered the ludicrous family-conspiracy theory which Luciano seemed to believe lay behind their broken engagement. Why had the most obvious explanation not occurred to him? Why had he not immediately grasped that she had found out about his stolen night of passion with her stepsister? And how could he possibly accuse the Linwoods of framing him?

But then, to be fair, she reflected, if Luciano had not been the thief, *who* had been? Having read the newspaper reports that covered his appeal in depth, she had been genuinely shocked by the number of irregularities that had undermined the original investigation of his case. It seemed that the police had targeted the man they saw as the most likely culprit and had failed to follow up conflicting evidence.

So, who else had had access to those doctored office accounts? A whole host of people, Kerry conceded, but none of them dubious characters. Her father did not even come into the equation, for he had no need to steal what he had every right to take. It would be just as crazy to consider Miles a possible suspect: she knew her step-brother inside out and would have staked her life on his integrity. Equally, Rochelle had not worked at Linwoods long enough during that period to have been involved.

At the time, the firm's chief accountant had been Kerry's uncle, George Linwood, who had since retired. His deputy then had been his son, Steven. That branch of the family was most noted for church activity and charitable endeavours. Even the office manager and the sales director had been distant Linwood relations. At executive level, Linwoods had always been very much a family concern. Could she credit that one of them might have been embezzling from the business? Certainly someone had, but she had come full circle, considered every potential candidate and come up with precisely nothing!

Miles opened the door of his elegant apartment. Tall and slim, he had classic blond good-looks similar to Rochelle's but his friendly hug immediately emphasised that that resemblance only ran skin-deep. 'How's my girl?'

'I've been better,' Kerry confided unevenly.

As her stepbrother took her into his spacious lounge and offered her a drink, she noticed that his eyes were red-rimmed with tiredness and that he was thinner than he had been when she had last seen him. But there was nothing new in that, Kerry acknowledged, for her stepbrother might work very hard but he also liked to party. A devoted follower of the belief that you were only young once, Miles had always enjoyed a frantic social life with a like-minded circle of mates and a succession of leggy girlfriends.

A soft drink clutched in her hand, Kerry plunged straight into telling her stepbrother about the arrears on Luciano's loan and the repossession order.

'What a bastard da Valenza is!' Miles exclaimed with a supportive heat that warmed her. 'But surely even he couldn't be serious about evicting the old folk?'

'He's got the law on his side and that's all he needs.'

'In his *pocket* by the sound of it!' Miles tossed back his whisky and immediately went to pour himself another. 'He got out of prison on a forensic technicality. They should've left him locked up!'

Kerry frowned. 'He did do five years. Considering that the missing money was replaced, that's a long time to serve for a first offence and if it's true that he's innocent—'

'Are you telling me that you actually *believe* the rubbish the papers have been printing?' Miles demanded with sudden raw derision. 'You'll not be feeling so generous when do Valenza throws you all out of the castle!'

Disconcerted by that attack, Kerry studied her stepbrother in surprise and dismay.

'Look, I'm sorry…I didn't mean to come down on you like that,' Miles groaned in immediate apology. 'I'm under a lot of pressure at the office right now.'

Kerry's troubled gaze softened.

'Let's concentrate on your problems,' he suggested. 'Any hope of the bank—?'

'No—'

'I wish that I was in a position to help but I've never been the type to save up for a rainy day,' her stepbrother told her with a grimace. 'Were you thinking of approaching your father?'

Kerry winced. 'He's never had any time for my grandparents.'

'And, between ourselves, Linwoods isn't doing very well,' Miles volunteered. 'The *Salut* chain is hitting us right where it hurts—'

'I think I saw one of their ads on TV the last time I was over—'

'They're selling wine like it's the ultimate cool lifestyle choice… Their stores are fitted out like fancy continental bars. They're taking our customers *and* undercutting our prices. How they can afford to do that on top of a rapid expansion and a nationwide marketing campaign I have no idea, but your father's giving me a lot of grief over it.'

'I know that working for Dad isn't easy.'

'I don't think you're following me…*Salut* is hammering us. We're already facing the prospect of closing our smaller outlets and cutting back on staff.' As Miles took account of the time, he frowned and got up. 'I'd better get changed for this dinner do.'

Fifteen minutes later, Harold Linwood arrived to pick

up his stepson. When Kerry answered the door to her father, a guarded expression tightened the older man's features. A stockily built man with greying hair in his sixties, he spoke to her much as though she was a distant acquaintance. It was even more embarrassing when Miles tried to suggest that Kerry could join them that evening and her father stiffened with visible irritation.

'I'm so tired, I couldn't face going out again,' Kerry cut in hastily.

When the two men had gone, Kerry compressed her tremulous lips hard. Why was it that she was still cut to the bone by her father's total lack of interest in her? Why was it that memory would always plunge her right back to her ten-year-old self? Unhappily, she was unlikely ever to forget overhearing her father talking to her stepmother on the phone from Ballybawn.

'How would I describe Kerry? Set beside Miles and Rochelle, she'll definitely be the runt of the litter. Expect red hair, buck teeth and specs. Yes, I *do* accept that I'm asking a lot of you, Pamela,' Harold Linwood had snapped, 'but how *can* I leave her here? No, I'm not exaggerating…the O'Briens are as nutty as fruitcakes…if I don't intervene now, the kid will go the same way her slut of a mother went!'

Exhaustion sent Kerry to bed long before her stepbrother's return. She knew she would need her wits about her when she met with Luciano again. Only she had no need to sleep on what she had to tell him! But wasn't it pitiful that *she* should still feel gutted and humiliated by *his* infidelity? For her grandparents' sake she had to fight Luciano with every weapon she had. If he truly had no suspicion that she had found out about his night in Rochelle's bed, he was about to be caught at a severe disadvantage. Surely that fact could be made to work in her grandparents' favour?

Luciano would not be able to deny that *he* had wronged *her*. Wouldn't he feel guilty? Didn't he deserve to feel guilty? All she needed was a few months' grace on that repossession order and one good summer season of visitors to prove that the Ballybawn estate could bring in sufficient money to start eating into those loan arrears.

Tomorrow was another day, Kerry reminded herself bracingly...

CHAPTER THREE

ARRIVING at the office at eight the next morning, Luciano found Costanza sniggering over Kerry's business plan.

'Have you looked at this yet?' the brunette demanded with positive glee.

'No.' Reaching for the file, Luciano set it back on the desk. 'I didn't ask you to look at it either.'

Today he would bring down the curtain on Kerry's hope that a compromise could be reached where the castle was concerned. How could she still be that naive? But then she had no real idea who she was dealing with, had she? A brooding smile of acknowledgement formed on Luciano's sculpted mouth. For her benefit, he had once subdued all that was tough, unsentimental and aggressive in his own nature. He had even once sunk to the level of seeking out a field filled with poppies to stage a romantic proposal. He still felt quite queasy at that recollection and he moved fast to suppress other equally disturbing images.

On the dot of eleven, Kerry approached Luciano's office door for the second time. Adrenalin was pumping through her, for the prospect of confronting Luciano with his lowest moment had steadily gathered more punitive appeal. He wanted the personal dimension? He was about to get it in spades!

'Let's keep this brief,' Luciano drawled before Kerry could even get the door shut behind her.

Unwarily, Kerry let herself look at him. A breathtakingly gorgeous guy in a charcoal-grey business suit. Once he had been *her* guy. That painful thought threatened to swallow every drop of her bravado. In an effort to banish that pain, she reminded herself of Luciano's most essential flaw: he was too handsome for any woman's good. Why should he confine himself to one woman when so many others were happy to share his bed without attaching strings? He got chased by her sex, he met with endless temptation, but that did not excuse what he had done to her. He had asked her to marry him, built up her hopes and then smashed her heart to smithereens.

Wounded blue eyes veiling in self-protection, Kerry straightened her taut shoulders. 'I'm afraid that you're not going to enjoy hearing what I have to say—'

'Just get to the point,' Luciano advised drily.

'Yesterday you claimed that you had no idea why I dumped you five years ago.' Kerry could not help savouring that word, 'dumped', and watching from below her lashes as he literally froze in receipt of it. 'But I find that hard to credit. Why didn't you just examine your own conscience?'

'It was *clean*.' At that hint that she was about to foist blame of some kind on him, Luciano's temper leapt straight onto a razor edge.

'The evening I returned your ring...I'm sure you remember...I'd just returned from spending the weekend at Ballybawn. You'd said you were far too busy to go with me—'

'I *was*.' His smoky drawl now had an audible roughened edge.

'Yes, you were certainly busy that weekend.' Kerry's tense mouth tightened even more with distaste as she steeled herself to continue. 'The day I got home, Rochelle picked one of your cuff-links up off her bedroom carpet and told me that you had slept with her the night before.'

Luciano closed his eyes on a soundless groan. 'Are you trying to wind me up with this silly spiel?'

His complete lack of guilty reaction infuriated Kerry. 'You think you can deny it, *don't* you? I bet you also think that I don't have any proof!'

Ebony lashes swept up on hard golden eyes. 'At this moment, you are walking a tightrope with me.'

The silence stretched, thick and heavy.

'Do we have to go through with this stupid pretence?' In spite of Kerry's valiant attempt to remain calm and unemotional, she heard her own voice taking on a sharp note of accusation that she could not control. 'Why after all this time can't you just own up to being an absolute rat and betraying my trust?'

'Rochelle told you that I'd slept with her? If you were stupid enough to believe that, why would I argue the toss now when I don't give a damn?' Luciano angled that derisive question at her with cutting clarity.

Kerry flinched and coiled her taut hands together in front of her. 'So...er...you're more or less admitting it—'

'Like hell I am!' His steady golden gaze flamed with outrage.

'But I even know what you're going to say...that Rochelle was lying and that she could've taken that cuff-link from the office!'

'You don't know what I'm going to say.' Luciano's response was one of dangerous, menacing quietness.

'Or maybe you're about to suggest that I'm making this all up in an effort to cover up that crazy family conspiracy you mentioned yesterday!' Kerry condemned with even more dismissive scorn, but she was trembling with the force of her own emotions and her voice was shaking. 'But I know for a fact that you *did* sleep with my stepsister that night!'

'*Dio mio*...I refuse to listen to another word of this!'

'Only *you* could have told Rochelle that I was still a virgin and why!' Kerry slammed back at him in agonised condemnation. 'And if I'd needed any further confirmation, you *lied* to me—'

'I have never lied to you.' Lean, arrogant face clenched hard, Luciano made that emphatic statement with conviction.

'—about where you were that night! I phoned your apartment and there was no answer. But when I called again the next morning, you insisted that you had been in all evening and that you must've been in the shower. But you *did* go out, you *were* at Heathlands, you *were* at my father's home that night!' Ashen pale as she had to force out those distressing facts, Kerry had to pause to draw breath.

By this time Luciano was so still that he could have rivalled a stone statue. But just as swiftly, he unfroze and his lean hands curled straight into powerful fists. Rage and frustration were eating him alive. He *had* driven over to Heathlands to see Harold Linwood that evening. He *had* lied about it. One of those harmless little untruths that only another guy could have understood, he rationalised in a fiercer fury than ever. And in the circumstances, who of an earthly ilk could have blamed him? What male in his right mind would have risked unleashing yet another painful three-act tragedy from Kerry with the news that he had quite accidentally found Rochelle...*home alone*?

Kerry's hands were coiled into tight fists too. Her entire being was concentrated on Luciano. At last, it had come: his moment of truth when at the very least he should be unable to meet her eyes. In a head-on collision his sizzling dark golden gaze sought hers in defiance of that belief. Her mouth ran dry and confusion claimed her.

'I *know* that you lied to me...' Kerry found herself repeating in case he had yet to get that message.

Luciano shifted a broad shoulder in a fluid shrug but rage was smouldering like hot lava inside him. After all he had said and done, she had still let Rochelle come between them. Even now, she was so gullible that she could not see the bigger picture. He knew only *one* Linwood capable of winding Rochelle up to stage such a stunt. And it had worked and the timing had been perfect, he acknowledged with savage bitterness. He had been arrested and Kerry, who might have become a very useful ally in the enemy camp while he fought to prove his innocence, had walked away from him.

'Don't you have anything to say?' Kerry muttered in growing bewilderment. 'Does that mean that you're ashamed of yourself?'

'No…' Luciano breathed with savage restraint. 'I'm just thinking that you got what you deserved—'

'What…*I*…deserved? Are you telling me that I *deserved* to have you go behind my back to carry on with my stepsister?' Kerry gasped strickenly.

'Don't you understand anything yet?' Luciano demanded with derisive force. 'Nothing happened between Rochelle and me that night or on any other occasion while we were engaged.'

'But you lied about being there that night!' Kerry almost shouted back at him in her distress.

Luciano subjected her to a withering appraisal. 'I was sick and tired of the way you reacted every time Rochelle came anywhere near me. I drove over to Heathlands to see your father. Rochelle said he was due home. I waited about fifteen minutes and then decided it would make more sense to see him at the office. I knew you'd go into a real mood if I told you that I'd seen her, so I took the easy way out and chose not to mention it.'

Kerry was trembling but her face was stiff with discomfiture. He was forcing her to remember how much friction her insecurity over Rochelle had caused between them and how her own constant need for reassurance had taxed his patience. 'It *couldn't* have happened like that—'

'It *did*.' The very indifference with which Luciano spoke shook her faith in her own conviction of his guilt. 'But it hardly matters now.'

But to Kerry it still mattered a great deal, and his explanation plunged her into confusion. Was it possible that Rochelle had lied to her? That it could *all* have been lies? That Luciano had decided not to mention his visit

to Heathlands simply because he knew that she would
have made a fuss when she learned that he had seen
Rochelle there? She refused to believe that, refused to
credit that she was listening to anything more than a
clever story.

'You o-owe me the truth...' Kerry stammered in turmoil.

'I owe you nothing but I'm not about to admit to
something I didn't do just to make you feel better,' Luciano countered with lethal cool.

'It's not a matter of making me f-feel better!' Tears
of frustration flooding her eyes without warning, Kerry
spun away, fighting to regain control of the tempestuous
emotions he had unleashed. But it was as if he had
yanked the very ground from beneath her feet. She
needed him to admit that he had been unfaithful. To
make her feel better? A choking sob clogged up her
throat but mercifully remained there. If she had to face
the unimaginable and terrifying alternative; that she had
ditched him when he had done nothing, how could she
live with that? How could she *ever* learn to live with
that?

'What...about....that...cuff-link?' she pressed in near
desperation.

'I was always losing them.' His attention welded to
her bent head and pinched profile, Luciano was rigid
with angry tension. He did not want to hear her stammer
or see her tears. He resented being made to feel like a
bully when all he wanted to do was get on with business.
'The fact that your stepsister knew that we weren't lovers? I imagine that she knew you well enough to make
an accurate guess. Now, let's leave the subject there.'

'I *can't*...' Kerry admitted jaggedly as she lifted her head, bright blue eyes full of anguished appeal.

'You must,' Luciano traded with icy cool. 'We have more important issues to deal with.'

Kerry could not dredge her mind as fast as he could from the past. 'Luciano—'

'To save us both from extending this meeting, I'll cut to the base line. The repossession order on the castle will proceed.'

Kerry stared at him in shock. 'You're not even giving me a chance to—?'

'To what?' Leaning back against the edge of his fancy desk, Luciano surveyed her with grim golden eyes and a cynical slant to his beautiful mouth. 'To witter on about great-uncles and the like and try to make me feel guilty about sins I never committed? Let's not pretend that you came here today with any intent other than to try and make me feel bad. Business is business, Kerry. Wake up and join the real world.'

As he spoke, Kerry had become so pale that the sunlight coming through the windows made her hair glitter like fire illuminating snow. For a minute, he thought she might be on the brink of passing out on him. His aggressive jawline clenched as he sensed his own readiness to move forward and catch her. No, he wasn't about to back down. Kerry had the fragile build of a fairy in a child's story book, and could not help looking pathetic when she got bad news. But he was no longer the stupid bastard who had once been possessed by a need to protect her from every hurt, *was* he? So why the hell did he feel sick to his stomach?

Utilising every atom of courage she possessed, Kerry

flung her head back, copper and russet ringlets cascading back from her taut cheekbones. 'I already live in the real world. I wouldn't have come here to try and persuade you to change your mind if I didn't. All I'm asking for is more time—'

'Kerry…' Luciano trailed his heated gaze from the fiery gleam of her hair just as the pink tip of her tongue snaked out to wet her full lower lip. Desire exploded like a burning flare in him and ricocheted through every hard angle of his big, powerful frame. He wanted her but only on his terms. What his terms would be he had no idea but he had no intention of allowing lust to interfere with business. 'I won't change my mind.'

'Do you realise how many people are depending on the castle to give them a living?' Kerry prompted sickly.

While Luciano shrugged, he took note of that point. It would be foolish to antagonise the locals before he had even decided what to do with the castle. In the short term, he would instruct that staff should be retained and that any business-related arrangements dependent on the estate continue without interference.

'So you didn't even glance at my business plan?'

'That's correct.'

'Am I allowed to ask what plans you have for Ballybawn?'

Luciano's expressive mouth quirked. 'I haven't made any yet.'

'My grandparents only occupy a few rooms…couldn't you let them stay on even as tenants?' Kerry pressed doggedly in a last-ditch attempt to find a compromise. 'The castle is very big. I could move them somewhere where they wouldn't get under anybody's feet.'

'How many ways are there to say no?' Luciano angled back his arrogant dark head, the better to study her.

'Is there n-nothing I can say…nothing I can s-suggest or offer to make you think better of forcing my grandparents to leave their home?'

He spread his hands in a negative motion and continued to watch her.

Burning colour began to banish Kerry's strained pallor. Never in her life had she been more conscious of anything than she was of his smouldering gaze wandering at a leisurely pace over her tense figure. The accelerated rate of her own heartbeat made her breath catch in her dry throat. Stressed as she already was, thinking straight became an even greater challenge. As his attention lingered on the swell of her breasts, an unsettling combination of angry bewilderment laced with a faint stab of forbidden excitement tugged at her. Her mind, she acknowledged in cringing dismay, had no control over her own body.

His insolent gaze skimmed back to her hot face. 'Are you offering me sex as an inducement?'

Utterly taken aback by that lazily voiced enquiry, Kerry gasped in furious rebuttal that he should dare to even ask her such a thing. 'Are you c-clean out of your mind?'

'Not at all. I've had an amazing number of offers in that line since I walked out of that court a free man,' Luciano told her with a shameless lack of hesitation. 'It seems that the very concept of a guy having been locked up and deprived of certain pleasures for five years appeals to the female imagination.'

'Not to m-mine!' Kerry slung him a scandalised look. 'Is this what you call sticking to the issue?'

'We've got nothing else to discuss—'

'H-h-haven't we? Well, I'm telling you now that I won't leave the castle unless I'm *carried* out of it!' Kerry declared tempestuously.

'Thank you for the warning but it really wasn't necessary. I could lift you with one hand. But I urge you *not* to encourage your grandparents into a similiar stand. For their sake, not for mine.'

Kerry trembled. 'I won't let you do this to them. I won't involve them but I won't go without a fight!'

'I enjoy fights. And if you're still around when I arrive to inspect my latest acquisition, be prepared to end up in my bed, *cara mia*.' Luciano met her enraged look of disbelief with a sensation of intense pleasure and anticipation.

'You'll regret saying that t-to me!' Kerry hissed like a spitting cat.

No, he didn't think he would. Warning his victim added a keener edge to the challenge. And challenges were the very spice of life to Luciano.

Stooping to snatch up the bag she had left by a chair— she had remained standing throughout their meeting— Kerry stalked forward to angrily reclaim the file that contained her business plan. 'You needn't think that you're getting the chance to steal *my* ideas!' she told him.

For the first time since he had emerged from that court room, Luciano had an urge to laugh out loud with genuine appreciation. *Really* laugh, as opposed to making a polite pretence. But the possessive pride with which she clutched the same file that had sent Costanza into whoops stopped him from laughing. He remembered how often her father had scorned her best efforts at Linwoods. He remembered that she had taken it on the chin and just tried harder.

But Kerry's next words killed that more generous thought-train stone dead.

'I'd have had more respect for you if you'd just admitted what you did with my stepsister!' Kerry bit out fierily as she yanked open his office door.

Brilliant golden eyes cold as ice, lean, bronzed features hard, Luciano shot her a look that chilled her to the marrow. 'I suggest you go home and start packing.'

The instant Kerry departed, he reached for the phone and called Rochelle.

Having failed to move Luciano an inch from his purpose, Kerry was in a daze as she travelled to the airport to catch her rearranged flight home. She had been full of hope, foolish hope, she conceded numbly. There was no escaping the suspicion that from her grandparents' point of view she had been the worst possible go-between. It might have been more sensible to *lie* about why she had ended their engagement. Her need to finally confront Luciano about Rochelle had overruled her common sense. Antagonising him had been a mistake.

Somewhere deep down inside herself, she discovered that she *had* expected Luciano to agree to some kind of compromise over the castle. Why that should be she had no very clear idea. Had he ever cared about her at all? Even a little bit? Had his interest in her then been as solely mercenary as Rochelle had insisted it was? After all, Luciano had never said he loved her and he had winced when she asked if he did. In fact he had shown her more emotion in their two recent meetings than he had ever shown in the past. Anger, derision...*dislike*. In fact dislike was too mild a description for the cold hostility she had sensed. She shivered. Why would Luciano feel that amount of animosity towards her? Unless in every way possible she had been guilty of misjudging him?

Miles had promised to meet her for a late lunch at the airport. 'You look like a ghost,' he told her, walking her into the nearest bar. 'I gather it went badly with da Valenza.'

Too worked up to trust herself to speak, Kerry jerked her chin in affirmation.

'I wish you'd waited up for me last night. I've hardly seen you,' her stepbrother complained. 'I've the feeling that you've been holding out on me.'

Painfully aware of just how much she was holding back, Kerry was momentarily tempted to go right back to the beginning and tell him everything that troubled her. Miles was the brother that she had never had and she knew that he was fond of her. But Rochelle was Miles's real sister and he was loyal to his sibling. Confiding that, five years ago, Rochelle had claimed to have slept with Luciano again would embarrass Miles and strain their friendship.

'Luciano said no. He wouldn't even discuss the possibility of any other arrangement.'

'You're dealing with the contemporary equivalent of a gangster, not Mr Nice Guy,' Miles contended. 'I hate to say it, but what did you expect?'

'I can't believe that you're *still* harping on about his Sicilian ancestors,' Kerry sighed.

Miles settled bloodshot blue eyes on her. 'I'm serious. When that money went missing from Linwoods, why do you think the police arrested him so fast? They checked out his background, came up with his mafia grandfather and they *knew* that they had their man!'

Uneasy though she was with his prejudice, Kerry just felt too stressed to argue with him. In any case, she knew why Miles had always had a blind spot of dislike where Luciano was concerned. Her father had had to promise Luciano a totally free hand at Linwoods before he could persuade the younger man to mount a rescue bid on his loss-making wine-store chain. Luciano's arrival had stripped Miles of his executive authority. Being hauled over the coals for his business expenses had set the seal on her stepbrother's resentment.

Miles gave her a pained look. 'You're still carrying a torch for da Valenza the size of an Olympic flame...'

Disconcerted, Kerry flushed. 'Of course I'm not!'

'If I say a word against him, you try to make excuses for him—'

'I always see both points of view. I'm like that with everybody,' she argued. 'It doesn't mean anything. I hate Luciano now.'

'I'm glad to hear that *because*...' her stepbrother grimaced '...on my way here Rochelle rang me, and guess what? Not content with making an ass of herself outside that court room on da Valenza's behalf, she's now dancing with delight because he's asked her out tonight!'

The blood drained from Kerry's shaken face. Although she told herself that that news should mean nothing to her, it was as though Miles had stuck a knife in her chest. She jerked a thin shoulder and dropped it again. 'S-so?'

'I just thought you ought to know.' Meeting her stricken gaze before she could veil it, her stepbrother averted his attention to his menu. 'He's a real slick womaniser but she's better equipped to handle him than you ever were—'

'Maybe they were always meant to be together...and I just got in the way.' Pride made Kerry force out those words, for her imagination was already tormenting her with an image of Luciano and Rochelle emerging from a church to a shower of confetti and good wishes.

'What a horrible thought!' Miles laughed out loud. 'If it got serious, I'd have to start pretending that I too believed that he had suffered a miscarriage of justice. I mean, let's face it, with the millions da Valenza's got now, we really would have to swallow our pride and throw down the welcome mat!'

Kerry occupied herself ordering a meal that she had no appetite to eat. 'Rochelle went to see him in prison...didn't she?'

'The experience gave her no end of a thrill. But, considering that my sister originally gave evidence against him, I was amazed that he was willing to see her,' Miles continued chattily. 'But then I suppose he can hardly blame us for his imprisonment, can he?'

Making an effort to concentrate, Kerry glanced up and muttered, 'Actually he seems to think that the Linwoods somehow framed him...but evidently, Rochelle doesn't suffer from that same stigma.'

'*Framed*...him?' Her stepbrother raised startled brows

in concert. 'Good grief! On what does our Luciano base that extraordinary suspicion?'

'I haven't a clue but, if he didn't take that money, obviously someone else at Linwoods did. He did say that he would fight until he had cleared his name,' Kerry reminded him. 'If he succeeds, the police will have to reopen the investigation.'

'They won't find any new evidence this long after the event. Da Valenza's got his precious freedom back. What more does the guy want?' Hailing the waitress, Miles ordered another drink and then excused himself from the table.

A few minutes alone were welcome to Kerry at that moment, for instead of her finding Miles's company a comfort his revelation that Rochelle was seeing Luciano that very evening had only cast her into deeper conflict with herself. Why was the very idea of Rochelle and Luciano being together hurting her so much? Was it her pride? Or even a rather shameful dog-in-the-manger feeling? No matter how badly Rochelle behaved, she always seemed to get what she wanted. But surely she herself ought to be used to that by now? In any case, how could she allow herself to agonise in *any* way over a guy set on evicting her grandparents from their only home?

Miles returned from the cloakroom full of jokes and entertaining stories. Just keeping up with his lively conversation helped Kerry to suppress her own emotional conflict. She boarded her flight home, more properly engaged in wondering just *how* she might still fight Luciano and stay on the right side of the law, for she was

fully convinced that her grandparents would not long
survive any move from Ballybawn.

The castle had been in the O'Brien family for over
five hundred years. Like most fortified tower houses in
Ireland, Ballybawn had a chequered past. The castle had
withstood hostile neighbours, seige and flames and had
been razed to ground level more than once. But throughout those challenging times, Ballybawn had remained in
family hands and had only ever been occupied by an
O'Brien.

Through poverty, war and famine her ancestors had
fought tooth and nail to retain their heritage even when
it was just a heap of rubble. No sacrifice had been too
great for them, Kerry reminded herself bracingly. In the
eighteenth century, the O'Briens had been reduced to
sharing a lean-to with their livestock in the shelter of the
ruined walls. Offered a fortune to sell their land, had
they surrendered an inch of it and snatched at the chance
of an easier life? *No way!* It had taken them forty years
to amass enough money to rebuild Ballybawn but
against all the odds they had pulled off that meteoric
achievement.

Gathering inspiration from that stirring fact, Kerry
told herself that where there was a will, there was a
way...

CHAPTER FOUR

'MOST thoughtful of Luciano, don't you think?' Hunt O'Brien passed the letter complete with oily fingerprints to Kerry and bent over the ancient generator again. 'Life will go on just as before for all our dear friends. '

Frowning in surprise, Kerry scanned the letter from Luciano's solicitor, which in the event of the repossession order being granted not only promised ongoing employment to O'Brien employees but also urged that estate businesses should continue to trade as normal. Her troubled turquoise eyes clouded. Luciano was willing to be generous to everyone involved with one notable exception: her grandparents. Were her grandparents being punished for their association with her? How could Luciano offer such a far-reaching assurance unless he intended to maintain the castle as a private dwelling?

'Next month, your grandmother and I will as usual be visiting Cousin Tommy,' her grandparent remarked. 'Tommy always enjoys the company. Perhaps we could make it a more permanent arrangement…what do you think?'

While making noncommittal sounds, Kerry thought that the elderly bachelor's other relatives might be distinctly dismayed if the O'Briens were to demonstrate a desire to become more than biannual guests in his Dublin home. Yet she was reluctant to rain doubt on her grandfather's fond hope when she had as yet failed to come up with any alternative. In just three days, the High Court would deal with the repossession order but there was no chance of a miracle in that line when Hunt O'Brien had refused to even try to fight the order.

Indeed, on that score Kerry had found the older man immoveable.

'I owe money I can't repay…I won't interfere with the course of the law,' he had sighed.

'But people would have a lot of sympathy—'

'No. I must do what's right and behave with dignity,' he had insisted.

The generator kicked nosily into life again and the old man beamed with pleasure. It had always been a source of huge satisfaction to Hunt O'Brien that Ballybawn Castle was not joined to the national electricity grid. Since 1897, Ballybawn had generated its own power from a complex water system originally designed by her great-grandfather. Mercifully the years when rain had been less than plentiful had been few. However, blackouts were not unusual and, owing to the finite nature of the output, the ground floor alone of the castle was wired for electric light.

Only when Kerry gave that brief letter a second perusal did it dawn on her that it could be the loophole and the very escape clause that she had been frantically seeking to buy some time. What if…*she* was to become an official estate employee? As long as she was signed up as such before ownership of the castle passed into other hands, she too would be protected from the threat of immediate eviction. Of course, it would *have* to be a job that included live-in accommodation. She would become the housekeeper, she decided. It had been some time since Ballybawn had rejoiced in such a luxury but the former cook's quarters were spacious, for Bridget, the previous occupant, had raised a large family there.

In the tiny estate office in the old stable yard, Kerry filled out an application form and backdated it for the files. Printing out an employment contract, she went off to find her grandmother. Viola, who had always maintained that flowers ought to stay in the garden to enhance the view, was fixing ground elder, dandelions and reeds from the lake in a vase in the great hall.

'If only it wasn't too early for the convolvulus to bloom,' Viola lamented.

'It still looks lovely.' Kerry gave the arrangement of what the unimaginative might have regarded as weeds an admiring appraisal, slotted a pen into her grandmother's hand and showed her where to sign on the dotted line.

'Have we engaged a new member of staff?' Viola asked, twitching the reeds to a more prominent position with careful hands.

'A housekeeper,' Kerry advanced, deadpan.

'Oh…how nice that will be!' Viola trilled with warm approval. 'I shall be able to give my menus to her instead of to you and inspect the linen cupboard again.'

Back in the office, Kerry filed her new employment contract and organised a tenants' meeting so that she would pass on the contents of the solicitor's letter, for naturally the estate tenants had been very concerned about their own future. Ballybawn was, after all, the centre of a thriving cottage industry. At the same time, however, Kerry's business enterprises had, through lack of investment capital, been based more on the principle of bartering and exchanging services than on market forces.

Thus, a local builder, who rented premises on the estate at a favourable rate, had over the years helped Kerry to create two holiday cottages from what had once been staff quarters at the rear of the castle. The imposing reception rooms in the Georgian wing used by Elphie Hewitt to showcase her own artistic talent were also rented out for parties and receptions. The castle gardens were maintained by a landscaper, who also ran a nursery on the estate. His plants were on sale in the stable yard, which also contained an artist's gallery and the studios of several local crafts people. In Kerry's hands, Ballybawn had become the trading heart of the community.

Three days later Kerry waited for her grandfather to emerge from the local court sitting, and when he reappeared he had tears shining in his blue eyes. She was too distressed by the sight of his pain to intrude by asking questions. As he climbed into the car, he paused to say heavily, 'The officials will be coming in to do valuations and such. We'll have a month to move…'

Exactly four weeks later, Luciano braked at a tiny junction that boasted an embarrassment of signposts.

Two of them pointed in opposing directions to Ballybawn Castle. Deciding against the potholed road with the discouraging central furrow of grass, he drove about five kilometres down the other before finding himself back at the same staggered crossroads. To say that he did not take that revelation in good part would have been an understatement. A journey that he had believed would only take him an hour had already taken him three.

Within minutes of taking the grassy lane Luciano was, however, rewarded with a fleeting glimpse of a gingerbread turret through dense thickets of trees. An imposing castellated entrance appeared round the next corner. While frowning at the huge cracks in the façade of the gateway, he received his first view of a castle straight out of a Gothic fantasy. A hotchpotch of improbable turrets and elaborate battlements broke the skyline. He was not impressed by the beauty of the limestone in the afternoon sunshine or the glory of the mature woodland that embellished Ballybawn because the very *first* thing he noticed was the giant tarpaulin that was lashed to part of the roof. As repairing the roof had been the main purpose of the loan he had advanced, righteous anger hardened Luciano's lean, dark features.

Shooting the Ferrari to a halt in the rough parking area below the trees, he headed up to the castle. Three huge Irish wolfhounds charged down the grass slope towards him in an ecstasy of over-excited barking. Any notion that he might be under attack was soon dispelled by the excessive enthusiasm of his welcome. Forced to repel the onslaught of lolling tongues and giant muddy paws from dogs who had clearly not enjoyed even the most basic training, Luciano uttered a ringing rebuke. The gambolling hounds went into confused retreat and he entered the castle's imposing porch alone. He looked in surprise at the furniture, walking sticks, boots and coats, not to mention the moth-eaten stuffed stag's head still ornamenting the wall. Evidently, regardless of the reality that Ballybawn was now *his* property, the O'Briens remained in residence.

Kerry heard the dogs barking and groaned out loud.

In the middle of baking for the visitors' tour booked for the next day, she paused only to brush the flour off her skirt before racing for the front entrance to see who had arrived. There she came to a sudden shocked halt the instant she saw the tall, powerful male poised by the smoke-blackened fireplace. In his leather jacket and faded jeans, luxuriant black hair tousled by the breeze, a slight hint of a stubble already darkening his aggressive jawline, Luciano had all the stunning impact of a punch in the stomach.

'I wasn't expecting you *this* soon...' Kerry admitted, mouth running dry, brain empty of inspirational openings as she thought in dismay of all the tasks she had yet to accomplish.

Not the slightest bit surprised by her appearance, for it had not once occurred to him that she would not live up to her threat of staying on in the castle, Luciano sent her a grim dark golden glance. 'Where are your grandparents?'

'In Dublin staying with a relative...I left them there yesterday.' Kerry sucked in a steadying breath, heart thumping hard inside her tight chest as she decided that that was really all the information he required at present.

Relieved of the prospect of being forced to deal with the O'Briens in person, Luciano flung back his arrogant dark head in interrogative mode. 'So what are *you* doing here?'

Self-conscious pink bloomed in Kerry's cheeks. 'I'm...I'm the castle housekeeper.'

As he received that declaration, black lashes with the exotic density of silk fans almost hit Luciano's hard cheekbones. Grudging appreciation grabbed him. It was perfect. Indeed, he almost congratulated her on making such creative use of his concession that estate employees would be retained until further notice. But if she had *already* rehomed her grandparents in Dublin, what was her game plan? She had to have an ulterior motive and a strategy in mind. Exactly what could Kerry hope to achieve by pretending to be his housekeeper?

Proximity. As Machiavellian designs came as naturally to Luciano as the art of breathing, he was quick to decide that her most likely objective was…*him*. Here he was, her former fiancé, now in possession of loads of cash and her ancestral home. So what if he was an ex-con deemed to have played away with her stepsister? Needs must when the devil rides…hadn't that once been one of Kerry's cute little sayings? She could only have assumed the role of housekeeper in the hope of catching him in a weak moment and marrying him. Forewarned of that fell motive, Luciano squared his broad shoulders, wide, sensual mouth curling. He would go to his grave before he caught wedding fever in her vicinity again.

In the buzzing silence, Kerry closed her restive hands together. She could only hate him for the sheer cruelty with which her grandparents had been stripped of their possessions. Unfortunately, hatred was not an emotion she could afford to luxuriate in or risk showing him. At most she had six to eight weeks before her grandparents would have to return from Dublin. In that time, Luciano would decide whether to sell on the castle or to put it to some other use. If she was lucky, he would continue to employ her in some capacity and she would be able to share her accommodation with the older couple.

Luciano gazed down at her with gleaming dark golden eyes. 'And what do your duties as a housekeeper entail?'

Bright turquoise eyes carefully veiled, Kerry tilted her chin. 'You're the boss...you tell me.'

'You can start by showing me to the main bedroom.'

'It's in the tower but, although my grandfather used it, I don't think it's suitable for—'

'Then the tower is where I want to be.' Luciano moved fast to crush any suggestion that he would settle for anything less than an O'Brien born to the privilege.

Kerry compressed her lush mouth and opened the door that closed off the spiral stone staircase and kept the worst of the cold draughts out of the rest of the castle. If he wanted to bath in lake water in Ballybawn's very oldest bath and freeze, that was his business. Or was it? Did she want him to be uncomfortable at Ballybawn? Her own best hopes depended on him retaining ownership.

'It's quite cold in the tower. My grandparents liked it that way. Grandpa thought it was healthier,' she admitted uneasily.

'I'll survive.' At the very top of the stone staircase that climbed four floors, Luciano strode past her into the mediaeval pannelled room which had a shabby four-poster bed as a centrepiece. A wonderful barrel-vaulted wooden ceiling soared above and he was impressed. The narrow casement windows gave a spectacular view of the rolling wooded hills backed by the distant blue mountains.

Folding her arms, her slim body taut, Kerry studied him while he stood there. Light gleamed over his cropped black hair and delineated the hard, bronzed lines of his classic profile. His sleek leather designer jacket moulded his muscular physique with the same fidelity as the denim jeans that hugged his lean hips and long, powerful thighs. Something hot and forbidden curled low in her tummy, tensing her up even more. In punishment for her own weakness, she dug her fingernails hard into the tender skin of her elbows.

Aware of her watching him with the fine-tuned senses that made him the very dangerous enemy that he was, Luciano pictured her sprawled naked across the bed. In his imagination, he saw her clear as day: glorious hair flaming in contrast against the simple white quilt, small, pouting breasts, pale, perfect limbs. Before he could dredge himself back out of that erotic daydream, the damage was done. His body clenched hard in urgent sexual response, and all the volatile impatience that lay at the heart of his forceful character surged to the fore.

'I still want you,' Luciano confessed without hesitation, ebony lashes low over the smouldering golden onslaught of his challenging gaze. 'And you want me just as much. Let's ditch the flirtatious foreplay and just go to bed.'

For the count of ten endless seconds, Kerry stared back at him with wide, disconcerted eyes and parted lips from which no sound emerged. He still *wanted* her? Even now, he could find her attractive? That startling revelation sliced right through Kerry's every defence. Immediately she felt different about that kiss at his office. If that had been prompted by a passionate impulse rather than a desire to humiliate her...what? *What?* There her disturbing thought-train screeched to a guilty, confused halt. How on earth could she be allowing herself even to think about Luciano in such intimate terms again?

'Time feels very precious to me right now. I intend to live every moment,' Luciano confided huskily, shrugging free of his jacket and tossing it in a careless, graceful movement onto a chair. 'Live it *with* me.'

He was the very last word in smooth and cool and he had been born knowing all the best lines, Kerry thought with angry pain. He might still be so heartbreakingly gorgeous that he could dazzle her but she now had the distinct advantage of knowing what a cruel and ruthless bastard he was at heart. He was the male who in the wake of the repossession order had allowed a valuer to come in to lay claim to the few saleable items that still remained in the castle...*everything*, from furniture right down to the family portraits, her grandfather's beloved books and even her grandmother's pathetic collection of damaged Chinese porcelain.

'I really can't believe you're talking to me like this after what you've done to my family over the last few weeks,' Kerry condemned unevenly, her face firing with colour when she found herself still having to fight to drag her attention from the magnetic lure of his gaze.

Luciano gave a slight wince that implied that she had clumsily touched on an indelicate subject. 'Debts have to be settled.'

'Yeah...*right*,' Kerry conceded on a rising note of helpless bitterness. 'So Grandpa was conned into acting like an old-fashioned gentleman and agreeing to a voluntary arrangement with your representative to meet those debts. Then, guess what? The valuer decides that Ballybawn is a tumbledown white elephant and undervalues it, so that even *after* you get the castle Grandpa *still* owes you money—'

'What are you talking about?' Luciano cut in.

'You've stripped my grandparents of everything but the clothes on their backs. You've got a few sticks of furniture, books, some paintings…maybe I could accept that if you were broke, but when you're filthy rich you've got no excuse to be that stingy and greedy!' Kerry slammed back at him in seething accusation.

Beneath that hail of abuse, angry colour burnished Luciano's proud cheekbones. Having taken no interest whatsoever in the finer points of how that debt was discharged, he had had no idea that his legal team had been quite that efficient, but he was damned if he was about to apologise or show the smallest sign of regret.

'I was fleeced by you and your family for four and a half years…did you or your grandparents ever lose any sleep over that fact?' Luciano enquired grittily.

In frustration, Kerry moved forward. 'I keep on *telling* you that I didn't know the loan repayments weren't being made—'

'Did it once occur to you that when I gave you that loan I was surrendering *my* dream of buying a vineyard in my own country? Or that, back then, I lent what was a lot of money on my terms…and a considerable sacrifice?' Luciano launched with raw force, hard, dark golden eyes scorching her with his contempt. 'No, it didn't, did it? In fact, you didn't even care enough to ensure that a loan made purely for *your* benefit was utilised or even repaid in a businesslike manner!'

The blood had drained from Kerry's fair complexion.

Genuine dismay had seized her but resentment soon followed in its wake. He had had a dream of buying a vineyard in Italy? It was the first she'd heard of that ambition! Why had he not shared that with her while they were engaged? Even worse, why was she only now being told that the wretched money had constituted a far greater proportion of what he had had then than she could ever have appreciated? Indeed, why had he offered the loan in the first place? That grand and generous gesture had been typical of Luciano's macho style but his silence on the true costs had been equally so.

'If you'd been more frank with me at the time, I wouldn't have allowed you to give Grandpa that money...I mean, it wasn't like anyone asked you to do it,' Kerry framed jaggedly. 'I understand your anger but—'

Luciano sent her a burning look of outrage. '*Accidenti*...how could *you* understand my anger?' he demanded, blazing dark fury flaring in his lean, strong face. 'Especially when I realised that you weren't *worth* the sacrifice!'

'Luciano...' Kerry forced out his name from bloodless lips, her throat convulsing and dry as a bone. 'Don't say that—'

'You were *useless* in every way that mattered!' Luciano derided with harsh emphasis. 'You had no loyalty and even less faith in me. You weren't even woman enough to share my bed—'

Kerry flinched. She was trembling, feeling sick, only standing her ground out of pride.

'*I* made all the allowances, *I* did all the giving, and at the end of the day you still let me down. You let a woolly-headed old man play ducks and drakes with my money...the final insult for me has to be the sight of that bloody big tarpaulin on the roof!'

At that, even though his attack had ripped her apart inside herself, Kerry pushed her head up high again. 'That woolly-headed old man is the same man that you *chose* to give your money to—'

'I expected to be around while it was being spent!'

'The roof on the tower and the roof over about half of the Georgian wing *were* replaced but there wasn't enough cash to do more than running repairs on the rest. Re-roofing an historic building is horribly expensive, so before you accuse anyone of inappropriate use of that loan I suggest you check out the actual cost of the work that was done.' Her narrow back ramrod straight, Kerry urged her wobbling legs to carry her out onto the landing. 'I'm going downstairs to make dinner.'

'Don't bother...I'll see to myself,' Luciano groaned, striving not to let his brooding gaze linger on her pale, clenched profile. He did not feel quite so good about hurting her as he had believed he would.

Too raw not to suspect his true meaning, Kerry had to resist a childish need to assure him that she was now a very efficient cook capable of catering to quite large parties. With that appalling word, 'useless', still ringing a cruel and savage indictment in her ears, she went down to the kitchen. No loyalty, no faith in him. Such charges struck at the very heart of all that she respected.

What faith had Luciano expected her to demonstrate in him after she had discovered that he had *lied* to her about being at Heathlands with Rochelle that night? What loyalty had he sought to encourage when he had accepted the return of her engagement ring with anger but *without* a single word of argument? And not once had he contacted her after his arrest, not once had he made a single tiny move that might have suggested that he ever wanted to lay eyes on her again for any reason!

In every way, Kerry had interpreted his behaviour and his silence as that of a guilty man: a male who knew he'd been unfaithful and could not be bothered protesting otherwise, a male facing serious criminal charges for embezzling from her father's business, who saw no point in trying to retain contact with Harold Linwood's daughter.

But what if Luciano was telling her the truth? What if he had not betrayed her with Rochelle and was indeed the victim of a legal miscarriage of justice? Succumbing to the gathering force of her own turmoil, Kerry chopped fresh herbs to a consistency finer than dust. *Yes,* she finally conceded with raging, hurting bitterness, Luciano's behaviour towards her after his arrest could be seen in a different light. He was arrogant, proud and as stubborn as a pig. When he believed he was in the right he did not compromise, he just dug his heels in harder. The challenge of owning up to actually needing someone whom he believed had wronged him could very easily have come between Luciano da Valenza and his wits. But in those circumstances that would not be *her* fault, would it be? A ballooning tightness clogged up her throat.

'Not even woman enough to share my bed'? That had been the lowest of attacks, she thought with pained bitterness.

Between the ages of ten and fifteen, Kerry had been

forced to listen to regular references to what a promiscuous tramp her own mother had been. Carrie had had at least three affairs during her stormy marriage to Harold Linwood and her father had never come to terms with the embarrassment his feckless first wife had inflicted on him. Nor had he ever been able to hide his fear that promiscuity might be hereditary and that Kerry would turn out to be man-mad too. Even her stepmother had enjoyed voicing stinging little barbs that emphasised her own superiority over her predecessor as both wife and parent, and Rochelle had reaped immense entertainment from telling all her schoolfriends that the mother who had deserted Kerry had been a nymphomaniac. Made to live with the degrading shame of Carrie's mistakes as though they had been her own, Kerry had promised herself that she would never give anybody reason or excuse to talk about her in similiar terms.

As a teenager she had been very shy and she had only had a couple of boyfriends before she met Luciano. Saying no to sex had never been a challenge. Indeed, until Luciano came into her life temptation had not even touched her. But the instant she experienced that reckless, dangerous desire to just let him do whatever he wanted to do with her terrifyingly willing body, all those years of cautious preconditioning had exercised their effect. For the first time she had been afraid that maybe, after all, she might be over-sexed the way her mother appeared to have been and at serious risk of making a total mess of her life. Saying no to Luciano had then acquired all the true fervour of a defensive battle campaign.

But after he had asked her to marry him she had ques-

tioned her own belief that she ought to continue exer-
cising the same restraint until that wedding ring was on
her finger. However, the unhappy truth of Luciano's
prior fling with Rochelle in Italy had then come to light
and put paid to all such self-doubt. Apart from anything
else, Kerry had just wanted to kill him for having a past
that had destroyed her present. Yet since then she had
not once felt a hint of the same crazy, tormenting desire
for any other man.

Miles truly did know her inside out, Kerry conceded
heavily. Humiliating as it was to acknowledge, she *did*
still have far too many powerful feelings for Luciano.
Why else was she allowing his unjust accusations to upset her so much? No, she would not think about that
bold sexual invitation of his, she would not surrender to
the weak, stupid side of her own nature that longed to
believe that she might still mean something to him. Even
as she gave way to that latter thought, she recognised
fearfully that deep down inside herself she had been hiding all along from the awareness that she wanted Luciano back.

She sucked in a steadying breath. Did that mean that
she believed he was telling the truth about not having
slept with Rochelle during their engagement? Or just that
she was willing to believe anything he told her that
might give her an excuse to be with him again? But *was*
he seeing Rochelle again? Or was her stepsister up to
her old tricks? Rochelle would have found out from
Miles that Kerry was over in London seeing Luciano
and her stepbrother. Rochelle's claim that Luciano had
asked her out might well have been a lie that she had
hoped her brother might pass on in all innocence for her.

Angry at the amount of hope that surged through her at that suspicion, Kerry made herself sit down at the kitchen table to work through the remainder of the drawer of unanswered letters which she had abandoned on the dresser almost six weeks earlier. The last thing Luciano needed in his current mood was to come on the actual evidence of her grandfather's indefensible refusal to deal with his own financial problems.

When she came on a larger than average envelope she frowned, for it was addressed to her and *not* to Hunt O'Brien. Why on earth had a letter for her been put away unopened? Possibly, her grandfather had only noticed the English postmark and had assumed it was yet another threatening communication from Luciano's lawyer. Slitting it open, she found another envelope inside directed to 'The Linwood Family' at her father's address in England and an accompanying brief note from her stepmother:

'If you take my advice, you won't follow this enquiry up.'

Curiosity heightened even more, Kerry removed a single sheet of headed notepaper from the second envelope. It was an enquiry from a London solicitors' firm, asking if the Linwood family had any connection to a Caroline or Carrie Linwood, who was also believed to have gone by the surnames of Carlton and Sutton. Kerry's tummy lurched. Was that *her* mother that was being referred to? Who else? Prior to marrying Kerry's father, Carrie had been calling herself Carlton. In fact, Carrie had preferred to use any name, it seemed, other than O'Brien, the one she had been born with.

She knew what the letter meant. Carrie was dead.

What else could it mean? Over four years ago, some solicitor had been trying to locate Carrie's relatives. She scrunched up the letter, pushed it aside with a trembling hand and wished that she had not noticed that the original envelope had been intended for her. Her shaken eyes gritted up with tears. Why had she never tried to trace Carrie? Why had she been so hard and unforgiving? Or was it simply that she been too scared of receiving yet another rejection from the woman who had walked away when she was four years old and never looked back?

As Kerry tried to stifle the sudden gasping sobs that overcame her with her hands, the kitchen door opened.

Luciano strode in, lean, dark features sardonic. 'I can't find an electric socket in the bedroom,' he delivered before he realised that she was in floods of tears.

Kerry dragged in a shuddering breath and dropped her head, hoping that he hadn't noticed. 'There isn't any…there's no electricity upstairs.'

No electricity upstairs. Consumed by total disbelief at that declaration but appreciating that further questioning on that score would seem inappropriate at that moment, Luciano hovered in rare indecision. Obviously, he had *really* upset her. She had always been maddeningly over-sensitive to his habit of straight talking. Did you really need to tell her she was useless? the uneasy voice of conscience asked him. His lithe, powerful frame emanating fierce tension, he approached the table much as if it had been an executioners' block.

'I was in a rough mood…I didn't intend to hurt you,' he stated with a graceful shrug of dismissal, knowing that he was lying, knowing that there was something in him that just wanted to lash out at her every time she came near him.

But that was entirely her fault, not his, Luciano assured himself. Any normal woman who had just looked at him with that amount of sheer physical longing would have hit the bed sheets with alacrity, for he had never subscribed to the belief that women were any less sexual beings than men. It had taken Kerry to make a drama out of his natural male reaction to that unspoken but obvious invitation of hers. And to ignore his proposition. And to duck the challenge of denying that, in spite of her prudish principles and prejudice, she did want him. As Luciano spoke, Kerry was frozen in her seat. He actually thought that *she* was weeping her head off over what *he* had said to her? Flattening her palms to the table, she leapt upright to settle scornful blue eyes on him. 'You don't have the power to hurt me any more!' she slammed back at him. 'I was upset about something private that has nothing to do with you.'

Luciano's furious golden gaze fell on the letter crunched into a telling ball. Without even thinking about it, he reached for it to satisfy his need to know what could possibly be more important than him.

'What do you think you're doing?' Throwing him an angry look of astonishment, Kerry snatched up the letter and dug it into the back pocket of her skirt.

At that point Luciano recognised the smell of charring food and he strode over to the range to look down without surprise at the casserole that had boiled dry and burned into the bargain. It was petty but the discovery that she was still as utterly hopeless at cooking as she had always been gave him a warm sense of consolation and continuity.

As she took in the same view Kerry's soft pink mouth wobbled and then thinned into a tight line of restraint. 'I'll make something else—'

'No, I wouldn't dream of putting you to so much trouble,' Luciano purred.

To her horror, she discovered she just wanted to hit him again. To hit him so hard she knocked him into the middle of next week and closed that smart mouth of his. She had been looking forward to his shock when she presented him with a perfectly cooked meal. Really, she had been very well rid of him, she told herself feverishly. Being married to a guy who could whip up fantastic dishes with the galling, flamboyant expertise of a seasoned chef but who very rarely had the time to do so would have been an endless nerve-racking ordeal.

'I'll eat out,' Luciano continued.

Unable to make even a stab at faking the concern of a housekeeper keen to feed her employer, Kerry jerked a thin shoulder. Had he still to appreciate how remote from civilisation Ballybawn was? There wasn't a restaurant within miles, but he could find that out the way he found out most things: the hard way.

'But before I do that, I'd like to see round the castle,' Luciano concluded.

'It'll be getting dark in an hour—'

'Then we'll use torches...or doesn't Ballybawn have those either?' Luciano countered silkily.

Ten minutes later Luciano was treated to a detailed display of the workings of the Ballybawn water-powered electrical system, which was housed in a lean-to below the trees. Kerry became quite animated as she described her great-grandfather's inventive expertise, while not seeming to notice that he remained distinctly under-whelmed. 'That we produce our own electricity is a very special part of living at Ballybawn,' she completed, pat-ting the ancient, rusting turbine with a fond hand.

'I won't live without electricity,' Luciano said with gentle irony.

'We've *got* electricity…just not upstairs.' Kerry an-gled a reproving glance at him as if electricity at any other level was an outrageous luxury he should be ashamed to even mention. 'And why would you need electricity in a bedroom? Oil lamps have been used at the castle without the slightest inconvenience for well over a hundred years.'

'I have a sneaking fondness for those little switches that magically give light in darkness. I also like to plug in lots of consumer products…cellphone charger, PC, satellite TV, music, digital phone—'

'You can use all those things downstairs. You can use the library as an office,' Kerry told him stubbornly. 'Or even one of the units in the stable yard. Grandpa allowed the yard to be connected to the mains because some of the tenants have to use equipment that consumes a lot of power.'

'Oil lamps are dangerous. I'm very surprised that you haven't had a fire.' Luciano wondered how he had ever convinced himself that she bore not the slightest resem-blance to her scatty grandparents. Only a fanatic would ask him to start using an oil lamp.

Fires littered the history of the castle, and as soon as her grandmother had become a little unsteady on her feet

Kerry had persuaded the older woman to move into a downstairs bedroom. However, nothing would have made her admit that to Luciano. He had owned Ballybawn for less than a day and *already* it seemed he was thinking about making sweeping changes that filled her with dismay and an urgent need to protect the castle's historic heritage.

As the inspection of Ballybawn continued, Luciano just sank deeper and deeper into shock. On his arrival, he had been too preoccupied to pay proper heed to what he was seeing of the castle. Throughout his imprisonment, however, he *had* confidently pictured Kerry living it up at his expense in some grand aristocratic home. For that reason, discovering the harsh reality of her lifestyle truly shattered him. Contemporary living standards had passed Ballybawn by. The O'Briens had existed with the primitive conditions of their ancestors but without the many servants who would have eased the privations of a household that had no labour-saving devices. The only means of heating the huge, cold rooms came from monster fireplaces, and what few electrical fitments he saw ought to have been given museum status and indeed, in his opinion, constituted a serious safety hazard.

Damp and decay were in full control of the wing once inhabited by Great-Uncle Ivor and the door had simply been shut on that part of the castle. While though in a more acceptable condition, the Georgian wing had become the showroom for what he could only have described as the *trompe l'oeil* artist from hell. Grandiose decorating themes that would have been more at home in a Roman villa, or, in one case, the dank tomb of an

Egyptian pharaoh, had turned the gracious rooms into the equivalent of a tacky theme park.

'These rooms are hired out for wedding receptions and private parties. I do the catering for some of the functions.' Kerry was frustrated by his brooding silence, her expectant eyes clinging to his impassive profile. 'Before my friend, Elphie Hewitt, made this her base, the paper was hanging in strips off the walls and there was no decent furniture. Grandpa didn't have the funds to redecorate but now these rooms are habitable again and they *are* better used than left empty.'

Having decided to save the atmospheric and charming heart of the castle to the last, and with the light fading fast, Kerry took him outside again at that point to walk the several hundred yards to the old stable yard. There Luciano gazed without surprise—for he was way way beyond surprise—at the superb architecture of buildings built to last and in infinitely better order than the castle itself. Kerry's ancestors had spent much more on housing their horses than they had on their own home. Without any apparent awareness of the incongruity, she then showed him round a holiday cottage that offered a first-class luxury comparison.

Her enthusiasm and pride in what she was showing him undimmed, Kerry led him back indoors. A parade of sad, shabby rooms followed. Some of the multi-paned windows sported little boards where panes were missing and rickety furniture was propped up on bricks and books. Nowhere could he see anything of any true value: just the obvious spaces and marks on the walls that revealed where pictures had once hung and where pieces of furniture must have stood before being removed to be sold. That she had spent five years struggling to maintain a castle in the midst of such pitiful poverty shook him even more. That she should want to fight to remain within the cold, damp, comfort-free walls struck him as certifiable insanity.

He also saw that she did not see what he saw. Love for her family home had blinded her to defects that screamed at him. He was asked to admire the great hall, which was embellished with collections of strange metal implements hung on wall-grids apparently made of rusty chicken wire, curtains that hung in rags of faded grandeur and a peculiar floral arrangement of weeds.

'That portrait is of Florence O'Brien. She's supposed to be the family ghost,' Kerry informed him with determined cheer.

Almost desperate to find something worthy of the appreciation she seemed to expect, Luciano duly studied the remaining primitive, smoke-stained oil above the massive hearth. He was disappointed yet again, for the canvas featured an unattractive redhead with protuberant, staring eyes which seemed to follow him round the room. He almost quipped that any self-respecting ghost ought to have long since shipped out for more impressive surroundings but thought better of levity. After all, Ballybawn *was* no joke and he did not feel like laughing: he had just been landed with the biggest and most expensive white elephant in the history of the world.

The tour finished in the tower, where he discovered that Kerry was still occupying the bedroom below his.

'I liked to be close to my grandparents in case they needed me,' Kerry muttered awkwardly. 'I'll move out tonight—'

'There's no need to do that.' Luciano expelled his breath in a slow, measured hiss. 'Look, your grandparents can keep all the contents of the castle. I don't want any of this stuff.'

Kerry gave him a surprised, questioning look. 'You... *don't?*'

'No.' As an expression of bemused gratitude covered her delicate features, Luciano was lacerated by raw discomfiture and he swung away in a restless movement to approach the window. Darkness was rolling in fast and the lake was becoming a mere reflective gleam of still water at the foot of the gently sloping hill on which the castle stood.

Even as relief swept through Kerry and she marvelled at his change of heart, she wondered what had brought it about. 'Does that mean that you've already decided what you're going to do with Ballybawn?'

He could set a match to it and put it out of five hundred years of misery, Luciano reflected with a complete lack of humour. He had taken her beloved castle from her and he didn't want it. Nor could he even begin to imagine what he might do with a castle that promised to be a money pit of nightmare proportions. Realistically, he had no need of a home in the Irish countryside and the amount of restoration required would ensure that investment from a business point of view would be wildly unprofitable. Regret was a rare emotion for him and shame rarer still. Yet what possible satisfaction could he receive from an act of revenge that he could only now appreciate had consisted of kicking the unfortunate when they were already literally down and out?

His objectives, Luciano recognised with grim reluc-

tance, had become set in stone while he paced his prison
cell like a caged animal. When he finally won his freedom, he had been too impatient to reconsider those tar-
gets. He had had no idea how impoverished the O'Briens
were. Nor could he ever have dreamt that Kerry and her
grandparents might be living in appalling conditions just
to keep a giant hovel in the family.

But then, if he was honest with himself, it had not
suited his purpose to acknowledge that the older couple
ought to have had their advanced age and needs taken
into compassionate account. He had refused to make a
more personal appraisal of their situation. Determined
not to be deflected from his driving desire to punish
Kerry, he had remained one careful step removed from
the whole unpleasant business of repossessing Ballybawn Castle. Now, he conceded grimly, he was paying
the price for being the ruthless bastard he had always
wanted to be: he was ashamed of himself.

Bewildered by her failure to respond to her question,
Kerry stared at Luciano. Although his back was turned
to her, nothing could have concealed the savage tension
etched in the rigid set of his broad shoulders. He seemed
troubled, angry...or did he? In her experience, Luciano
was outspoken when anything annoyed him. When he
went silent he unnerved her, for she found herself worriedly awaiting a sudden explosion of temperament. Yet
what could he have to be angry about? He had got the
castle, hadn't he? What more could he want?

In an abrupt movement, Luciano turned, golden eyes
glittering below the dense screen of his lashes, lean
strong features taut with indefinable emotion. 'I'm going
out...I don't know when I'll be back.'

As he followed that announcement with immediate action, Kerry was taken by surprise. From the entrance hall, she listened to the telling screech of car tyres quarrelling with gravel as he reversed his sports car at speed and drove off. What on earth was the matter with him? The reproachful eyes of her grandfather's wolfhounds reminded her that she had yet to feed them their third meal of the day.

It was only later while she was making up a fire in Luciano's bedroom that she allowed herself to think again about that disturbing letter relating to her mother. No matter how upsetting it might be to learn how and when Carrie had died, she needed to know the facts for her own peace of mind and, what was more, her grandparents had an even greater right to learn what had happened to their only child. After a snack in place of the ruined evening meal, she sat down to write a reply explaining that she was Carrie's daughter. Afraid that the solicitor might refuse to advance information without further proof of her identity, she enclosed a copy of both her birth certificate and her mother's. Ashamed of the manner in which she found herself listening out every moment for Luciano's return, she climbed into her grandfather's twenty-five-year-old car and drove down to the village to post the letter.

Only when she was getting into bed did it occur to her that she had responded to a letter that had been sent over four years ago as if it had arrived only the day before. She would wait a couple of weeks and if she'd heard nothing from the solicitor she would try phoning the firm. Where had Luciano gone? Why didn't she just face it? Hard as she found it to comprehend, he had

seemed almost impervious to the charm of Ballybawn.
Had he decided to sell the castle? Was that why her
grandparents were now to retain all the contents? Her
heart sank.

Having had to drive a very long way before he finally,
accidentally, came on a bar where only the most basic
of meals was on offer, Luciano returned to Ballybawn.
As it was barely eleven, he was surprised to find only
the light in the entrance hall burning and Kerry nowhere
to be found. Was she out or in bed? The sight and sound
of a triple-decker sandwich of snoring wolfhounds in a
giant, shaggy mat on the tower landing below his suggested that she had retired for the night. Utilising the
torch from his car, he passed on up to his own room,
where a big fire cast leaping shadows on the panelled
walls. He imagined her hauling those logs all the way
up the steep spiral staircase and he grimaced. For a
woman who had done him wrong she had an inspired
grasp of how to make him feel bad.

He explored the *en suite* facilities and all hope of a
shower died fast. History rather than modern plumbing
had triumphed and an ancient discoloured copper bath
tub sat below the stone window. There was no doubt
about it, Luciano decided. An almost biblical amount of
personal suffering and discomfort featured in life at Ballybawn. He turned on a tap and water that had a brackish
green tinge and remained resolutely cold gushed out.
Without hesitation, he headed for the holiday cottage and
its irresistible parade of mod cons. With very little persuasion, he could have stayed the night there glorying
in the joy of unrestricted electricity, but promptings he

was reluctant to examine sent him back to his tower bedroom.

By his bed he found a dog-eared copy of an old guide book about the history of Ballybawn. To remove his mind from the reality that, in spite of the fire, he was cold, he began to read and it was riveting stuff. Buckets of bad luck had pursued the O'Briens from their earliest beginnings, for in every war and rebellion they had supported the losing side. In the seventeenth century, he read that, 'Florrie', Florence O'Brien of the staring eyes, had drowned herself in the lake after finding her bridegroom carousing with her maid and her restless spirit was said to wail in mourning whenever an O'Brien woman was on the brink of marriage.

In the sardonic act of wondering whether or not that little book had been left out quite by accident for his perusal, Luciano flung it aside. He had decided to view his sojourn at Ballybawn as a much-needed period of enforced relaxation in a novel and bracing environment, and in the morning he was calling in every builder, plumber, glazier, roofer and electrician he could find.

It was wonderful what a difference a few hours could make to one's convictions, Luciano mused. His loan to Kerry's grandparents had not been misspent: it had been eaten alive by pressing need. All he had to do was figure out a cool way of backing himself out of the tight corner he had put himself in so that he could give them back the home from hell. Of course, he would have to make at least part of it habitable, not only because it was a crime to put tenants at risk but also for his own occasional visits and comfort. Kerry would be *very* grateful. He would figure as the soul of forgiving generosity.

While he wondered how long it would take him to seduce her into his bed to keep him warm, a noise intruded on his concentration: it was a dog howling. Springing out of bed in exasperation, Luciano strode from his room stark naked to give the dog the benefit of his opinion on baying to the moon. However, having opened the door, he discovered too late that the canine contingent had sneaked up a level and had just been waiting their chance. All three hounds hurtled past him in their frantic eagerness to gain entry to his room. He watched in astonishment as the dogs flopped down on their bellies and shot below the bed at impressive speed.

'You're not staying,' Luciano warned them.

Somewhere in the distance, he heard another, longer bout of that same keening cry and it provoked a chorus of anxious doggy whines in response. It was a woman crying and with such solid walls and doors the sound could only be carrying up to his room through the chimney. Kerry was sobbing her heart out and frightening the dogs.

'I wouldn't give you house room,' he told the spineless animals shivering beneath the four-poster as he pulled on his jeans at speed. 'You're supposed to be guard dogs and you're hiding just because of a stupid echo!'

Heading barefoot down to the floor below and fast chilling in the unbelievably icy temperature of the stairwell, Luciano thrust open the door and strode straight into Kerry's room. It was in darkness but the torch illuminated her bed.

'I can hear you crying...' he murmured with a buoyancy he only just managed to keep out of his voice. 'It's not reasonable to expect me to listen to that and do nothing.'

'Wha…at?' Kerry mumbled sleepily, pushing herself up on one elbow and then squinting against the unkind beam of light engulfing her.

'Don't waste your time trying to convince me that you were asleep, *cara*,' Luciano urged.

'Well, I'm not asleep now because you woke me up,' Kerry answered in bewilderment as she reached for the matches to light the storm lantern by her bed. 'Why did you *do* that?'

Luciano spread wide impatient arms in emphasis. '*Dio mio!* I could hear you crying from the floor above—'

'But I haven't been crying.' What on earth was he doing in her bedroom in the middle of the night? And why was he spouting some cock-and-bull story about having heard her crying when she had been fast asleep?

As the glow from the lantern began to slowly cast dim light, Luciano lowered the torch that had been blinding her. Taken aback to then note that his lithe, lean masculine frame was only clad in jeans, she studied his bare brown torso where lean, corded muscle rippled below smooth, bronzed skin and a riot of short dark curls sprinkled his chest. Involuntarily, her gaze wandered over his sleek, taut midriff and lingered. Suddenly, it was hard to breathe and she could feel her wretched face burning like a bonfire with embarrassment.

'You…were…crying,' Luciano ground out in exasperation, brilliant golden eyes probing her blushing visage for evidence.

'Over you again…I suppose?' Kerry found it almost soothing to recognise that on one level Luciano had not changed a jot: he was the centre of his own world and he had always assumed that he was the centre of hers too.

'I heard you, but if you want to deny it, go ahead. But I would be obliged if you would remove the dogs from under my bed—'

'Sorry…?' Kerry frowned.

'You heard me.' Luciano dealt her a fulminating look before he left the room.

Not content with waking her up, he was now acting as if it was her fault that the dogs were in his room, but he must have *let* them in! Scrambling angrily out of bed and safe in the knowledge that her nightie was about as revealing as a shroud, she sped up the twisting stairwell and stalked into his room.

'*Out!*' she launched at the trio of long, pointed noses peering out guiltily at her from below the high bed. In any other mood, she would have laughed at the picture the dogs made, for Finn, Bab and Conn might be the size of little ponies but they were still only puppies. One by one the littermates emerged, cast a last look of regret at the fire they were used to sleeping beside and slunk out.

'Just keep your door shut,' she advised Luciano sharply, bright blue eyes enhanced by the furious flush on her cheeks. 'And stay on *this* side of it…don't wake me up in the middle of the night with daft stories!'

Aggressive jawline clenched while his brilliant gaze continued to scan the extraordinary voluminous confection of white cotton and lace covering her from throat to toe, Luciano breathed, '*Dio mio!* It was not a daft story. I heard someone sobbing—'

'It's a windy night and the rafters creak and groan.' Now painfully conscious of his wondering appraisal of her antique nightdress, Kerry stiffened, feeling foolish. As she realised that she would have given her right arm to have startled his expectations of her with sexy satin instead, she was so angry with herself for even caring that she added with withering scorn, 'Or maybe our fabled Florrie is haunting you…Florrie's *got* to have it in for unfaithful men!'

That she should throw that same charge at him again sent dark fury hurtling through Luciano. Before she could walk out, he sent the door crashing shut with the heel of his hand. 'Is hit and run all you're good for? Or have you got the backbone to face facts?'

Already regretting having tossed that incendiary final comment, Kerry was disconcerted by his furious reaction and forced to a halt. She folded her arms with a jerk. 'There's nothing wrong with my backbone—'

'But there's a lot wrong with that narrow little mind of yours!' Lean, strong face grim, Luciano's dark golden eyes smouldered over her. 'Do you think if some previous lover of yours had shown up the way Rochelle did when we were engaged that I would have reacted in the same way as *you*? That I would have resented and blamed you for a past encounter that nothing could change? You let her come between us. You encouraged her behaviour by overreacting to her every move—'

'I didn't see you rejecting her!' Kerry accused heatedly, his every censorious word cutting through her defensive barriers.

'I told her to cool it…but, believe it or not, it wasn't a crime for her to speak to me in an office environment.

She likes to play games and you were a very responsive target. The minute she appeared, you started behaving like a jealous kid,' Luciano derided. '*Porca miseria*... our engagement seemed to mean nothing to you. Then you wanted some perfect fantasy guy who had never lived until he'd met you—'

'No, I didn't!' Struggling to control the tempestuous surge of her emotions, Kerry sent him a stark look of reproach. 'I just *needed* to know that you loved me. Without that, I couldn't feel secure and I couldn't believe that you could find me more attractive than her...'

Luciano had stilled and faint perceptible colour had burnished his hard cheekbones. His shimmering golden eyes were no longer seeking to strike aggressive sparks off hers but veiled by his dense black lashes. In the tense silence, he parted his lips as though he was about to say something, then seemed to think better of it and sealed them closed again.

Biting pain scythed through Kerry at the confirmation of what she had long suspected. He had never loved her. He had liked her, perhaps fancied her a certain amount too, but that had been about it. 'Were you really naive enough to think that I would eventually inherit my father's wine stores?'

A preoccupied air about him, his arrogant dark head came up, a questioning frown etched between his winged brows. 'Of course not. When I told your father that I was going to ask you to marry me, he went out of his way to inform me that you wouldn't be featuring much in his will. I was angry that he should imply that I would care either way.' Belated comprehension hardened Luciano's fabulous bone structure, outrage narrowing his gaze. 'Is that what you thought?'

Her eyes fell from his in sudden shame.

His pride was lacerated by that insult to his integrity. 'How stupid can you be?' Luciano demanded. 'I was *so* crazy about you I lost my wits! For what other reason would I have gone looking for a poppy field in which to propose?'

Kerry froze, lifted her lashes, focused on his enraged dark features and had not a doubt in her head that she was hearing the whole, the absolute and ultimate truth: *I was crazy about you.* That declaration rang like a jubilee chorus of bells in her ears, for it freed her from a suspicion that had murdered her self-esteem. In the grip of those heightened emotions, her eyes shining, she moved closer. 'So why couldn't you have told me that then? It would've made such a difference.'

'You shouldn't have needed to be told.' Luciano was furious that temper had betrayed him into making that revealing admission but he was already getting distracted by her proximity. It disturbed him that even in that weird tent thing she was wearing she still looked incredibly feminine, and then his glittering gaze zeroed in on her full, soft mouth and a different kind of tension altogether seized him.

'Were you ashamed of it?' she whispered in confusion.

'What is this? An interrogation?' But Luciano had already lost his angry focus on what for him had been the main issue of his integrity.

'I just want to know…' Kerry collided unwarily with his drugging golden eyes and was caught and held. It was so quiet in the room that all she could hear was the rush of her own breathing and the crackle of the fire in the hearth.

'Know what?' Luciano framed thickly, lifting his hand to let his forefinger trace the voluptuous curve of her lower lip, all recollection of the previous dialogue wiped from a mind taken over by far more primal images.

Although it was the merest, briefest touch, her heartbeat went haywire. Locked into his mesmeric scrutiny, she quivered with the force of the longing that had come out of nowhere and taken her prisoner. Her breasts stirred, the sensitive tips abraded by the coarse cotton of her nightdress, and a dulled ache clenched tight at the very heart of her. The slow, heavy pulse in the atmosphere made the tip of her tongue steal out to moisten her dry lower lip in a nervous flicker.

In one sudden movement, Luciano reached for her, spreading his hands to her narrow ribcage to propel her right off her feet, up into his arms, so that he could bring his hard, hungry lips crashing down on hers. A muffled gasp of shock sounded in her throat but the explosion of inner heat that seized her when his tongue probed the moist recesses of her tender mouth with ruthless masculine expertise only made her cling to his broad shoulders, her head swimming, all awareness of time and place torn from her. When she surfaced from that devastating kiss, Luciano was in the act of tumbling her down on the bed.

Molten golden eyes flaming over her, lean, dark, handsome features taut with desire, he breathed in a roughened undertone, 'Share my bed tonight. Let me make love to you...'

CHAPTER FIVE

IN A daze, Kerry stared up at Luciano with warm, vulnerable eyes. *I was crazy about you.* Like a magic key those words had unleashed a flood of hope and happiness inside her, washed away the bitterness, left her barely knowing whether she was on her head or on her heels.

His wonderful smile sealed that effect. 'Ever since you walked into my office last month, I've been burning for you, *cara mia*,' Luciano admitted.

Deep down inside, Kerry melted like snow in hot sunshine. He came down on the bed beside her and lifted her back into his arms. He made her feel like a doll, for she was awesomely conscious of his strength and masculinity.

'Is that a fact?' she muttered unevenly.

He anchored one hand into her bright fall of curls to tip her head back, and studied her with intense golden eyes. 'I've imagined this so often, I can't believe it's real.'

'It's real…' Gathering her courage, Kerry smoothed her fingertips shyly along the hard plane of one proud cheekbone. Her heart raced so fast at that contact, that sweet freedom to touch again, that she trembled.

'No…you, me and a bed could never feel real,' Luciano quipped, turning his cheek into her palm to catch her forefinger between his lips and suck on it with an erotic intent that startled her even as it sent an equally

surprising little *frisson* of heat feathering through her.
As he took in her widened eyes, he laughed huskily. 'I
do believe I'm going to shock you tonight.'

For Kerry it was as though time had slipped, bringing
back the male without the hard, abrasive edges, the male
who could still be tender. She couldn't take her spell-
bound attention from his lean, strong face; it was as if
that cold indifference might never have been. He pressed
his lips to the tiny pulse flickering like crazy at the base
of her fine collar-bone. He tasted the delicate skin there,
lingered, finding pleasure points she had not known existed, and her head fell back, her whole body thrumming
and almost painfully responsive to his every caress. She
sank her fingers into the luxuriant depths of his black
hair and struggled to breathe.

Cooler air brushed her skin and she tensed as she realised that he had already undone the buttons hidden below the lace on her nightdress. Lifting his tousled dark
head, he took her willing mouth with a raw, passionate
urgency that made her heart race and then he stood her
up between his spread thighs. With sure hands he slid
the nightie from her taut white shoulders. As the heavy
fabric fell in a heap, a tide of colour washed her fair
skin and she crossed her arms over her nudity in instinc-
tive concealment.

'*Per meraviglia...*' His dark deep drawl ragged with
emphasis, he caught her hands in his and parted her
screening arms again. His slumberous golden gaze
roamed over her pale curves with unashamed masculine
appreciation. 'You're my every fantasy.'

'No need to get carried away,' she mumbled.

'I intend to get *very* carried away,' Luciano intoned, tugging her back to him.

He curved his hand to her pouting breasts and watched her jerk against him in quivering response. A whimper of sound broke low in her throat. She pushed her sensitised flesh into his palm, tormented by the throb of her distended nipples. He bent his head there and closed his mouth round a tender pointed bud and her breath rasped in her throat at the sweet gathering torment of sensation beginning to cascade through her. She could feel her own body slipping away from her, eager and wanton, ready to go out of control, and it was almost as scary as it was exhilarating.

'Luciano…' As his handsome dark head lifted and she collided with shimmering golden eyes, she trembled against the hard, muscular wall of his chest. 'Is this going to mean anything to you?'

She heard herself say it even though she didn't want to say it, and then she wanted to die for herself, lose herself in some dark, deep hole where she could convince herself that she hadn't voiced that so obvious and pathetic leading question. The taut silence that followed chipped away at her nerves like a chisel.

His brilliant eyes narrowed. Closing his arms round her again, he swept her off his hard thighs and set her back against the tumbled pillows instead. He smoothed the tangled curls back from her white brow. 'It means more than you would *ever* believe, *cara.*'

Which told her precisely nothing and she knew it, knew it even as he sent a lean brown hand trailing with innate provocation down over her slender thigh to distract her. But she couldn't prevent the leap of her own response any more than she could stop herself from reaching for him and dragging him down to her by his shoulders so that she could clumsily find his beautiful mouth for herself again. And finally she understood what *really* wanting was: all caution, all pride sacrificed in the desperate hope that something better would come of it.

'You're still mine...that's why,' Luciano informed her with scorching assurance as she let him come up for air again, her lips red and moist from the wild hunger of his.

He sprang off the bed in a fluid, graceful movement and arched his narrow hips to unsnap his jeans.

Far too critical of her own flaws to be at ease half-naked, Kerry scrambled beneath the sheet. 'What does being yours...er...entail?'

'Being a total sex slave for my pleasure...' Sheer provocation in his gleaming gaze, Luciano surveyed her with a smouldering satisfaction he made no attempt to hide. 'And not looking away when I take off my jeans...'

An uneasy laugh was dredged from Kerry, for she had been about to do exactly that. She lay there all of a quiver, wicked heat coiled at her feminine core, making her shift against the cool sheet. Suffering from not a single inhibited bone in his magnificent body, he peeled off those jeans with deliberate slowness and he watched her like a hawk. Studying him with an attention that had become distinctly fixed, Kerry tried and failed to suppress her nervous tension, for, while he was gloriously, breathtakingly male, he was also hugely aroused.

He slid into the bed and leant over her with wicked amusement still brimming in his clear dark golden eyes. 'You can scream now if you want to.'

'Stop teasing me…'

'Your innocence is the hottest, sweetest turn-on I've ever had,' Luciano confided, plundering her lush mouth with a hard, deep, explicit kiss that left her reeling. 'Also the biggest threat—'

'Threat?'

'Take my five years of abstinence and your virginity *and*…we'll work it out,' he promised thickly, his hands cupping her hips to bring her into firmer contact with his throbbing sex. 'But I can't promise it won't hurt…a little.'

'Hmm…' Kerry mumbled, only to gasp out loud as he rolled her back from him to explore the straining peaks of her breasts.

Every nerve-ending already primed with anticipation, her body was still supersensitised to his touch. She lay back, wanton with longing, shivers of desire rippling through her, the dulled, tightening ache between her thighs making it impossible for her to stay still. When he burned a passionate trail down over her unbearably tender flesh, a driven little moan parted her lips. Every feeling was intensified. The warm, clean male scent of him flared her nostrils, so familiar even after so long that her very senses rejoiced in him.

Her hands found the corded smoothness of his shoulders and then clutched into his thick hair, her hunger climbing with shameless greed and impatience. She wanted, *needed*…and he knew what she needed. He traced the moist, swollen heart of her and with intoxicating expertise roused her to a fever pitch of desire. She cried out in sensual shock, for the pleasure was mindless and unrelenting, and before very long the surge of her own hunger was more than she could bear.

'Oh...*please*...' she begged, hardly knowing what she was saying, her hips writhing, her whole being pitched on a tormenting edge.

'Want me?' His lean, strong face rigid with the control he was exerting over his own impatience, Luciano gazed down at the hauntingly lovely face that had somehow continually, infuriatingly superimposed itself over every other feminine image he had tried to rouse an interest in. Having her just once would end that, set him free.

'So...much,' she admitted.

Hot, hungry golden eyes locked to her with laser-force intensity. He came over her, spread her slender thighs with precision, took a deep, shuddering breath and plunged into the slick, wet heat of her. An agonised groan of pleasure was wrenched from him.

The sharp stab of pain made Kerry jerk and grit her teeth together. But the wonder of that intimacy, the sensation of him filling her, the wild surge of her own hunger for his driving maleness overwhelmed that discomfort. Instinct made her arch up to him and it was his undoing. What control he had wrested from him by that minor encouragement, he sank into her harder and faster and set a raw pagan rhythm to satisfy his own overriding need. White-hot excitement gripped her. Her heart hammered, her breath emerged in quick, shallow gasps. He drove her to a mindless peak where her body crested and splintered in a dazzling, electrifying charge of fulfilment. As she cried out in ecstasy, his own climax took him in a savage, shattering wave. His powerful body shuddered violently as he poured himself into her.

His first conscious thought was that she had to be the only woman in the world worth waiting five years for. He buried his face in the silky disarray of her hair and drank in the warm intrinsic scent of her and closed both arms round her tight. As she continued to tremble from the effects of her own release, he recognised that he had been very lucky. He had almost blown it but someone somewhere had decided to be merciful and make her wonderfully responsive.

'I never dreamt…it would be like that,' Kerry whispered shakily.

Luciano lifted hands that he noted to his dismay were unsteady and curved them to her flushed cheekbones. He encountered wondering blue eyes. 'It'll be better the next time, *cara mia.*'

While it dawned on him that in his original scheme of things there was not to *be* a next time and he endeavoured to explain his own mental shift in gear, his attention was stolen by the sight of the contraceptives still lying on the chest by the bed. The packet seemed to glint in smug reproach at him. He hadn't used anything to protect her. Startled by that realisation, he tensed.

Kerry wrapped her arms round him and gave a blissful sigh, and he basked in her naive appreciation and shrugged off his concern. Just this one time, this one special time, he had been careless but he wouldn't be again, he told himself. He rolled over, carrying her with him, and draped her over him with care to hold her close.

'I feel sleepy,' she whispered, her face buried in his shoulder, utter contentment embracing her because she knew that she loved him and nothing could have con-

vinced her at that moment that taking a leap of faith had
been wrong.

'No rest for the wicked.' Luciano hauled her up to
him again to ravish her reddened mouth with renewed
hunger. It was just sex, he reminded himself, nothing he
had to make rigid rules about.

In the night he woke up, shaking and perspiring from
the dreams that still taunted him with the knowledge of
how unsafe life could be. As usual, he had believed he
was back in his cell, angry and disturbed voices crying
out in the night, inmates banging on the steel doors,
while he fought the sensation of being trapped and helpless in a nightmare that never quit. But then the peaceful
silence of the room enclosed him. He focused on the
dying glow of the fire and the woman sleeping beside
him and the agonising tension in his muscles eased.

He tugged Kerry closer, and as she gave a drowsy
murmur he kissed her awake. 'I need you,' he breathed
roughly. He despised himself for admitting that but not
enough to deny his sudden, overpowering craving to remind himself all over again that he was free and able to
lose himself in one of life's most primal and basic pleasures.

Even though she was exhausted, Kerry woke up early,
for rising ahead of her grandparents was her usual routine. Luciano had one heavy arm as well as a hair-
roughened thigh draped possessively over her. She was
uncomfortable but tender appreciation softened her eyes
as she looked at him. *At last* he was asleep. She smiled,
for she ached in places she had not known a woman
could ache: he was a wildly insatiable lover. She was
still stunned by the effect of all that pleasure and aston-

ished by the extent of her own abandonment. But she felt no regret, no, not an ounce of regret, for she had been reassured by the undeniable depth of his need for her.

She lay surveying him: the blue-shadowed roughness of his stubborn jawline, the outrageous length of his black lashes that were the only femininising influence in that lean, strong-boned face of his and the bronzed vibrance of his skin tone against the white linen. He was, without a single doubt, absolutely gorgeous. He could also, without a single doubt, have broken that five-year abstinence with some very much more beautiful, sophisticated and experienced woman than she was. But instead he had come back to *her*. That had to mean something. If she still had feelings for him, why shouldn't he still have feelings for her? She had to rise above her own negative habit of thinking too little of herself, she thought fiercely.

Easing inch by careful inch out from beneath Luciano's hold, Kerry crept out of bed. She would make him breakfast. She just had this overpowering need to spoil him. Making do with the very basic bathroom facilities on the ground floor, she then trawled through her sparse and dated wardrobe to find something more presentable to wear than her usual jeans. It was too cold for a dress but the soft blue cotton shift she put on flattered her and she tugged on a cardigan with it.

Luciano wakened in a state of relaxation new to him. He looked for her. She wasn't there. It annoyed him that he should be annoyed that she wasn't there. He hoped she wasn't making him breakfast because he knew he would end up trying to eat it even if it was inedible. His active mind soon switched to planning the future, for the previous night had supplied a very satisfactory framework. To a certain extent, he had misjudged her, he acknowledged grudgingly. Kerry had neither played a part in framing him for the crime for which he had been falsely imprisoned, nor played fast and loose with the money he had given her grandfather. When he still wanted her, why shouldn't he keep her in his life? Why the hell should he make a big deal of that?

It *would* be on his terms: he would spend the occasional weekend at Ballybawn. The hire of a helicopter and a pilot would be essential. As for the castle, he would concentrate on the original and oldest part of the building. Once repairs had been done and he had put in a power shower, a jacuzzi and under-floor heating, it would be an unusual *pied-à-terre* but perfectly acceptable. Of course, he would have to be frank and tell her that marriage wasn't on the cards this time. Whatever, she would not lose by the arrangement. He would turf her friend, the artist with the Egyptian fixation, out of the Georgian wing and have it renovated for her grandparents' occupation. He would also make Kerry his estate manager. He pictured her waiting here for him on Friday evenings…smiling at the door or in the jacuzzi.

Humming under her breath, dogs at her heels, Kerry balanced the tray on her hip and opened the bedroom door. 'I bet you're hungry,' she said chirpily.

'Funnily enough…' As Luciano absorbed her hopeful, brimming smile, he hesitated on the instant negative he was about to utter.

She set a tray on his lap. He stared down at the picture-perfect cooked breakfast in astonishment, for he was convinced that nothing that looked that good could taste bad. 'This is fantastic...'

'A few years back, I did a couple of catering courses,' Kerry confessed with wry amusement. 'At one time I thought of opening a small restaurant here but in the end I appreciated that there wasn't the demand for it.'

'Restaurants are a very high-risk venture,' Luciano murmured approvingly, adding a kitchen to his refurbishment plans as he ate. 'We have to talk.'

Meeting his level dark golden gaze and remembering the night hours that had passed along with the incredible passion, Kerry was consumed by an attack of shyness. 'What about?'

'Us...where we go from here.'

Although she thought it much too soon for any such discussion, Kerry said nothing, for she suspected that Luciano was quite incapable of just letting their relationship drift. He had always liked everything organised, controlled and structured.

Lounging back against the banked-up pillows, Luciano studied her with a quality of cool gravity that made her tense. 'I've got to be honest...I'm not going to marry you—'

'For goodness' sake...' Her fingers clenched convulsively into the over-long sleeves of her cardigan which she had been unconsciously fiddling with and her face flamed. 'Give me some credit. I'm not expecting you to be thinking about marriage right this minute—'

'But that's not what I'm telling you. I'm saying that I'm *never* going to think of marriage,' Luciano delivered steadily. 'I find you very attractive and at this moment

in time I still want you in my life, but we can't go back
to where we once were. That's gone.'

A deep inner quiver had convulsed Kerry's insides.
She could feel the colour and the warmth draining from
her, for when he had said 'never' in that cool tone of
emphasis it sent a chill down her spine. When he felt
the need to impose rigid boundaries within hours of their
new intimacy, it degraded what she had believed they
had shared to the lowest possible physical level.

'Agreed that the past is way back and we're both
bound to have changed…' Valiantly, Kerry swallowed
hard on the thickness in her throat. Broken things could
be fixed and the past could be reclaimed. Didn't he know
that? 'But I don't see why we have to talk about this
now—'

'I don't want any misunderstandings. Come here…'
He stretched out a lean, imperious hand and she was so
tense she had to force herself forward. As her fingers
were engulfed in his, he tugged her down beside him
and anchored one arm round her slight, taut shoulders.
'That's better. I have plans for Ballybawn.'

'Oh…?' She loved him, Kerry reminded herself bracingly, and it was very early days. Naturally, he wasn't
about to plunge right back into where they had been five
years earlier but he might have done her the justice of
appreciating that that had not been her expectation either. Instead, whether he realised it or not, he had made
it sound as though her sole ambition was to marry him.

'I shall renovate it—'

'Restore…the word's restore,' Kerry corrected, trying
to still the little shake in her voice, for she was conced-
ing that she needed to be honest with herself too and

admit that she naturally *did* still want to marry him. She wondered if in some ghastly immature way she had already made the mistake of letting him see just how much he still meant to her. Was that what had inspired his wounding determination to tell her that everything was over before they had even really begun? For wasn't that what he *was* telling her? That their present relationship was a temporary thing that could go no place at all?

There was nothing worthy of restoration in Luciano's opinion but, having breezed past what he had regarded as the most sensitive point without a word of protest from her, he had relaxed. 'I'll make you my estate manager,' he informed her. 'You can bring your grandparents back from Dublin and they can live in the Georgian wing—'

'But my friend, Elphie, is using—'

'I'll make it well worth her while to move out. A few coats of paint and we'll never know she was there in the first place. Once I've had a few improvements made, Hunt and Viola will be very comfortable there.'

'That's a very generous offer.' But Kerry was too agitated to stay seated any longer and she got up to pace away a couple of steps before turning back to look at him. 'We'd be your tenants, then.'

Pure mockery fired Luciano's golden gaze. 'I don't think I'll be regarding *you* in quite that light. You won't be living in the Georgian wing with your grandparents— except of course when I'm not here. But when I am here I'll want you with me in the main part of the castle, which I will restore for *our* benefit.'

In a daze of uncertainty, Kerry stared at him, her heart

beating so fast it felt as if it was at the foot of her throat. 'Are you talking about us…er…living together?'

'No, I'm talking about me flying back here to spend weekends with you…obviously I couldn't make it *every* weekend, though.' Luciano's besetting sin of needing to dot every 'i' and cross every 't' had kicked in.

'I…I see.' And Kerry did see, she truly *did* see, and what she saw made her very much regret spoiling him with breakfast in bed. She would be his mistress, perhaps not even as much: a casual lover for whenever he felt like a country weekend with sex included. She wondered why it had not dawned on him that her grandfather might feel it rather inappropriate to live off the equivalent of what he would see as his granddaughter's wages of sin. How could he think that she would even consider such a demeaning arrangement? How could he have got her so wrong? And what was she planning to do about it?

Her attention fell on the door into the bathroom and lingered while she wondered if he had yet to sample the facilities. 'Let me run you a bath—'

'Forget it…the plumbing is shot. Last night, I used the shower in the holiday cottage—'

'There's nothing wrong with the plumbing. In fact you were depriving yourself of a very special bathing experience.' Kerry let the bathroom door half close behind her and switched on the bath taps, calling, 'You just need to run the water a while.'

When Luciano finally took the bait and pushed open the door to see what she was doing, she was waiting to dart behind him and stretch up on tiptoe to cover his eyes with her spread hands. 'Close your eyes,' she urged in a playful tone.

'Kerry…what the—?'

'You're not allowed to look,' she murmured sweetly.

His imagination racing straight to an erotic interpretation of that declaration, Luciano smiled and allowed her to turn him round and back him until his thighs brushed the edge of the bath. Without hesitation, Kerry then planted her palms on his muscular chest and thrust with all her might to off-balance him.

Taken entirely by surprise, Luciano could find nothing to grip to regain his balance and he went backwards into the copper tub with a gigantic splash. As he vented a savage expletive at the sheer shock of the freezing cold water and his eyes shot open in disbelief, he found Kerry staring down at him with a look of scornful satisfaction in her gaze.

'Another Ballybawn invention, Luciano. The water is pumped up from the lake. My great-grandfather firmly believed that his longevity derived from his daily refreshing dip in lake water. Unfortunately since then the pipes have silted up a little but, to be frank, you deserve to bath with pond-scum!'

'*Santo cielo!*' Luciano heaved himself up out of the slimy green water with a shudder for if there was one thing he could not bear it was to be less than clean. 'If you think *this* is funny—'

'It wasn't meant to be.' There was fierce condemnation in Kerry's eyes. 'It was my answer to the kind of relationship that you just had the cheek to offer me! How could you try to use my attachment to my grandparents and what used to be their home as a means of persuasion? You're wasting your time because I won't ever sink so low that I become some woman you sleep with when you feel like it—'

'That was *not* what I suggested!' Luciano launched back at her in a blistering rage as he snatched at a towel to wind it round his magnificent bronzed length. 'Whether I like it or not, your grandparents are involved in what happens between us and the onus is on me to make some provision for them—'

'Having evicted them, your sudden concern for them comes rather late in the day!'

'Don't let your pride come between you and your common sense.' Brilliant golden eyes hard, Luciano made that warning with icy clarity. 'You won't get a better offer than the one I've just put on the table.'

'But I'm not up for grabs or offers,' Kerry proclaimed with furious distaste. 'Last night was a mutual mistake. So, you decide what you want to do with Ballybawn and leave me out of it. Right now, I just work here!'

'Is that a fact? If you *just* worked here by now I would've sacked you for screaming at me like a shrew, so don't attempt to hide behind that cop-out!'

'Oh, so you would have sacked me…you never could stand the smallest criticism,' Kerry could not resist asserting, watching him go rigid at that less than tactful reminder. 'But you're great with the threats. Only you're wasting your time threatening me because I've already lived through the *worst* you can do—'

'Kerry—' In the act of fighting an angry desire to carry her bodily back to bed solely in the hope of silencing her, Luciano snatched in a deep restraining breath.

'—the day Grandpa came out of that court room humiliated and ashamed of the level debt had sunk him to! You could afford to show compassion. That you didn't should have been my warning. But one way or another, *I* will look after my grandparents and I don't need you to do it for me.'

Angry that his generous attempt to make amends had been tossed back in his teeth, Luciano dealt her a cool appraisal. 'To date, you haven't contrived to look after them very well, have you?' he pointed out drily.

At that crack, Kerry turned white. 'You have a point. Obviously I was wrong to respect Grandpa's right to be treated as if he could manage his own affairs.' Spinning on her heel, her eyes filled with guilty conflict, she paused halfway across the bedroom to pick up the breakfast tray. 'By the way, there's a half-bath in the cloakroom on the ground floor. From now on, please just treat me like a housekeeper—'

'*Per meraviglia!* You can't act as though last night never happened—'

'Oh, I won't do that,' Kerry countered tightly. 'I'll just remind myself that you're not the guy I once thought you were and I don't think I'll be tempted to cross the boundary lines again.'

As the door shut in her wake, Luciano swore with savage frustration. He had been too honest with her and he had hurt her pride, but he refused to lie and it *would* have been a lie to pretend that the clock could be turned back. He would never forgive her for her lack of faith in him five years earlier.

But even as he reminded himself of that truth, he also found himself wondering for the first time whether he might have expected too much from her. She had only been twenty-one, unsure of herself and, in spite of their engagement, a lot less certain of him than he had ever appreciated. In fact, he had pretty much ignored her insecurity over Rochelle except when it affected his own comfort. After all, what male did not receive a vicarious thrill from having two attractive women vying for a share of his attention? He winced at that belated moment of truth with himself.

Furthermore, what had been the chances of Kerry crediting that he was innocent of theft when all the Linwoods, including her domineering father and employer, had judged him guilty? Or, perhaps even more to the point, how much loyalty could he have expected her to offer him when she had been deliberately led to believe that he had embarked on a fresh liaison with her stepsister?

Kerry was much too busy to have the time to dwell on her thoughts. With a dozen visitors due to arrive at ten for a tour of the castle followed by morning tea, she had plenty to do. But she felt hollow inside as if Luciano had ripped everything out and thrown it away. Wishful thinking had blinded her to the passage of time and the intrinsic complexity of the male she was dealing with. When had she allowed herself to forget Luciano's cold, contemptuous attitude towards her in London?

Five years ago she had misjudged Luciano, and last night he had taken her virginity before suggesting a demeaning joke of a continuing relationship: no commitment, no future, only humiliating dependency while he controlled virtually every aspect of her life. She tried to imagine living at Ballybawn, working for him, reliant on his goodwill but also sharing his bed when he was in

Ireland. Agonised but angry hurt cut through Kerry, because he could not have made a more offensive offer had he tried. It would just be a convenient arrangement for casual sex. Scarcely a proposition likely to appeal to a woman who had once hoped to marry him. Yet again, Kerry was being forced to face the reality that Luciano was still very, very angry with her and now she was also realising that he might well be set on levelling the score. That he had just succeeded beyond his wildest dreams was a truth that she hoped to have the strength to keep to herself.

An hour later, sluiced clean of lake water but still unamused by the recollection, Luciano discovered that he could not even charge his laptop in the library because the lead would not plug into the elderly electrical socket. He was in the act of turning the air blue with Italian invective when he glanced up and froze in astonishment at the sight of the crowd of strangers watching him from the doorway.

Kerry stepped forward. 'This is Mr da Valenza, the new owner of Ballybawn Castle.'

She had brought in a bunch of tourists to gape at him as if he were a zoo animal! He couldn't believe she was doing that to him! What was more, Luciano recognised with raw incredulity, the visitors were awarding him a concerted look of disapproval as if nobody other than an O'Brien had the right to own the castle. Much as if he had not been there, Kerry went on to talk about the woodcarver responsible for the bookshelves and draw attention to the superb plasterwork ceiling before leading the group out again. Luciano frowned as he studied the same shelving and ceiling, noting for the first time and with some surprise that, although in need of professional attention, both were indeed worthy of note.

Kerry only breathed again when she was back in the corridor. At their entry, Luciano had looked up, lean, dark, handsome features impatient, golden eyes bright with annoyance below black spiky lashes. Her heart had jumped as though he had squeezed it, and so powerful and instantaneous had been the surge of tormented longing inside her that she had felt dizzy. In remembrance, she trembled and almost lost the thread of her speech in the next room. A little subconscious voice that she would have done anything to silence whispered that perhaps she had been too hasty in rejecting his proposition. How, after all, did she attach conditions when she had given herself so freely only hours before? But if Luciano could not even leave the vague possibility of a future open, what point was there in risking such hurt again?

But wasn't she already hurt? To be plunged from happiness back down into despair and regret and self-loathing again? Last night she had not required reassurance, for she had believed in her heart that Luciano was on the way back to being hers again. How much more gullible could a woman be? To place sexual desire on a level with caring? To ignore the obvious fact that what she had once withheld, he had smoothly persuaded her to surrender?

Yet hadn't Luciano also said that the onus was on him to make provision for her grandparents? A statement that suggested he had rethought his attitude towards the O'Briens. Ought she to dismiss out of hand an arrangement that would allow the older couple to return to their home and live there in comfort? But then even had she wished to accept that offer, it would be an impossible situation. No way could she openly live with Luciano in her grandparents' vicinity!

Having watched the minibus of tourists depart, Luciano went off in search of Kerry. She was not in the kitchen. But as he turned to leave again, he noticed a familiar crumpled sheet of notepaper lying on the tall dresser. He was going to look, he *knew* he was going to look. Telling himself that nobody left really private correspondence lying around, he studied the letter that Kerry had been crying over the day before. His wide, sensual mouth compressed.

Kerry walked in and stopped dead at the sight of him. 'I suppose you're about to complain about the tour but you did say that business-related ventures should continue here—'

'When did the letter about your mother arrive? Yesterday?' Luciano cut in.

'Didn't you even think twice about reading it?' Kerry swept up the letter and added it to the box of correspondence she had been sorting out for her grandfather.

'I wanted to know why you were upset.' Luciano rested his gleaming golden gaze on her in level challenge. 'I'm sorry you got the news like that.'

'You think it means that she's dead too…?'

Luciano nodded his head in reluctant confirmation and watched her bright head lower to hide the pain and disappointment in her expressive face.

'I used to think that no news might well be good news where your mother was concerned,' Luciano confided bluntly.

'That's an awful thing to say…' Tears pricking the

backs of her eyes, Kerry spun away. 'Just because your mother kept you and raised you in spite of everyone's disapproval!'

Yet even as she upbraided him, Kerry was unhappily aware that her fond childhood fantasies of a loving mother returning to reclaim her had not survived what she had learnt about Carrie as she grew older. Her mother had been an only child and very much loved but almost from the moment she had become a teenager she had gone off the rails and had brought her parents nothing but grief. She had been expelled from several schools. There had been a scandalous hushed-up affair with a married man and a miscarriage as a result of it. At the age of eighteen, Carrie had left home without a word of warning and it had been more than ten years before she came back again.

'Your mother, Carrie, has considerable charm,' Hunt O'Brien had once told Kerry with great sadness. 'But regardless of who is hurt, she will always do exactly as she wants and what she wants changes with the wind. As she won't consider how her actions affect others, she can be very destructive towards herself and towards those who try to depend on her.'

Not a young woman likely to miss the burden of a child once she had become a divorcee, not a woman likely to agonise much over her own failings or indeed those she left behind, but a woman who lived for the day and the hour and her own self.

'But then *my* mother was excessively fond of babies and small animals. No puppy or kitten was ever turned from the door and I fell very much into the same category,' Luciano countered, forcing Kerry out of her self-

preoccupation as he drew her back against his lithe, muscular frame with confident hands. 'She accepted her lot
in life because she was very humble. When my father
set dogs on me, she was more shocked that I had *dared*
to approach him.'

Kerry's eyes widened to their fullest extent and she
flipped round to look up at him. 'Your father set *dogs*
on you?'

'They chased me…they didn't bite,' Luciano extended, seeking to make light of an event he had not
intended to share.

'I don't care…how did it happen?' Kerry prompted
fiercely.

'At school, I was taunted for being the good count's
little embarrassing mistake: he got drunk one night and
honoured my seventeen-year-old mother with his atten-
tions. When I was eight, I began hanging around outside
the walls of his villa and I was soon peering over them,
hoping to see him. My grandfather died and one day
inevitably I went over the wall…and the rest as they
say…is history,' Luciano concluded with a look of
mockery that in no way matched the roughened edge
that had entered his deep, rich drawl.

'What happened?' Her blue eyes were soft. 'Stop being macho about it.'

'Tessari was in his garden and I went right up to him
and asked him if he was my father. He panicked, denied
it and put his dogs on me to get rid of me…' His aggressive jawline clenched, golden eyes darkening and
hardening. 'The next day, my mother was told to leave
our home on the Contarini estate—'

'Oh, no, that was wicked!' Kerry exclaimed.

'My father was afraid of a scandal that might embarrass his lady wife and himself and, since giving my mother financial help would've been seen as an acknowledgement of paternity, he was careful from the day of my birth to keep his hands firmly in his pockets,' Luciano told her with a raw derision that made her flinch. 'We moved to the city, where we almost starved until my mother found work.'

Some of his history she had known but she had not heard it from him. She had read a more sensationalised account of his background in a newspaper a couple of years earlier and she had marvelled then at how much he had contrived *not* to tell her even when she had been engaged to him.

'Why did you never tell me who your father was and what he did to your mother and you?' she asked, her regret on that score unconcealed.

'Because Roberto Tessari wasn't my father in any way that I could respect. He was a hypocrite and a coward—'

'But he *did* help you to fight to prove your innocence after you were imprisoned,' Kerry reminded him gently.

'Guilt…the fact that fate laughed in his face and he never had another child…the need of a dying man to make peace with his maker…who knows?' Luciano shrugged, chilling indifference etched in his bronzed features. 'My mother was only thirty-three when she died from pneumonia. She was never strong but to keep us she had to clean houses and take in washing. Roberto Tessari trashed her life. Do you think I could ever forget that?'

'No…I suppose not,' Kerry conceded in a rather wob-

bly undertone, her throat convulsing because she ached
for the pain that he was so determined to hide from her.

'I've depressed you so much you're crying—'

'No, of course you haven't and I'm *not*—'

'Finally…you're crying over me, *bella mia*.' Luciano
awarded her a brilliant smile of approval. 'And all I had
to do was tell a sob story and touch your heart.'

Even as Kerry recognised the skill and determination
with which he cast off unhappy memories and centred
all attention back on to her, her mouth ran dry in receipt
of the megawatt effect of that wickedly attractive grin.
The hands he had loosely linked behind her slid down
to her hips and curved her into connection with his lean,
hard physique.

Her breath caught in her throat while intelligence
urged her to retreat. In defiance of that awareness, she
wanted him just to grab her and kiss her: that way she
wouldn't have to think about what she was doing. But
Luciano had never made things that easy. Glittering
golden eyes held hers in thrall. Her heart rate speeded
up, constricting her breathing. A *frisson* of heat curled
like a cruel betrayer in the pit of her stomach before
settling into a dulled, throbbing ache between her thighs.

'Touch your heart *and*…?' Luciano teased with
husky, knowing intimacy, tipping her forward a little
more, long fingers flirting in provocation with the hem
of the dress that had ridden up the backs of her slender
thighs. 'Isn't self-denial painful?'

Helplessly, controlled by the fierce yearning of her
own body, Kerry leant into him. She was wildly aware
of every hard, sexy angle of his big, powerful frame
against hers. Tiny little tremors of desire slivered

through her. It was a revelation to her that even after the night that had passed he could still make her feel like that. 'Kiss me…' she muttered, her fingers spearing up into the black depths of his hair.

'I couldn't possibly make a move on my house-keeper.' Brilliant dark golden eyes struck hers in ruthless challenge. 'On the other hand, if you're my lover…'

Rage, longing and wonderment engulfed Kerry all at once. At such a moment, only Luciano would have tried to exploit her weakness with calculated cunning. In response, she put into practice what he himself had taught her. On tiptoe to overcome the disparity in their heights, she pressed her lips to the wide, sensual curve of his firm male mouth and with the tip of her tongue conducted a more intimate exploration. The fractured hiss of his breathing and the raw tension tautening his muscular length against her were her reward.

'I created a witch last night,' Luciano growled in roughened acknowledgement of his own error.

He banded strong hands to her hips and lifted her up to him so that he could devour her lush mouth, over and over and over again with explicit, hungry demand. The plunge of his tongue between her lips set Kerry on fire with excitement. She couldn't think, she couldn't breathe, couldn't get enough of his passion. With a muffled groan, he anchored her legs round his waist and lowered her down onto the edge of the table. In that position, she was agonisingly aware of the hard thrust of his arousal and every pulse in her entire body jumped with frantic energy until her own fevered craving became more than she could bear.

'Luciano—'

'Not here…not like this,' he muttered thickly.

Acting on instinct, Kerry rocked forward into needy contact with his bold erection.

Surprise and appreciation shimmered in Luciano's hot, hungry gaze and suddenly he no longer wanted to wait for the comfort of a bed. The depth of her desire excited him. She wanted him the way he had always wanted her to want him: without defence or conditions. He hauled her back to him.

'I just want you…' she heard herself confess shakily, possessed by the fierce need driving her but unnerved too by her inability to fight it.

'How much?' he prompted, sliding up her dress and hooking his fingers into the band of her cotton briefs.

'You're driving me crazy—'

'And making you reckless. I like that…I *really* like that, *bella mia*,' Luciano admitted, sexily grazing the delicate skin of her throat with his teeth and sending such a powerful surge of heat to the moist heart of her that she whimpered out loud.

The complete and glorious havoc that he could wreak with his mouth and his hands deprived Kerry of any true grasp of the sequence of events over the next few minutes. The belated awareness that she was half-naked beneath her dress startled her but she was way out of control by then and pitched to a wild high of anticipation. When he pulled her to him and entered her hard and fast, the sensation was so intense, so exquisite, she wanted the moment to last forever until he withdrew and surged into her again with renewed force and it was even more sublime. She cried out, lost in him, drowning in the fierce passion of his dominance. He sank his hands below her hips to deepen his penetration. As he slammed into her damp inner sheath, her raw excitement reacted with the explosive heat coiled at her inner core and pitched her into a shattering climax. In the heaving, gasping aftermath while she still clung to him, the sound of his cellphone ringing was a piercing intrusion.

'It might be something important,' Luciano finally groaned, retaining a possessive hold on her as he answered the call.

Still in a daze, Kerry pressed her hot face into his shoulder until she heard his caller speak as clearly as if she had been standing in the same room.

'Are you missing me yet?' a woman asked in a teasing tone of intimacy.

It was her stepsister's voice, unmistakably Rochelle in seduction mode, Kerry registered with sick distaste. Detaching herself from Luciano in one sudden movement, she jumped down off the table. She almost cringed at the sight of her discarded panties lying on the floor and walked past them on unsteady legs. The madness of passion had evaporated to leave Kerry reeling in shock and shame at her own behaviour. She had thrown herself at Luciano, encouraged him every step of the way. What had happened to her proud boast that she would not be a woman whom he slept with when he felt like it? It was sheer insanity to get involved with a male still in regular contact with her stepsister. No way was she lowering herself back into some degrading competition for Luciano's attention!

Only minutes later, Luciano strode into the great hall, where Kerry was clearing away the evidence of the morning tea she had served there earlier. Her every tiny movement made her shamefully conscious of her partial nudity below her dress and she could barely muster the courage to look up when she heard his entrance.

Lean, bronzed features hard, Luciano came to a halt. 'Don't do this to me again,' he breathed impatiently. 'Surprise me...don't say a single word about Rochelle phoning me.'

Kerry had nothing to say. If he was expecting a jealous fit, he was in for a disappointment. That Rochelle was still confident enough to purr down the phone to him like a lover hurt and humiliated Kerry. But she had also decided that she had been lucky to receive that wake-up call to her own wits. Why was she allowing Luciano to make a fool of her? Within twenty-four hours he had contrived to devastate her faith in her own intelligence.

'OK, never let it be said that I can't take a hint,' Luciano drawled with sardonic bite. 'So we just had casual sex again—'

Kerry shot him a stricken appraisal. 'I don't *do* that sort of thing—'

'You just *did*,' Luciano contradicted in a wrathful undertone. 'You let me screw you on the kitchen table. Isn't it time you dropped the prudish euphemisms?'

As hot colour stained her fair complexion, Kerry tore her shaken attention from the threat of his glittering gaze. 'I won't...I *can't* discuss this with you.'

'Yet you just had sex with me—'

'Will you stop talking to me like that?' Angry mortification and a sense of being out of her depth lent Kerry's voice a shrill edge that made her flinch. 'For goodness' sake, I'm supposed to be *working* for you—'

'That was work? Your eagerness to meet my every need goes way beyond the average employee's commitment,' Luciano derided. 'But whatever turns you on… I'll have lunch at one and dinner at seven. I'd also like a list of the most reliable local builders a.s.a.p.'

'Builders?' Glancing up in surprise, Kerry collided unwarily with sizzling dark golden eyes that made her mouth run dry. 'But why?'

'If you're playing housekeeper, act like one,' Luciano suggested drily. 'Questions of that nature fall into the impertinent category.'

Reddened mouth compressed, Kerry carried her laden tray past him. 'As does your familiarity…so keep your hands to yourself from now on.'

Luciano almost smiled at that sally. He was very confident that within a very short time he would be enjoying exactly the kind of lifestyle with Kerry that he had envisaged. She couldn't resist him. Passion had triumphed in the kitchen. Her resistance was crumbling and his terms *were* attainable. In the meantime, he would forge ahead with his renovation plans for the castle to demonstrate that what he had promised to do, he would do to the letter.

One week later, Ballybawn was surrounded by newly erected scaffolding and workmen were busy both indoors and out. Kerry helped her friend, Elphie, to pack the last of her possessions from the Georgian wing into the van that the other woman had hired for the occasion.

'I'm looking forward to moving into my new showroom this weekend,' Elphie said cheerfully. 'Did I tell you what a prime location it's in? Luciano has been very generous. I'd have moved out for a lot less compensation than he's giving me!'

'I'm just glad you're not upset about having to move at such short notice—'

'I'm convinced that I'll do better business in the town. My father is even more pleased that his tenancy agreement for the farm has been renewed,' the chirpy brunette confided. 'In fact, from our point of view, Luciano da Valenza just about walks on water. I suppose it's pretty tactless of me to tell you that—'

Kerry forced a smile. 'Not at all—'

'I know how hard it's got to be for you to watch someone who *isn't* an O'Brien rescue Ballybawn. However, any worries I had about your ex-fiancé went the minute I heard the wonderful rumour that your grandparents would be moving back in as tenants!' In the awkward silence that followed, Elphie settled her inquisitive gaze on Kerry's flushed face. 'I heard that Luciano could be planning to resettle them in the Georgian wing—'

'And what if I told you that there were rather more personal strings attached to that possibility?' Kerry was shaken that Luciano could have been so indiscreet and furious that yet more pressure was being put on her.

'If the other end of the string was attached to Luciano... in your place, I'd jump for joy,' the other woman declared with frank amusement. 'He's drop-dead gorgeous and willing to go to enormous lengths to accommodate your grandparents. If you're looking for more than that from a guy you once ditched, you could be waiting a very long time.'

Kerry paled at that blunt appraisal.

Elphie climbed into the van and grimaced. 'I tried to hold that little lecture in but I just *couldn't*. You're breaking your heart over him anyway. What do you have to lose? Are you still speaking to me?'

'Just about,' Kerry breathed before her childhood friend drove off with an airy wave.

Was she so transparent? Kerry had never been the type to confide easily in friends and it embarrassed her that her unhappiness had been noticed. Since the day she had shamed herself by acting like a wanton hussy in the kitchen, it had been surprisingly easy for her to avoid seeing much of Luciano. During the day the castle was swarming with workmen, and the architect in charge of the restoration usually joined Luciano for the lunch that she provided. In the evenings, Luciano had professed a desire to escape the dust and upheaval by going out to eat.

But the very fact that he had actually commenced work on Ballybawn had thrown Kerry into total confusion. Did the arrival of the builders mean that, regardless of her refusal of Luciano's proposition, her grandparents could still become his tenants? Or did it mean that Luciano was determined to put *her* under such a sense of obligation that she might well end up agreeing for the older couple's sake? He was ruthless enough to use that kind of pressure on her and she knew he was.

But Elphie's frankness had turned Kerry's thoughts in a rather different direction. Was it really her pride and her fear of being hurt again that was coming between her and even the chance of happiness? What relationship came with the guarantee of a future? If she truly loved Luciano, just being with him again was all that should matter, she reasoned tautly. Why had she hidden behind the excuse of how her grandparents might feel about her engaging in a less conventional relationship? Hunt and Viola O'Brien had a remarkable ability to turn a blind eye to anything that threatened their comfort. If she was content, they would neither comment nor interfere.

Kerry went back indoors with her mind clearer than it had been in many weeks. As she entered the great hall, surprise stilled her in her tracks, for a woman was standing by the hearth.

Fixing feline green eyes on Kerry, the stunning blonde sauntered forward. 'Hi…long time no see, and no regrets either,' her stepsister, Rochelle, declared in her usual withering style.

CHAPTER SIX

'WHAT are you doing here?' Kerry asked before she could think better of it, for Rochelle's appearance at the castle had left her reeling with shock.

'That's none of your business. I travelled with Costanza and she tells me that you're now working here in a *domestic* capacity.' Having treated Kerry to a scornfully amused appraisal, Rochelle smiled with satisfaction. 'Luciano's being *so* tough with you and I can't tell you what a turn-on that is for me. I wouldn't place too much hope on the Cinderella story coming true at Ballybawn either...no way will I ever play an ugly sister!'

Mortified colour burning over her cheekbones, Kerry wished and not for the first time that she could match her stepsister's quick, annihilating tongue. Furthermore, much as Kerry would have liked to note that Rochelle's beauty had faded since their last meeting five years earlier, Rochelle defied the belief that too much drink, too many late nights and too great a fondness for men left their punishing mark on a woman's looks. Rochelle rejoiced in creamy skin, a mane of naturally blonde hair and a fantastic figure, enhanced by a very short leather skirt and a clingy white gypsy top.

'Neither am I in search of some mythical prince,' Kerry murmured tightly, her heart sinking as she found herself making the familiar demeaning comparision between her stepsister's attractions and her own. Red corkscrew curls and ordinary features could not compete with glorious golden hair and classic beauty. Nor could her own small, very slim body hold a candle to Rochelle's sexy curves and long, shapely legs.

'Oh, you definitely *were* five years back,' her stepsister sneered. 'But today I genuinely feel sorry for you.'

Kerry raised a brow. 'And why would that be?'

'Well, you've missed the boat once again with Luciano…why else would he be flying me in on his private jet? You're such a loser, Kerry,' Rochelle mocked. 'You've had a clear field with him for more than a week and I bet you did nothing but whinge at him.'

'I'm not going to listen to this stuff.' Kerry turned on her heel.

'It's so sad that you're about to lose all hope of ever regaining the family castle as well…'

Kerry hesitated and then spun back. 'What are you talking about?'

'According to Costanza, Luciano has just received an offer to name his price to *sell* Ballybawn and make a massive profit,' Rochelle delivered with smug superiority. 'Now, you tell me, would Luciano turn down a chance like that?'

The revelation that Luciano might be considering some very tempting offer to sell her grandparents' home to strangers made Kerry's slight figure tense in rigid rejection. 'I believe that he *would* turn it down,' she contended. 'If he wants to sell, why would he be having all this work done to the castle?'

Rochelle widened derisive green eyes in apparent wonderment. 'Oh, dear…oh, dear…you just don't get it even now, do you? Luciano's out to take *everything* that you value away from you. I saw his desire for revenge weeks ago…where have you been? On a different planet?'

In receipt of that chilling assurance from her worst enemy, Kerry lost every scrap of colour. If she was honest with herself, that same fear had occurred to her the instant she laid eyes on her gorgeous stepsister: surely Luciano could only have invited Rochelle to Ballybawn out of a desire to hurt and humble his former fiancée? Was he planning to conduct an affair with Rochelle right under her nose? Her tummy lurched and she started feeling sick.

Did she even have the right to get upset about Rochelle's arrival? After all, she herself had turned Luciano's proposition down flat and had been avoiding him to the best of her ability ever since. In fact, when she had told him to treat her as an employee, she had made it very clear that she wanted nothing more to do with him. At that point, Kerry had made a mortifying discovery about herself: she might have said that but she certainly hadn't *meant* it! No, she hadn't meant a word of it, so where did that leave her?

Costanza strolled in and acknowledged Kerry's presence with an inclination of her elegant head. 'Luciano would like to see you and your stepsister together.'

'*Kinky!*' Surprised but full of bubbling confidence, Rochelle sashayed past Luciano's PA into the library.

Angry, terrified curiosity made Kerry follow in the blonde's wake.

A stray shard of sunshine gleaming over his luxuriant black hair and accentuating his smooth, hard cheekbones, Luciano was poised by the window. In his formal dark grey business suit, he looked incredibly attractive, and her stepsister's greeting was effusive. Over the top of Rochelle's blonde head his glittering golden eyes scanned Kerry's pale, set features and veiled. He was angry with her but too proud to show it. Time was very precious to him yet seven days when they might have been together had already been wasted and he found it hard to forgive her for again subjecting him to the maddening ache of unsated desire. He had finally reached the conclusion that she must still have doubts about his past fidelity and he had decided to settle that issue head-on.

'You must be bored out of your mind here with only Kerry the nag for company,' Rochelle quipped. 'In fact I bet you're wondering what you did to deserve so much punishment, but rest assured, I'm here now and we're going to have fun—'

'Rochelle…' Lean, strong face sardonic, Luciano said flatly, 'All fun aside, you need to know why I asked you to come to Ireland—'

Rochelle lowered her lashes with a mock innocence that suggested that she scarcely required an explanation on that score. 'I…*do*?'

'I want you to tell Kerry what happened between you and me thirty-six hours before I was arrested five years ago,' Luciano drawled, taking both women aback with that request.

Rochelle's lashes stopped fluttering like fly swats. 'You're kidding me…you've got to be—'

'No, I'm not kidding.' Luciano surveyed the bewildered blonde with cool dark eyes.

'I get it.' Rochelle giggled. 'You want to remind Kerry just how stupid she was—'

'I wouldn't have put it quite like that.'

As confused as her stepsister had initially seemed by Luciano's demand, Kerry's attention skimmed from Rochelle's malicious smile to Luciano's hard, bronzed profile. 'Will someone tell me what's happening here?'

'Wise up and wake up,' Rochelle advised her. 'I

filched those cuff-links I showed you from the ware-house where Luciano had left them. Naturally, he *didn't* sleep with me that night the way I said he did. In fact he was an award-winning hero of restraint. When I brought him coffee stark naked, he refused to be tempted and he left the house!'

Kerry gaped at Rochelle. 'You brought in the coffee *naked*—?'

'You're supposed to pick up on the main issue,' Luciano intervened with driven impatience. 'Which *is*… that your stepsister lied to you the following day.'

'And if you're expecting me to feel bad about having lied to you, you can think again.' Rochelle gave Kerry a defiant glance. 'Make love not war—'

'I wasn't a child of the sixties and neither were you,' Luciano incised. 'Who suggested that particular timing to you?'

Rochelle frowned. 'Sorry…I don't know what you're asking me.'

'Someone *told* you when to stage that scene for Kerry's benefit and encouraged you to lie in the sure knowledge that those lies would destroy my relationship with her,' Luciano countered flatly. 'Who was it? I deserve all the facts.'

Fully intent on that exchange, Kerry snatched in an uneven breath.

'I suppose you do, and it hardly matters this long after the event.' Rochelle gave Luciano an apologetic look of appeal and shrugged. 'It was Miles—'

'*Miles?*' The sharp interruption was Kerry's. 'Why are you accusing Miles of being involved in the dreadful lies you told me about Luciano? That's nonsense…Miles would never have tried to hurt me like that!'

'Miles thought Luciano was bad news for you,' her

stepsister derided. 'And I thought *you* were bad news for Luciano. Great minds think alike.'

'That's enough, Rochelle. You can go now.' Luciano swung open the door and stood back. 'Costanza's waiting for you outside. She'll ensure that you get back to London.'

'Go…you want me to *leave* again?' Rochelle questioned in open disbelief.

'I can think of no reason why I would want you to stay.' As Luciano made that crushing statement, Kerry studied him with an astonishment similiar to her stepsister's.

'I don't understand,' Rochelle said tautly.

In the tense silence, Luciano maintained his cool, level scrutiny.

'How can you treat me like this after all I've done for you?' Rochelle demanded with stark incredulity. 'Only a few weeks ago, I risked getting charged with perjury when I spoke at that appeal hearing on your behalf…I'm the woman who dared to admit that I'd signed a statement that I *knew* was incorrect five years ago—'

'You're also the same woman who stood by that false statement in my original trial and let her lies contribute to my imprisonment for crimes I didn't commit.'

That harsher condemnation of her own past behaviour visibly shook Rochelle.

'And *why* did you lie?' Luciano dealt the stricken blonde a contemptuous appraisal. 'You lied out of spite and vanity because I rejected you!'

Assailed by unexpected discomfiture, Kerry found herself averting her attention from the shocked humiliation etched in her stepsister's shattered face.

'I get it,' Rochelle gasped accusingly. 'You only brought me here to play this scene for Kerry's benefit!'

'Yes, you finally get it,' Luciano confirmed without a shade of remorse.

Before she left the room, Rochelle hung back to stare at Kerry with outraged green eyes. 'Since what you've just witnessed is what you'll suffer too, be warned,' she said bitterly. 'In fact, start running now because you needn't kid yourself that he's not going to kiss you off with the *same* treatment or worse somewhere down the road!'

Only when Rochelle departed did Kerry realise that she was trembling.

'Satisfied?' Luciano enquired silkily.

'I think you scare me,' Kerry whispered truthfully.

Luciano reached for her clenched hands and wound them slowly into his. 'I wanted you to know for sure that I was telling the truth. Bringing Rochelle here was the only way I could be certain of that.'

'But ever since you came out of prison...well, haven't you encouraged her to think that she might mean something to you, that she was at least a friend of yours? I saw how shocked she was today,' Kerry muttered uneasily. 'It almost looked as if you've just been using her—'

'I did string her along to get the information I needed. Why not?' Luciano shrugged, his beautiful, sculpted mouth firming. 'Do you really think I would have got it any other way?'

'But I believed the explanation you gave me about that night in any case. You didn't need to drag Rochelle here and make a fool of her like that...' Kerry searched his lean, dark-angel face, clung to the vibrant gold of his intent gaze and closed that latter thought out. Her throat ran dry on the tide of sheer longing threatening her composure. He had brought Rochelle to Ballybawn solely to dispel any doubts that she might still have had about his trustworthiness. Shouldn't she be pleased that he had made that amount of effort on her behalf and that he had not yet given up on her?

'Five years ago, your stepsister helped to screw up my life. What she just got in return was a very minor slap on the wrist, *cara mia*,' Luciano delivered.

'Certainly, she had no qualms about lying about Miles the way she did.' Kerry was struggling to overcome her dismay at the extent of that ruthless streak of his by reminding herself that the blonde was a persistent and shameless liar.

Luciano tightened his lean, strong hands over hers. 'I know Rochelle and she wasn't lying. I never did have much time for your stepbrother, Miles, and now it seems I had good reason to feel that way—'

'She's definitely lying about Miles! I'd trust him with my life. He would never do anything that would cause me distress,' Kerry insisted.

As Luciano absorbed the look of sincere faith in her eyes, a flame of raw resentment currented through his big, powerful frame. When had she ever had that kind of trust in him? And what had Miles Linwood ever done to deserve that amount of loyalty? For days he had been patient, he had given her time to adjust, but now the anger he had been holding back was stirring. She wasn't the only woman in the world, although the way he'd been behaving of late, anyone could've been forgiven for assuming that she was.

'When did you last hear from Miles?'

'I hear from him all the time…we're still very close. I stayed with him when I was over in London seeing you,' Kerry confided.

His brilliant gaze hardened. 'I don't want you to get in contact with him again.'

Kerry's brows drew together. 'But—'

'Either you're with me...or you're against me,' Luciano spelt out with chilling softness. 'There's no safe middle path. If you plant yourself on the Linwood side of the fence, don't expect to have me in your life as well.'

Kerry paled. 'Is that a threat?'

He lifted her hand and pressed his mouth into the centre of her palm before trailing it down to the tender, delicate skin of her inner wrist and making her insides melt with heat and her knees shake under her. 'It's whatever you want to make of it, *cara mia*,' he breathed with a ragged edge to his dark drawl as he sank his other hand to her hip and eased her into contact with his long, powerful thighs. 'Did I ever tell you that I only have to look at you to get so hard I ache?'

'No...' Sharp, sweet craving was rising in her like a dangerous tide. That close to him she was just a mass of jumping, sensitised nerve-endings, achingly aware of the familiar scent of his warm skin and the strength of his lean, tensile muscularity. But most of all she was aware of the virile male thrust of his erection beneath the fine wool of his trousers.

'Tomorrow I'm leaving for London to see my legal team. I don't know when I'll be back here...no more games, Kerry.' In a move as controlling as though she had been a floppy rag doll, Luciano drew her hands up to his shoulders and linked them behind his neck.

'I haven't been playing games...' The temptation to plaster her weak, wanton self to every inch of him that she could reach was more than Kerry could resist. He didn't know when he would be back? How had he contrived to grasp that nothing he could say to her could have more impact than that particular one?

With an appreciative laugh, Luciano hoisted her up, curving a strong arm below her slim hips to support her as he splayed her knees round his waist and leant back against the desk to keep her balanced. His dark golden gaze smouldered over her. 'Prove that to me…satisfy that ache I'm suffering from now, *bella mia*—'

'*Here?*' Kerry queried shakily.

'No, the door doesn't lock…upstairs.'

'I can't, *we* can't…there are workmen all over the place!' Kerry protested.

Fabulous bone structure rigid, Luciano slid her down the length of his magnificent physique, unlaced her hands from round his neck and planted her back onto her own feet. 'So?'

'They'd guess what we were doing!' Kerry was in an agony of guilty mortification.

She could barely credit that she was even having the conversation with him: she could not recall the moment when her ability to resist him had evaporated and she had succumbed to her own weakness. Had it been the instant she realised that Rochelle meant nothing to him? Without a doubt the sure and final knowledge that he could find her more attractive than Rochelle had played a part in destroying her defensive barriers.

'*So?*' Luciano was not in the mood to be reasonable.

'In a country area like this, single women are expected to respect certain standards of behaviour. I'm sure you think that's old-fashioned but then we're not in the city and I suppose I'm not brave enough to ignore those standards and offend people and have them talk about me.' Cheeks warm with embarrassment as she completed that speech, Kerry looked back at him with turquoise eyes that carried a sincere plea, for she had been as honest as she knew how.

Straightening to his full, commanding height, Luciano vented a sardonic laugh. '*Dio mio*…many thanks for the news that if we were married sex in the middle of the day would be acceptable!'

'That isn't what I meant—'

'And that neighbourhood standards predate Noah's ark…a discouraging announcement for a new resident. Perhaps I should be considering the very advantageous offer I've had for the castle.'

Kerry stilled in dismay. 'So it's true, you *have* had an offer…it's not just something Rochelle dreamt up to upset me!'

'Yes, it's true, and naturally I intend to take a closer look at it. In my experience only actors in movies ask anyone to name their price to sell, and if I'm getting an open-ended offer of that magnitude I'd like to know who it's from and *why* it's coming my way—'

'You don't know who's trying to buy the castle?'

'Someone hiding behind an investment company in the Caymans. I need to find out why anyone in their right mind would be willing to pay *any* price to own Ballybawn—'

Kerry studied him in surprise. 'I should think that's obvious…someone wealthy has come out here on one of our tours and fallen in love with the castle. But you're not seriously saying that you would think of selling… *are* you?'

Just half an hour earlier Luciano would have said no, but in the space of a moment the anxious look in her expressive gaze changed his mind. He entertained himself with the possibility that some rich, decrepit old guy might have visited Ballybawn and fallen madly in lust for his little redheaded blushing guide. That possibility grew less entertaining by the second when it dawned on Luciano that Kerry might well go to the highest bidder. Just how far would she go to regain the family castle? Shouldn't he have asked himself that question *before* he made the crucial mistake of using Ballybawn as the ultimate bribe? That was the instant when Luciano knew that she would have to make a choice between him and her home. Nothing less would satisfy him. She had to choose. He did not want Kerry in his bed solely because he owned her ancestral hovel…since when had he got so particular?

Alarmed by his silence, Kerry closed her hands together tightly. 'Luciano…?'

'I *am* considering selling—'

'But you promised—'

'That was over a week ago and you said no. I believe I'm at liberty to do as I like with my own property,' Luciano pointed out smoothly. 'But I stand by my assurance that if you stay in my life I'll take care of your grandparents' needs.'

He was reneging on his original proposition. Kerry decided that that was a judgement on her and exactly what she deserved for sinking low enough to even think of accepting that degrading offer to become his weekend trollop. Tears burned at the backs of her eyes and all over again she hated herself for the mistakes she had made, but all of a sudden she hated *him* even more! He had moved the goalposts when he had no right to do so!

Thrusting unsteady fingers through the vibrant curls clustered on her brow, Kerry gave him a furious look of condemnation. 'Shall I tell you something? Dismal as it is to appreciate that a guy can still be so narrow-minded, you had more respect for me *before* I slept with you than you have now!'

'Santo cielo—'

'No, you needn't bother spluttering Italian at me because I know what I know!' Kerry slammed back at him in angry reproach. 'I didn't ask for anything and I didn't expect anything from that night I spent with you. But you couldn't leave it at that. No, you were too worried that I might have expectations. So, you put me down and treated me like some gold-digger who was only with you in the first place for your money!'

'That is not how I behaved—'

'Don't you dare try to tell me that you didn't do what you *did* do!' Kerry railed back in passionate protest. 'You insulted me, you hurt my feelings, and you threw back what I gave for free in my face!'

Luciano was pale beneath his bronzed skin, his dark golden eyes hooded, his strong jawline clenched. 'To date you've asked for everything that's happened here—'

'And how do you make that out?'

'You stayed on after the repossession. Of course, I would've come and found you even if you hadn't,' Luciano acknowledged with brooding dark humour. 'But you didn't put me to that inconvenience.'

'Well, it's never too late to learn my lesson, is it?' Kerry was further mortified by that reminder. 'I can move out just as quickly!'

Luciano swore under his breath and strode forward to close a staying hand over her slight forearm. 'That's not what I want—'

Kerry yanked herself free. 'Maybe what you want doesn't carry the weight you think it ought to—'

Shimmering dark golden eyes assailed hers. 'If you

walk away from me again, that's it! If I feel more comfortable now with a relationship that I more or less pay for, who are you to say that's wrong? Surely you're not trying to pretend that once you gave me something better, something more permanent?' he derided with harsh emphasis. 'I've had five years to think about how much your love was worth once romance gave way to reality—'

At that hard statement, Kerry's tummy knotted. 'You're not being fair...I thought you'd been unfaithful—'

'Why can't you just be honest? Five years ago you put your pride, your family, your reputation, everything before me where I put you *first* and I can't forget that. But no way will I let you put a pile of ancient bricks ahead of me in importance as well!' Luciano growled with raw clarity. 'So let's leave the castle out of our deal and see where that takes us.'

'That's where we differ.' Her gaze dropped from his to conceal her pain but her voice was torn by strain. 'I don't want to feature as part of some "deal".'

'That's the only way you can be with me. It's your choice. After I've dealt with business in London, I'm flying on to Italy.' Breathtakingly handsome face taut with stubborn purpose, Luciano settled grim golden eyes on her. 'You've got forty-eight hours to make your mind up and then I get on with my life with or without you.'

Chagrined colour drenched her cheeks and then receded again. To an ultimatum that blunt there could only be one answer and Kerry lifted her red-gold head so high that her neck muscles ached at the stress she was putting on them. 'You can bet on it being *without* me.'

Bitter frustration thundered through Luciano but he was as angry with himself as he was with her. For some inexplicable reason he had gone from being a male who rarely put a verbal foot wrong with a woman to a male who could barely open his mouth without causing offence. He knew when non-negotiable commands worked and when they didn't. Ensuring that Kerry had no room to manoeuvre even to save face had only made a negative response more likely.

On wobbly knees, Kerry marched herself out of the library. Outside the door, she stopped and hugged herself, suddenly cold to the marrow. What was she doing? What was she playing at? She loved him but love was not an excuse to make a stupid sacrifice of herself. But what was *he* doing? What was *he* playing at? That night she had lain in his arms he had been tender—yet, since then? Even by the next morning he had been backing off again, raising the barriers, imposing offensive limits…like a guy on the run? A guy who might be scared of getting hurt again?

Her strained eyes brightened and then dulled again. She could not imagine Luciano being afraid, for his life had always been tough. Once that knowledge had been the secret strength that helped her bear the thought of his being in prison: she had believed that, no matter what, he would survive. Yet she had never allowed herself to consider how he might be altered by that ordeal.

He had changed in more than the superficial ways which she had noted when she first walked into his impressive London office. Although he was more open about his emotions than he had ever been during their engagement, that seeming candour was deceptive, for he was infinitely harder and colder. As he withdrew even Ballybawn from the uncommitted sexual 'deal' he had originally suggested, it was almost as though he preferred to demand terms that she would refuse. After all, she was not some fancy-free single woman able to fly off at a moment's notice to Italy, and within weeks her grandparents would need her on a daily basis again. Possibly, Luciano believed that a few weeks would suffice to conclude his interest in her. Painfully conscious of her own vulnerability, she was scared that she could no longer rely on her own judgement, for her stepsister had hit a bull's-eye when she warned Kerry that Luciano would eventually turn on her too.

When the phone rang in the sitting room, Kerry answered it in an abstracted mood. The first sentences voiced by the caller confused her until she recognised the man's name, and then a weird little shiver ran down her spine. It was the solicitor phoning in response to her own written enquiry about her mother little more than a week earlier.

'I'm sorry, could you repeat that?'

'I can confirm that, as you feared, your mother *did* pass away some years ago,' the solicitor told her with measured clarity. 'But I do have more positive news for you. You have relatives on your mother's side—'

'I know all my relatives.' Heavy disappointment had made Kerry's shoulders slump, for, although she had guessed that her mother had to be dead, an obstinate little spark of hope had stayed lit.

'Were you aware that your mother's marriage to Harold Linwood was *not* her first marriage? At the age of nineteen your mother entered another marriage, which also ended in divorce.'

'Are you sure of that?' Eyes widening in astonishment, Kerry was transfixed.

'In the course of that marriage, your mother also had other children—'

'I beg your pardon...?' Kerry gasped.

'—and I have been asked to tell you that you have three older sisters. They have been searching for you for some years and are eager to meet you.'

The telephone almost dropped clean out of Kerry's nerveless fingers.

'Your sisters are also keen for this matter to remain private and confidential and I must ask you to be discreet.'

'Huh…' Kerry was nodding like a marionette at the other end of the phone. Her brain refused to process the very great shock she had just been dealt and the trauma was in no way eased by a man who contrived to speak as though his revelations were an everyday event.

'An open ticket for a flight to London is waiting for you at Shannon Airport. Please call me when you intend to travel. You will be met off your flight and taken to the hotel where your sisters would like their initial meeting with you to take place.'

Sisters? Kerry's thoughts lagged behind the travel arrangements being suggested. Her mother had once been married to someone other than Harold Linwood? Children had been born of that union…three little girls? But if that was true, where had those other daughters been all this time? Where in particular had they been during the early years of Kerry's life? And why had her parent been incorrectly styled on her marriage certificate as a single rather than a divorced woman?

The barrage of questions she attempted to ask was blocked by the solicitor's polite explanation that her sisters would prefer to exchange personal details with her at their first meeting. At his request, she noted down his phone number and actually allowed him to ring off before regaining sufficient brain power to call him back to declare that she would fly to London the following day.

Three…sisters? Sisters related to her by blood. *Three* of them! Frantic excitement bubbled through Kerry. All her life, she had felt very much alone even when surrounded by Linwoods, even when living with her grandparents, who inhabited a world quite removed from more mundane reality. Three older sisters had been searching for her for several years. *Searching* for her, Kerry savoured, feeling extraordinarily important and wanted as she recalled that heart-warming piece of information.

Bursting at the seams with her news, Kerry found that she was heading back to the library before she even realised what she was doing. Why was she even considering telling Luciano? Why the automatic surge in his direction? Ashamed of herself, she hung back. Wasn't she fortunate that she had learned about her sisters at a time when she was desperate for something other than Luciano, who was tearing her apart, to concentrate on?

She phoned Miles and, on the brink of sharing her discovery about her family background, remembered her sisters' somewhat puzzling request for discretion. Her stepbrother seemed very preoccupied. He made an audible effort to sound cheerful at the prospect of her impending visit but generally seemed in unusually low spirits.

Before she could lose her nerve, she went off to find Luciano to inform him that she would be taking time off.

'Yes, I can see why a jacuzzi would hit the right spot…' the architect Luciano had brought in as a consultant was confessing with a companionable shudder at the cheerless stone interior of the bathroom adjoining Luciano's bedroom.

'A…*what*?' Kerry exclaimed from behind the two men. 'Only a vandal would rip out an early copper bath and put an anachronism like a jacuzzi into a sixteenth-century tower house!'

Dark golden eyes landed on her in a sudden glancing volatile collision. 'A non-functional bath is a waste of space.'

'It's living history—'

'Perhaps I don't want to *live* history,' Luciano gritted between even white teeth.

With a harried excuse, his architect went into retreat.

'I just wanted to check that it's all right for me to be away for a couple of days. I'm off to London too—'

Luxuriant black lashes narrowed over Luciano's reflective gaze and he almost smiled. 'You can travel with me tomorrow.'

Kerry wondered if there was a bedroom on his private jet. It was a ghastly, demeaning thing to have to admit but she was not sure that she was up to resisting his powers of persuasion in a confined space. 'No, thanks. I've…er..already made my arrangements.'

Luciano's lean brown hands flexed straight into fists and then more slowly out of them again. 'Why has London suddenly become an attraction?'

Kerry made the first excuse that came to mind. 'I want to see Miles—'

'Even knowing how I feel about you seeing him?' Luciano ground out in a lethally quiet enquiry.

The very sound of that chilling intonation made her feel as if he had raised a tripwire against her knees. Inside herself, she discovered a truly terrifying desire to sacrifice Miles, sacrifice anything and everything, just to steal a little happiness with Luciano. But at what cost? That was just a silly girlish dream, Kerry labelled with anguished understanding, for she would never abandon her grandparents.

'Yes, even knowing how you feel about that,' Kerry confirmed flatly.

Luciano did not trust himself to speak. He walked away with the same hard, self-contained cool and acceptance that he had practised when he was threatened with knives in prison. He showed nothing and he refused to brood. But he could no longer comprehend why he had been wasting time considering the castle's deficient plumbing when he could sell Ballybawn for an enormous, comforting profit. He told himself that, in the best of Irish traditions, he was feeling on top of the world. In the mood to celebrate his wonderful freedom from all female ties and expectations, he got so drunk that night that he ended up toasting Florrie O'Brien's gloomy portrait in the great hall.

'I shall die single too!' he swore in Italian before he fell to thinking about Paola. Paola Massone, who would make a suitable wife in every way, who would ask nothing from him but the means to shop until she dropped. Paola, who rejoiced in every possible feminine and practical attribute but to whom he remained inexplicably impervious.

When he slammed the door on his exit, he did not notice that Florrie's canvas fell off the wall. He did not notice that a trio of shivering wolfhounds were hiding under his bed again either. He did dimly recognise that eerie sobbing sound again but he knew it to be the wind whistling down the chimney, for as he was all too well aware Kerry cried over all sorts of things but never, ever over him.

CHAPTER SEVEN

THE car that picked Kerry up at a London airport the following afternoon had a large envelope lying on the rear seat that carried her name like an invitation.

Tearing open the envelope, Kerry extracted a single sheet of paper which contained a concise history of her mother's life. The amount of pre-planning that her sisters appeared to have put into her reception was starting to amaze Kerry.

The account opened with the information that Carrie had at some stage changed her name from O'Brien to Carlton and continued with the details of her mother's first marriage to a man called Sutton. Kerry learned about the birth of her eldest sister, Freddy, now a woman in her thirties, and winced when she read about the extramarital affair during which Carrie had fallen pregnant again by her lover. Her husband's subsequent discovery that his wife's infant twins were not his children had led to a nasty divorce. Freddy had been raised solely by her father. The twins had been separated; the older, known as Misty, had been placed in the care of foster parents, the younger, named Ione by her adoptive family, was raised in Greece.

Carrie had returned to using the name of Carlton and had pretended to be a single woman when she married Harold Linwood, who had had no idea of his bride's past. A few years after leaving Kerry behind in Ireland,

Carrie had died in a London boarding house and by that time she had been an alcoholic.

Entering the grand and intimidating central London hotel where she was to meet her sisters for the first time, Kerry was extremely nervous. Outside the designated top-floor suite her heart began beating so fast at the foot of her dry throat that she felt dizzy. Just an instant later as the door shot open in answer to her knock she was engulfed in a hug by a tall, laughing redhead and an animated hum of female voices surrounded her.

It was a minute or two before Kerry was fit to absorb impressions and separate the voices.

'I'm Misty Andracchi, the older twin,' the redhead informed her with a grin.

'Ione Christoulakis...I'm three minutes younger and Misty never lets me forget it!' A tiny, exquisite blonde beauty kissed Kerry on both cheeks.

'And I'm Freddy al-Husayn, the eldest...' A smiling pregnant woman with honey-blonde hair swept up in an elegant style came forward last.

'We were excited to death when you wrote to the solicitor right out of the blue!' Misty confided. 'After four years, we'd given up hope of anything coming from those enquiries. We'd found a baby photo of you in Mum's things and we knew you existed but we had no way of finding you until we discovered that Mum's second husband was called Linwood. We had all the Linwoods we could trace contacted to see if we could establish any link with our mother's second marriage.'

'I'm afraid the letter took rather a long time to reach me,' Kerry said awkwardly.

'It doesn't matter, we're just overjoyed that you're

here now.' Misty grasped both Kerry's hands in hers, her eyes bright with satisfaction. 'I have to be frank with you and admit that we already know an awful lot about you because we had some checks made. We had to be sure of your identity.'

Taken aback by that admission, Kerry stiffened. She had already noted the glitter of precious jewellery, the designer garments and the expensive air of confident gloss that suggested that her siblings were all rather more privileged in life than she was herself.

'Our second biggest surprise and joy was discovering that we *still* have grandparents living. Oh, Kerry, we can't wait to meet Hunt and Viola O'Brien!' Freddy confided with delighted anticipation. 'That was the best news ever—'

'We ought to tell you something about ourselves first.' Ione seemed to grasp Kerry's bemused sense of dislocation. 'We're all married and our children range in age from nine years right down to six months old. So you're an aunt as well—'

'This is almost too much to take in all at once. I've been alone for a long time.' Kerry's voice wobbled a little, for she was touched by the affectionate acceptance that each woman had offered her yet she could already see the obvious differences between her sisters. Misty was the first to speak up, a natural leader with a lively personality. Freddy was quieter and more thoughtful. Ione with her husky Greek accent was more of an enigma, but, though she might have less to say, she had a lovely, warm smile.

Freddy patted Kerry's shoulder in an understanding

gesture. 'You've had a horrid struggle trying to manage on your own—'

'But you're not on your own now. You have us and *all* your problems are over,' Ione assured her.

'Which…er…problems would those be?' Kerry questioned uncertainly.

Misty winced…. 'Obviously we *know* that Luciano da Valenza evicted our grandparents from their home and that you've been forced to work for him—'

Freddy frowned. 'We don't think that your ex-fiancé has any excuse for the way he's behaved since he came out of prison.'

'He certainly sank very low in his treatment of you and our grandparents!' Ione opined in angry disgust.

Kerry was surprised by the extent of her siblings' knowledge of her circumstances and frankly dismayed by their opinion of Luciano. Keen to give them a more balanced view of recent events, she tried to explain. 'Five years ago, Luciano gave just about everything he had in the world to Grandpa in a very generous loan. I know that Grandpa and Grandma have had to leave the castle *but*—'

'Stop panicking. Nothing that's happened is your fault,' Ione asserted. 'Sit back, relax and watch *us* in action. Our husbands agree that Luciano da Valenza needs a lesson.'

'What are you talking about?' Kerry asked in honest bewilderment.

'To be vulgar…' Misty pulled a comical face '…we're all loaded. Freddy is married to an oil-rich Arab prince, I'm married to a very wealthy businessman and Ione is a billionairess in her own right. Our combined resources make us very powerful and we can put huge financial pressure on da Valenza's empire. In fact we could ruin him—'

In receipt of that recitation of facts, Kerry lost colour and felt distinctly queasy.

'But first we want to ensure that da Valenza sells Ballybawn castle back to us...whether he wants to or not,' Ione declared.

Misty nodded in agreement. 'In fact we've already made him an offer that he had better not refuse.'

'How can you threaten Luciano when you don't even know him?' Kerry demanded in disbelief.

'Does that bother you? Surely you would be much happier with him out of your life?' Misty was studying Kerry in surprise. 'You ditched him five years ago and it looks to us as if he's come back looking for revenge. If he has, we can stop him in his tracks by hitting him where it hurts—'

'Don't you dare!' Before Kerry was even aware of formulating those angry words in her mind, they had leapt off her tongue. 'If you make any move against Luciano, I'll fight you every step of the way. If you want to blame someone for our grandparents being forced out of Ballybawn, blame me for not managing to make a profitable enterprise of the estate!'

'You're in love with Luciano da Valenza...' Ione murmured in a shaken tone of discovery.

Making no attempt to hide her disconcertion, Misty groaned out loud. 'We didn't know...'

Kerry was still very much on the defensive. 'Well, now you *do* know.'

'I'm afraid we've been talking at cross purposes.'

Misty's discomfiture was clear. 'We assumed that Luciano was making you unhappy.'

'We're your sisters and we care about you, so I think we also need to admit that we have access to confidential information…and we're trying to warn you that in our opinion you can't trust Luciano da Valenza,' Ione stated uneasily. 'He's a very clever and dangerous man who is already hurting your family.'

'I'd have to know you a lot longer before I could think of you as family and I won't ever forgive you if you try to hurt Luciano. You have no right to threaten him and no justification either. He was planning to take care of Grandpa and Grandma…you've got him wrong.' Kerry found it hard even to voice those words, for she was hurt and distressed and alienated all at the same time. Without warning, her meeting with her sisters had gone horribly wrong and all the bright promise of a continuing relationship with them had evaporated before her eyes.

Misty groaned out loud. 'I can see that we've come across as interfering but we weren't aware that you were involved in a relationship with Luciano—'

'Yes, and I'm not ashamed of that either.' Kerry lifted her head high. 'Look, I think I'd be more comfortable leaving now. We all have a lot to think about. I'll tell our grandparents about their three new granddaughters so that when you go to see them—as I assume you plan to do—you won't come as too much of a surprise to them.'

'From now on, we'll be responsible for taking care of their needs.' Freddy gave her a warm, reassuring smile. 'You don't need to fret about them any more.'

Ione rested rueful green eyes on Kerry. 'I'm sorry that

we've made such a hash of our first meeting with you. Hopefully we'll do better on the next occasion, little sister.'

'Maybe when sisters are already grown up, it's too l-late to be meeting for the first time!' Before her pent-up emotions could make her stammer even worse, Kerry walked out of the suite.

Without caring where she went and in too much turmoil to stand still long enough to decide, Kerry left the hotel and walked through the busy city streets. What she had learnt from her newly discovered sisters had sent her into shock. It was clear that Misty, Ione and Freddy were behind that mysterious offer to buy Ballybawn at any price. Naturally. Who else would value Ballybawn as much as her own flesh and blood? Her half-sisters were as linked to O'Brien history and their ancestral home as she was herself and it was hardly surprising that they should blame Luciano for their grandparents' plight.

Hadn't she once blamed Luciano too? When had she stopped blaming him quite so much? Just when too had she started believing that no matter what happened her grandparents *would* be coming back to live at Ballybawn? For, in a moment of frank acknowledgement, Kerry recognised that she did have total faith in that reality and complete trust that Luciano would bring it about. Did that mean that she had been playing games with him as he had accused her of doing? Hanging out for a better offer from him? Why was what went on in the back of her own mind as big a puzzle to her as it might well be to him? Mingled tears of pain and reluctant amusement stung Kerry's eyes.

If ever anything had served to increase her understanding of herself, it had been the disorientating experience of her own automatic recoil from her sisters' threats against Luciano. In the space of seconds, her siblings had seemed more like the enemy than her own kin. She had not been able to bear that they should talk of harming Luciano in any way.

Her sisters seemed so confident of their right to stand in judgement over Luciano. How could they understand the forces that had made Luciano the tough guy that he was? Right from the moment of his illegitimate birth, nothing had come easy to him. His grandfather had been a hard-drinking bully and his mother had been virtually illiterate. Luciano had never been praised for his hard work at school because his parent had felt threatened by her son's unsettling ambition to make something more of himself. In short, Luciano had always had to forge his path in life alone and without support.

And it was that knowledge that made Kerry ache for him most of all. At the height of his success in the business world when he had been only twenty-eight years old, Luciano had been charged with theft and imprisoned and everything he had achieved had been taken from him. His career, his reputation, his financial security, even his fiancée, Kerry conceded with an agonised sense of guilt.

He had been too proud to reach out to her then and she had not thought enough of herself to keep faith in him. Convinced that he had fallen back into Rochelle's arms, she had found it that much easier to believe that he was a fraudster as well. After all, the whole Linwood clan had believed that and, heartsick with the pain of

losing him—as she had believed—to her stepsister, she
had not had sufficient trust in her own judgement to dare
to think anything different.

But Luciano had loved her...he had *loved* her then.
That awareness just tore Kerry apart and her throat
closed over with anguished regret for what she could not
alter. It was way too late now to see how her low self-
esteem and his arrogant self-sufficiency had weakened
their relationship. However, the past did not have to
make the present, Kerry reminded herself fiercely. Nor
did she have to repeat the same mistakes or behave as
if nothing she could do could change anything.

Just when Luciano had regained his freedom and the
right to live his life again, her sisters were threatening
to ruin him. She had to warn him. She had to ensure
that he understood exactly who he was dealing with and
what he was up against, and that he backed off. This
need clear as day before her, she pulled out her mobile
phone and punched out the number of his London office.
She was eventually put through to Costanza.

'Luciano is booked up until six,' his PA confirmed.

'I have important information for him. I *know* who's
behind that offer for Ballybawn.'

'I'm sure I can find a space for you somewhere,' Costanza conceded.

Kerry smiled, glimpsed her own reflection in a shop
window and stilled. Her smile fell away while she stared
because she looked wild: her face coloured hectic pink
from hurrying at a breakneck pace through the streets,
blue eyes big with anxiety, springy red-gold curls on end
from her efforts to tidy her hair with her fingers. At best,
with all the stops pulled out, her hair done by a stylist

and with full cosmetic assistance, she could make pretty. Yet regardless of that reality, Luciano had chosen her over Rochelle and yet *still* she hadn't had the courage to give their relationship a second chance!

Her imaginative older sisters had tried to persuade her that Luciano was out for revenge. But Kerry believed that that suggestion was nonsensical. Understandably, her siblings felt very protective towards the grandparents they had yet to meet. It was not surprising either that her sisters preferred to blame Luciano entirely for the old couple's present predicament. But to be fair, what businessman did not insist on collecting his debts? Nor could it be deemed Luciano's fault that her grandfather, in ignoring all efforts to find an earlier solution to his indebtedness, had acted as his own worst enemy.

Indeed, in Kerry's opinion, a male willing to go to great expense to transform Ballybawn into a comfortable home for an elderly couple who could never repay his generosity could hardly be suspected of possessing a vengeful nature. Luciano's refusal to confirm that he would retain ownership of the castle did not change her mind on that score either. How could she fault him for demanding that she choose between him and the estate? That she put him first? Wasn't that natural? Of course he didn't want to think that she might choose to be with him solely because he owned Ballybawn!

Yet only a few days ago, Luciano had not seemed to care what might motivate her. That he had moved on from that point to demand more from her was encouraging, that he had discovered that he had scruples whether he wanted them or not was even better, Kerry told herself with determination. And on this occasion she *could* be there for him, this time she was in a position to put him first and her family second and prove her trust. This time she would dare to be different and break the mould!

'Have I misjudged you?' Costanza asked with a searching look when she collected Kerry from the reception area of da Valenza Technology. 'Or have you finally worked out that it's safer to be on the winning team?'

In the act of entering Luciano's office, Kerry paused. 'I'll leave you to make up your own mind about that.'

As the elegant brunette spread the door wide, Kerry clashed with Luciano's intent gaze: bold, beautiful golden eyes set between black spiky lashes, framed by a lean, bronzed masculine face with features as pure and perfect in symmetry as those of a dark angel. A dark angel of the fallen variety, for it wasn't possible, it had never been possible, to look at Luciano and not react to the sinful sizzle of his sex appeal.

Now she no longer even tried to pretend that she could be impervious. In response to the hard look of challenge he angled at her, her entire body tingled and her heart pounded and an unholy charge of excitement raced through her slight, taut frame. It shouldn't have been that way and she was ashamed that it was but she was finally accepting that loving Luciano roused certain instincts in her that she could not fight. She loved him and she wanted to be with him and she could not stand back and do nothing when his interests were in jeopardy.

Luciano surveyed Kerry with cloaked eyes that concealed the raw satisfaction charging him with an adrenalin high. She had changed her mind. She was coming to Italy, he just *knew* she was coming to Italy with him and that he had won. Costanza might have been taken in by the excuse that Kerry had miraculous access to the identity of the secretive party eager to buy the castle but he had not been fooled.

'I'm sure you'll remember reading that solicitor's letter asking about my mother. I replied to it.' Kerry drew in a sharp, short breath before continuing. 'Well, the solicitor contacted me and confirmed that Mum was dead but he—'

'I'm sorry,' Luciano drawled with roughened sincerity.

'It wasn't a surprise,' Kerry sighed. 'But the solicitor also informed me that my mother's marriage to my father was her second. When she was barely out of her teens, she had married another man and she had three other children. I have half-sisters, and at their request I came to London to meet them today.'.

His winged dark brows had drawn together. 'Why didn't you tell me all this before I left the castle?'

'Because I didn't know anything about my sisters and I wasn't ready to talk about them...I think I didn't quite believe in their existence until I saw them in the flesh this afternoon.'

'Three more older versions of you,' Luciano mused.

'We don't look much alike, as we have three different fathers between us. I suppose you're wondering why I'm taking up your time telling you about this—'

'No.' Luciano took it for granted that she would come to him to tell him about any major event in her life and, if anything, he was annoyed that she had kept that information from him while he was still in Ireland.

'My sisters threatened you—'

'Threatened me? How?' Luciano rested back against his desk so that he towered over her a little less and his sculpted mouth quirked. Her *sisters* had threatened him? He almost laughed out loud. What the heck was she talking about? Yet there was something touching about the genuine concern that had tensed the delicate lines of her triangular face.

'I'm afraid that they're very annoyed about our grandparents having been forced to move out of the castle and from what I can work out they're rich enough to cause trouble for you—'

'In terms of probability, I would consider that unlikely, *cara*.'

Recognising that he was not taking her warning seriously, Kerry named her siblings. At the sound of the name Andracchi, Luciano began to frown in recognition. When she mentioned the fact that her eldest sister was reputedly the wife of an oil-rich eastern prince, Luciano straightened and threw back his wide shoulders. 'You can't be serious. *Dio mio*, are you trying to tell me that your three sisters *are*—?'

'And Ione…the youngest next to me—'

'Is called Christoulakis. She's the Greek heiress who married Alexio Christoulakis. *Santo cielo*…you must have heard of the three of them before!' All Luciano's relaxation and amusement had come to an abrupt end. 'Even I know that some society gossip columnist christened Misty Andracchi and her sisters the Three Graces for their charitable fund-raising activities—'

'Well, I hadn't heard of them, and my sisters weren't very charitable about you,' Kerry confided with a gri-

mace. 'In fact they seemed to be blaming you for everything that's gone wrong at Ballybawn, which isn't
fair—'

'Obviously very prejudiced ladies, and whoever said
life was fair?' An absolute rage of furious, frustrated
disbelief was nibbling at the edges of Luciano's steely
control. Just when Kerry was on the very edge of becoming wholly and absolutely his, providence threatened
to snatch her away again. She had three very wealthy
sisters, who would no doubt do whatever was in their
power to separate Kerry from him.

She could only have spent an hour at most in their
company and already his presence in her life had come
under attack. That knowledge so inflamed Luciano that
it was a second or two before he could even cool down
enough to consider what it was that her siblings might
find so very objectionable about him. He did not have
to consider that issue for long. On the face of it, he was
prepared to allow that he might not look like the ultimate
catch. He was not only an ex-con but also the bastard
who had had the misfortune to collect a debt that ensured
their long-lost grandparents became homeless. With luck
like that, Luciano reflected grimly, he might as well
shoot himself. Andracchi, Christoulakis and the Arab
prince Jaspar al-Husayn would make formidable oppo-
nents. Luciano was convinced that even on a bad day he
could take any one of them but he was less sanguine
about his prospects were all three to band together.

'It's my sisters who are behind that offer to buy Ballybawn. They want to give it back to Grandpa and
Grandma,' Kerry told him. 'So you just say yes to that
offer now and sell—'

'*Sell?*' Luciano ground out with incredulity. 'That's your home we're talking about—'

'It doesn't matter *who* gives the castle back to my grandparents. My sisters will do it. My sisters are dying to gallop to their rescue,' she emphasised tautly. 'You no longer need to worry about my grandparents—'

'But I own Ballybawn,' Luciano breathed with a raw edge to his delivery, outraged to have his life-changing bout of generosity tossed back ungratefully in his teeth.

'Yes, but you don't need Ballybawn and it's not as if you ever really wanted it or even fell madly in love with it,' Kerry reasoned ruefully. 'So you might as well sell the castle back to the family for the best offer you're ever likely to get.'

'You're telling me to sell out to your sisters—?'

'Yes. It'll keep them happy and give them less reason to threaten your business interests. I'm certain that they'll back off if you let them have the castle.'

Raw dark colour accentuated the hard slant of his blunt cheekbones and his brilliant eyes blazed gold. 'I am not afraid of your sisters or their husbands—'

Kerry stretched up and framed his lean, powerful face with spread fingers, blue eyes full of troubled appeal. 'Just for once in your life, don't be macho and aggressive. Try to think like a woman and be cool-headed and sensible…'

His beautiful mouth quirked.

'You know what I mean. Why look for trouble when you don't have to?' Kerry reasoned feverishly. 'You have no fight with them—'

'Don't I?' Long brown fingers drifted through the tumbled fall of her curls and slowly knotted there, his hot, hungry gaze resting full on her. 'I had a quarrel with your sisters the instant they tried to come between us, *bella mia.*'

Her delicate face clouded. 'You wouldn't believe how excited and happy I was when I realised that I had sisters…and meeting them at first was wonderful.' Kerry swallowed hard, for it was too upsetting to recall the special sense of connection which she had initially experienced in her siblings' company. 'But it all just fell apart when I realised how they felt about you…'

Luciano knew he ought to tell her that her sisters had probably spoken out of the best of intentions: their protective concern for her versus their distrust of him. He knew he ought to point out that she had no true experience of how normal family members interacted. Caring relatives did interfere in each other's lives but Kerry's father had never had the interest to do so.

Conscious that an essential spirit of fair play and decency ought to have prompted him to speak up, Luciano remained stubbornly silent. He much preferred to mull over the amazing fact that Kerry had turned her back on her own sisters for *his* benefit. Her first loyalty had lain with him. Automatically and instinctively, she had rejected their arguments against him. She had also rushed across London to warn him that her siblings were behind the offer for Ballybawn. What had he done to deserve that loyalty? Not a lot, Luciano was prepared to concede. But he knew how best to conserve his own good fortune. Removing Kerry from all possibility of further contaminating contact with her troublemaking sisters loomed large on his immediate agenda.

'We're going to Italy together,' he murmured gruffly.

Kerry felt a dreamy smile curve the softened line of her lips. 'Yes...but—'

His big, powerful frame tensed against her. 'No buts—'

'I'll need to go to Dublin first and see my grandparents. I'm also dining with Miles this evening—'

'Phone him...I have a stronger claim on you, *cara*.' As Luciano's breath fanned her parted lips, she trembled. She wanted that hard mouth of his on hers so bad it was a literal pain to be denied it. 'We'll see your grandparents together tomorrow. We'll stop off on the way to Italy—'

'Miles is waiting at his apartment for me. I can't let him down like that.'

Brilliant eyes narrowed, Luciano set her back from him with ruthless cool.

The shock of separation from that lithe, powerful length of his hurt even more. Her body ached, the wanton heat and dampness at the very heart of her reacting with shameless disappointment to his retreat. Her colour high, Kerry stepped back from him on unsteady legs. The amount of power he had over her shocked her but she was determined not to give way to his demand that she cancel her evening with her stepbrother. Even though her every shameless skin cell urged her to spend that same time with Luciano?

But when would she next be in London? In addition, she no longer had a home of her own to which she could invite Miles whenever she might choose. As she finally appreciated just how dependent she would be on Luciano in the future, her innate streak of caution almost went into panic overload. Suppressing her uneasiness, she backed away and secretly cringed over the fact that she had to bite her tongue to prevent herself from suggesting that she saw Luciano later that evening.

'I'll call you later,' Luciano drawled.

When Miles opened the door of his apartment, he was in the middle of a tense conversation with someone out of view. Turning back to Kerry with a hangdog air, he muttered rather indistinctly, 'Sorry about this.'

Kerry had entered his sitting room before she understood why he was apologising. His sister, Rochelle, was poised by the fireplace, her green eyes alight with defiance. 'Look, this was my idea, *not* my brother's...OK? Satisfied, Miles?'

As Miles closed the door again in craven masculine retreat, Kerry was very tempted just to walk right back out of his apartment again. 'I can't imagine what you could have left to say to me.'

Rochelle planted her hands on her hips. 'That I'm not the competition you needed to worry about...your real challenge is Paola Massone—'

'I have no idea who you're referring to, nor do I want to know.' Kerry gave the aggressive blonde a weary appraisal and decided that there was something a little immature about a woman of twenty-eight who chose to wear a skirt so short that the slightest bend threatened to expose her panties.

Her stepsister lifted the gossip magazine lying on the coffee-table and then slung it down again in emphasis. 'Read this and *weep*! I bet Luciano hasn't mentioned wedding bells to you this time around. Now that he's rolling in the dosh and the vineyards, he's got much fancier game in mind for the bridal role. Paola's got the looks, the social status and she's Italian too...and her daddy and Luciano are planning to make world-class wine together! Now, isn't that sweet? Top that little lot if you can!'

'Is that it? Are you finished now?' Kerry prompted hopefully.

'Just about. Of course, if you had any pride, you wouldn't settle for being his tart now when you were once engaged to him,' Rochelle remarked with soft, stinging scorn.

Only as her stepsister began to leave did Kerry find herself finally asking the question that she had always longed to ask the other woman. 'Are you in love with Luciano?'

Rochelle gave her a pained appraisal and winced. 'Why are you always so wet? I want to shag him every time I see him...that's *all*!'

'And just for that...you wrecked our engagement?'

'The guy was mine first. All right, so he was drunk and it was only one weekend, but he had no business getting engaged to you when he couldn't even be bothered using my phone number! Are you satisfied now?'

'Yes.' Kerry was thinking how very ironic it was that Rochelle should have been as jealous of her as she had been of Rochelle.

Ripe mouth pursed, her stepsister departed, slamming the front door in her wake.

Kerry found Miles seated at the breakfast bar in the kitchen, a bottle of whisky in front of him and an empty glass.

'So where are we going tonight?' her stepbrother

asked with feverish brightness, his words slurring as he clambered down off his high stool with exaggerated care. When he attempted to straighten, he swayed unsteadily. While she watched in dismay, he burst out laughing and grabbed the edge of the worktop to stay upright.

Miles was so drunk that he could barely stand and Kerry had no intention of leaving the apartment with him. 'I'll make us something to eat here.'

'I'm not hungry.' He lifted the bottle to help himself to another shot of alcohol.

Don't you think you've had enough? Kerry swallowed back a reproach that she knew would only rouse his resentment. Miles might be a party animal but she was dismayed that he could be in such a condition at only seven in the evening, particularly when he had invited her to dine with him. He looked rough in more ways than one as well. Usually immaculate in appearance, he was in dire need of a shave and a clean shirt, and his complexion was downright haggard.

'But I'm glad you're here.' On a sudden impulse, Miles engulfed her in a clumsy hug.

With firm hands, Kerry pressed him back onto the stool before he fell over.

'I'm in a mess,' he mumbled heavily.

Her concern increasing, Kerry murmured, 'What kind of a mess? Is my father giving you a hard time?'

'Yeah…everybody is and it's not about to get better, it's likely to get worse.' Miles went off into another burst of what struck her as inappropriate laughter. 'Linwoods is bleeding to death while those bastards at *Salut* steal our customers!'

'Linwoods has come through tough times before.' Kerry found some eggs in the fridge and decided to make omelettes in the hope of sobering him up with food. She was so relieved that she had not been tempted into cancelling her visit, for it was obvious that Miles was much in need of a caring shoulder.

Her stepbrother's sensitivity had always drawn Kerry to him. Although on the surface he seemed to have the same bold bravado as Rochelle, he had neither his sister's thick skin nor her resilience. He found it hard to work for a man as harsh and critical as her father could be and he seemed to see every disappointment and setback at the firm as a personal failure. When Luciano had been arrested for stealing from Linwoods, Miles had been stressed out of his mind for weeks afterwards.

At ten, Luciano called her on her cellphone. By then, she had managed to persuade Miles to go for a shower but it had been an uphill battle that had taxed her patience.

'So where are you?' Luciano enquired lazily.

'In Miles's sitting room.'

'How very exciting, *cara mia*,' Luciano purred with a satisfaction he was quite incapable of hiding. 'I'll pick you up after nine tomorrow morning. Are you missing me?'

'Nope…not in the slightest—'

'I *know* you miss me,' Luciano asserted.

Involuntarily, she grinned. 'So why ask?'

'I can't stay to chat. I have dinner guests,' Luciano sighed.

A minute later, Kerry asked herself why the news that Luciano was entertaining should make her feel like Cinderella after the stroke of midnight. When she had finally gone to see why Miles was taking so long to rejoin her, she discovered him lying face down snoring on top of his bed and understood very well why she felt like Cinderella. Bored but not ready for bed, she finally succumbed to the lure of the magazine which Rochelle had left on the coffee-table.

Paola Massone, Kerry learned from the pages of the relevant interview, was a tiny, very attractive brunette. The photograph of Paola emerging from an exclusive restaurant with Luciano some weeks earlier gave Kerry an unexpected and unpleasant jolt. Smooth and sleek in a well-cut dinner jacket, with a smiling Paola's possessive little hand pinned to his sleeve, Luciano looked utterly devastating. And when Kerry read the accompanying interview, her teeth ground together.

'We expect to be married within the next year but we're not in a rush,' Paola had declared to the world in print. 'Luciano and I enjoy a perfect understanding of our shared future and I am content to wait until he decides that the time is right.'

No, she was not about to throw a jealous, suspicious fit over that article, Kerry told herself wryly. Lots of women talked nonsense about rich, handsome men in magazine interviews and it was hardly Luciano's fault that the brunette had decided to earn herself some publicity by making attention-grabbing statements. Furthermore, she trusted Luciano…*didn't* she?

The following morning, Miles greeted Kerry with profuse apologies for his behaviour and insisted on making her breakfast. His lively mood astonished her, for she had been certain that he would be suffering from too severe a hangover to even rise from his bed to see her off.

'Since I can hardly pretend not to know *why* my sister was breathing fire yesterday, what's the latest on you and Luciano?' Miles enquired chattily.

Kerry coloured. 'I'm going out to Italy with him.'

'I'm happy with that if it makes you happy.' Miles gave her a rueful scrutiny. 'Of recent, I *have* been having second thoughts about who else might have taken that cash from Linwoods.'

Kerry studied him in surprise and then smiled. 'I'm glad.'

'It was easier to believe that Luciano had committed the fraud because he wasn't one of us. But I'm starting to think that it might have been Steven—'

'Steven Linwood...our cousin?' Kerry frowned but, although she was taken aback by the direction his suspicions had taken him in, she was pleased that he had moved beyond his prejudice to doubt his former conviction in Luciano's guilt.

'He's your cousin, not mine,' Miles reminded her.

'But you and Steven practically grew up together. How can you suspect him of stealing?'

'Do you think I want to? And, if you ask me, that was Luciano's biggest handicap when that theft was uncovered. Steven is such a likeable guy that nobody was willing to suspect him. But as it looks less and less likely that Luciano was responsible, we have to ask ourselves nasty questions. As deputy accountant at the time, Steven had the most opportunity to cook the books.'

'Yes, but—'

'Don't forget that with his father ill, Steven was pretty much in full charge,' Miles added.

Kerry thought about her cousin, Steven. He was older then she was and she thought of him as a kind, unassuming man, but he was not someone whom she could feel she had ever known well because he was naturally quiet and reserved. 'It was Steven who noticed the money had gone missing,' she objected. 'He'd hardly have blown the whistle on himself!'

'Why not? Can you think of a better way to throw suspicion on to others? After all, with an audit in the offing, Steven would've known he couldn't hide the discrepancies in the accounts for much longer!' Miles grimaced. 'But I just feel sick at the idea that he might have stolen from the firm.'

The limousine that picked Kerry up from her stepbrother's apartment that morning was empty. Luciano rang her on a car phone. 'Kerry—?'

'Where are you? Are you meeting me at the airport instead?'

When he expelled his breath in an audible hiss, she knew that she was about to be disappointed. 'No. An important meeting had to be rescheduled for this afternoon. I'll join you in Tuscany tomorrow.'

'*Tomorrow*? I wanted you to meet my grandparents again—'

'I know…but let's face it, they won't notice I'm missing,' Luciano murmured gently.

Kerry flew to Dublin on a commercial flight and when she landed a car was waiting to whisk her out to the shabby but spacious house in Howth that her grandfather's cousin, Tommy, inhabited.

Hunt O'Brien greeted Kerry with unusual animation. 'I'm lunching with a literary agent this week,' he announced with pride. 'He's Tommy's great-nephew. I hope to recoup the family fortunes with my lifetime's work.'

'That should be very interesting...but you really don't need to worry about having your books published.' Kerry was quick to pour cold water on that idea, for she dreaded the prospect of her grandfather's touching faith in his own work being destroyed by a blunt rejection. After all, a series of history volumes written over a period as long as half a century could not possibly be contemporary enough in outlook to win praise.

She bent down for her grandmother to kiss her cheek and murmured a compliment about the elaborately worked but faded embroidery stretched across the wooden sewing frame. It was one of several pieces that the old lady often simply pretended to stitch since arthritis had affected her hands.

Kerry asked her grandparents to listen carefully to the important news she had to tell them. She avoided stating outright that their only child, Carrie, was dead and concentrated instead on explaining that her late mother had given birth to three other daughters some years before her own birth.

'My goodness...only Carrie could have kept that a secret,' Viola O'Brien commented with a wondering shake of her white head.

'I do think that your mother ought to have considered mentioning that we had more than one grandchild,' her husband remarked. 'Perhaps she meant to tell us on her last visit and forgot.'

'Most unfortunate. Those poor girls have not had a single birthday card from us,' her grandmother lamented.

Even while residing with her grandparents Kerry had received only one or two cards herself, but she saw no need to point that out. To the best of her ability, she described Misty, Freddy and Ione. Her grandmother displayed enthusiasm at the mention of great-grandchildren and said she would look forward to inviting them all to stay at Ballybawn.

Kerry was surprised by that assurance, for she had not yet told the older couple that they would be able to live at the castle again.

'Luciano telephoned me last week,' Hunt O'Brien whispered to his granddaughter in a careful aside. 'He's desperate to find someone to look after the old place—'

'We shall have to instruct the housekeeper to air all the beds.' Viola smiled at that prospect before giving Kerry an anxious look. 'You did say that we would have a housekeeper, didn't you?'

Thinking of Misty's claim of how very, very rich all her sisters were, Kerry nodded. She was surprised that Luciano had already told her grandfather that he and his wife could go home to Ballybawn and very pleased that he had made that soothing promise in advance of her own trip to London. Her grandmother mentioned that she was looking forward to attending the Leopardstown races the following week and her grandfather confirmed that they would be ready to come home only after the National Book Fair had taken place in early July.

'I'm…I'm going to Italy with Luciano for a few weeks,' Kerry admitted tautly then.

'Now I understand why Florrie has been crying so

much in recent years,' her grandmother pronounced with satisfaction. 'Our granddaughters were getting married and we didn't know it. I think an Italian honeymoon trip is a charming idea, darling.'

Kerry tensed and flushed brick-red. While she endeavoured to come up with the words that would disabuse the older woman of the belief that she and Luciano were in the midst of planning a wedding, her grandfather began to describe his own boyhood trip to Rome. His host took up the topic of foreign travel with enthusiasm. Recognising how clumsy any bald announcement of continuing singledom would be at that point, particularly with her grandfather's cousin present, Kerry fell silent in mortified discomfiture.

Luciano phoned her when she was travelling back to the airport. 'My jet awaits you on the tarmac, *cara*,' he quipped. 'Check out the sleeping compartment during the flight. There's a surprise for you.'

Flying out to Tuscany in style and treated like royalty by the cabin staff, Kerry discovered that the compartment was piled high with designer garments in her size. She opened boxes, unzipped garment bags, came upon a whole embarrassing collection of whisper-thin lingerie. Biting her lip, she held up a white stretchy shirt-dress against her slim body and stared in the mirror. She had only packed an overnight bag for her visit to London yet it had not even occurred to her to wonder what she would wear in Italy. She was alarmed by her own uncharacteristic lack of practical forethought.

Yet Luciano had given no promises in terms of timing or exclusivity. He had made no commitment to her either. His gift of expensive clothes, however, truly shook her. A rich male bought fancy togs for his mistress, didn't he? Did he rush out and spend a small fortune on an entire wardrobe for his latest girlfriend? No, he did not, she answered for herself. A new lover might be offended or even seriously embarrassed by such generosity. But a mistress, or a woman whom Luciano was determined to treat as his mistress, just had to accept what might be considered payment for her sexual services.

On that cheering thought, Kerry skimmed off her unexciting navy trousers and jacket and used the compact shower adjoining the cabin to freshen up. The lacy lingerie felt wicked against her naked skin. The white shirt-dress clung as close to her slender curves as a caress and she knew just how much he would appreciate that effect.

Was Luciano worth more to her than the sisters whom she would never get to know while he was around? Her guilty eyes shadowed with regret. But choice had been torn from her the same moment that she accepted that she still loved him and indeed loved him a great deal more than she had five years earlier. She had had to lose him to appreciate him. She had had to live five years without him to realise just how boring, lonely and empty life could be.

She had not required Ione to tell her that Luciano was a very clever and dangerous male. She had always known that. He was absolutely ruthless and he had worked very hard at trying to conceal that trait from her, only he had never succeeded. The dark, stormy, shadowy side of his hot-blooded nature had always secretly excited her, for he was so very different from her. Nor had

Ione needed to warn Kerry that Luciano was already hurting her family by coming between her and her new-found sisters. The way her siblings felt about Luciano, that separation had been inevitable. After all, no woman painfully conscious that she had once had insufficient faith in the guy she loved would hesitate to range herself squarely by his side when she got a second chance.

And it *was* a second chance, Kerry reminded herself. She did not require bribery, persuasion or payment in any shape or form to share Luciano's bed. The very idea was laughable when in spite of her every attempt to convince herself otherwise, she still burned to lie under and over him again and behave like a shameless hussy. In fact being a mistress promised to be a lot of fun. If anything, *she* would be taking advantage of *him*... endless, wonderful, enjoyable advantage...and she could hardly wait.

CHAPTER EIGHT

As THE limousine climbed the steep road Luciano never once removed his steady gaze from the Villa Contarini, which dominated the lush valley.

The magnificent seventeenth-century palazzo built by the first Roberto Tessari sat high on a hillside thick with oak woods and clumps of black cypress. It was not a building that proffered a warm welcome, it was a living stone monument to Tessari power and money. At the foot of the long, sweeping driveway, Luciano told his chauffeur to stop. Just beyond the walls he had scaled as a boy he alighted from his limousine, determined to savour his right to walk up through the superb gardens which had been his father's pride and joy. In the drowsing heat of early evening, the aroma of the flowering oleanders lay heavy on the still air.

Impatient to find Kerry, he crossed the immaculate marble terrace that bounded the imposing front entrance. He felt good. Everything had fallen smoothly into place, everything was just as he wanted it to be, for he had never pictured being at the villa without Kerry. He snapped off a single white rose that had been allowed to curl round a pillar carrying the weathered bust of some mythical sea creature and went inside. The interior was silent, for he had given the staff the evening off. The arrival of Luciano da Valenza, the bastard son of Stephanella, in the grand villa of his titled forebears was a special occasion to which he wanted no witnesses. His steps echoed round the big porch.

In the vast hall that stretched before him, huge portraits hung in serried ranks on the walls. Although he had never set foot in the Villa Contarini before, he could name virtually every face depicted on those canvases. As a teenager, he had devoured all the books that documented the history of the Tessari family and depicted their treasure house of a home. In one portrait he now recognised the lineaments of his own hard bone structure reflected in the stern visage of his paternal grandfather. But the resemblance meant nothing to him, for it was many years since he had experienced a need to belong to any family tree and he averted his attention with cool disdain from the painting of his own father.

Yet the claustrophobic silence still began to make him feel oddly uncomfortable. His own reflection in a giant mirror startled him and he frowned. In rebellion, he jerked loose his tie, cast it on a marble side-table and unbuttoned his shirt collar. This was now his home: he should make himself at home. But it did not feel like home. But then for longer than he cared to recall nowhere had *ever* felt like home to him. When he had left the Contarini estate as a child he had never again allowed himself to become attached to a place.

A slight sound alerted him to the awareness that he was no longer alone and he swung round, light as a dancer on his feet for all his commanding height and powerful build. Kerry was poised at the foot of the imposing staircase, an uncertain smile wavering on her soft mouth. Her sweet familiarity twisted something inside him. The dying brilliance of the sunlight cascaded down through the tall landing window above and turned her hair to a fiery, curly halo and illuminated her skin to a pale gold that glowed against the perfect white of her dress. His hunger to possess her again was immediate, ferocious, primal…

In the suffocating silence Kerry stared back at Luciano, her heart going bang-bang-bang, her mouth running dry as a bone. His charcoal-grey pinstripe suit was conventional in colour but the sharp cut was all Italian designer style and gave him the suave, sardonic aspect of a sexy gangster. He had strolled down the hall with a lithe grace of movement that would have made a lion on the prowl look clumsy. She had watched him peel off his tie and throw it aside, luxuriant black hair gleaming as a slice of light fell on his bold, bronzed profile. Simultaneously, her bones had turned to water. He just took her breath away.

The stunning golden eyes Luciano levelled on her released a flock of butterflies inside her tense tummy. Her legs were so rigid that her knees began to wobble. He had an effect on her very similar to a chain reaction, she acknowledged in dismay. Embarrassment claimed her when she registered that her nipples had tightened into stiff little points pushing forward within her bra and possibly even visible to him through the fine, clinging material of her dress.

His brilliant gaze arrowed over her, lingered around chest level, his dense black lashes lowering and then skimming up with all male enjoyment to watch the wave of slow, hot colour climb her face.

With a flourish, he presented her with the rose. 'Did the staff look after you?'

The petals felt like soft, smooth silk beneath her appreciative fingers. 'Yes…I was shown to my room—'

'My room too,' he slotted in lazily.

At that reminder, Kerry ran even more out of breath. Some timbre in that throaty drawl of his teased at her spinal cord like a honeyed caress. 'Then I was served with afternoon tea in a very opulent drawing room. It's a very large building and rather intimidating…'

'Do you realise that you're whispering? We're alone here. Feel free to shout…even *scream*,' Luciano suggested huskily while he settled his hands to her slim hips and lifted her up onto the second last step of the stairs. 'Don't let the Villa Contarini inhibit your natural instincts—'

'Doesn't it inhibit you?'

'You must be joking, *cara mia*.' Lifting a seemingly casual hand, Luciano let his fingertips trace the fine line of her throat and watched her automatically tip her head back to invite his touch.

With the same measured cool, he tugged free the first button on her dress and watched her snatch in a sudden driven breath. 'I want to look at you here before the sunlight goes…the way I often used to imagine you…'

'Imagine me…?' Kerry could barely get breath into her constricted lungs.

'While I was in prison I pictured you in many ways in many places. You're not ready for the details, which makes it more exciting for me because you have no idea what I plan to do at any given moment,' Luciano pointed out with a roughened edge to his dark, rich drawl.

'F-fantasies?' Only the one word escaped Kerry, for

as soon as the stammer emerged she clamped her lips closed.

'What do you think?' The second button came loose, the parted edges springing back to expose the upper slopes of her breasts and the pronounced rise and fall of those pouting swells as her breathing grew more quick and shallow.

'Shouldn't we g-go upstairs?' she heard herself gasp.

'This is *my* fantasy but I can promise you that you are about to receive more pleasure than you have ever dreamed of…trust me, *bella mia*.'

Kerry was trembling. As the fourth button gave, she saw his molten golden gaze drop to the flimsy white bra which only accentuated the prominent pink buds below the lace. Her own sense of anticipation was so intense she was ashamed and she shut her eyes tight, for she was a total slave to the treacherous, maddening ache between her thighs that only he could satisfy. The dress fell away from her warm, damp skin and she hovered in an agony of expectation, the rose falling forgotten from her flexing fingers.

'You can't wait…I like that,' Luciano savoured. 'But I will *make* you wait.'

Her dazed blue eyes opened on him, her pupils darkened, dilated.

While Luciano surveyed her with possessive satisfaction, the surge of his own desire gripped him with almost painful intensity. A delicate beauty in silk lingerie, finally his to enjoy, and nothing had ever felt so good or given him such a raw sexual buzz. One provocative glimpse of her slender, quivering body adorned only in narrow bands of lace prevented him from lingering on the uneasy acknowledgement that it was taking him longer to work her out of his system than he had foreseen. He reminded himself that he was in Tuscany to unwind and he was taking time out from the real world only to lose himself in pure erotic pleasure. And never had the pursuit of pleasure exercised greater appeal than it did at that moment.

'I can't believe I'm standing here like this...' Kerry was already shocked by the discovery that it was a turn-on to be half-naked in front of him while he remained fully dressed in his business suit.

'Not for long...' Luciano pushed the cups of her bra out of his path and teased her straining nipples with expert fingers until she moaned out loud. He could feel the tiny little ripples of desire pulsing through her taut frame. Suddenly he didn't want the fantasy, the stupid, impractical fantasy of having her every which way on the stairs, he wanted to carry her upstairs and make love to her in a bed where he could torture her at length in comfort. In defiance of that weakness, he clamped her to him and let his tongue penetrate between her eagerly parted lips with a hungry need to imprint himself on her that was already threatening to rise out of his control.

Kerry was dizzy with longing, weak with desire. She had surrendered all self-will before he even got her dress off. When he let his fingertips skim a provocative sweep of the thin, taut expanse of lace between her trembling thighs, she jerked and cried out, for the slick, wet heat of her feminine core was unbearably sensitive to his merest touch. Her breath sobbing in her throat, she clutched at him with desperate hands to stay upright and buried her burning face in his shoulder.

'*Please…*'

He decided that he would do the staircase scenario some other time, scooped her off her feet and carried her on up to the gilded double doors that provided an entrance to the master bedroom off the landing.

'You make me weak,' Kerry confided unsteadily.

Luciano tensed at that word that had always had the power to fill him with rare unease. He was always waiting for weakness of some kind to make a sneak attack on him and he knew he would waste no time in rooting it out like the sickness it was. But wanting to spend at least six non-stop weeks in bed with Kerry was just rampant lust, perfectly normal for a sex-starved male, *not* a sign that he was getting unhealthily hooked on her again. And by the time he left Tuscany in—what?—maybe three, four months, he would be fully cured of the belief that she had any appeal whatsoever. Reassured by that conviction, he stood over her, pitched off his jacket and pulled off his shirt to expose his impressive, hair-roughened pectorals and sleek, smooth brown stomach.

'Weak…weak…weak,' Kerry mumbled in helpless addition.

'Stop saying that,' Luciano commanded in a raw undertone.

When he chose that same moment to discard his boxer shorts, she stretched back against the pillows and just burned for him. He came down beside her, all thrusting masculine heat and driving energy, but he lay kissing her with loads of arousing restraint. He closed her hand round his bold, smooth shaft and groaned out loud and shuddered when she explored him with an unashamed hunger that she found insanely exciting. But then she found everything that he did next and every move that he made even in response to her insanely exciting.

'I can't wait,' Luciano confessed raggedly.

She was way beyond talking, on an edge so high that when he finally plunged into her the flood of glorious pleasure shockwaving through her took her by storm. She hit a peak very fast, drowned for long, timeless moments of bliss in her own helpless release. But before she could even begin to recover, he flipped her limp length over, tugged her up on her knees and slowly, smoothly entered her again without even losing his pagan rhythm. She could not believe what she was allowing him to do but her own excitement triumphed over her. 'We shouldn't—'

'I *have* to,' Luciano growled and sooner rather than later he sent her over the edge of ecstasy all over again and any urge to reason with him evaporated.

When the world had settled again, Kerry lay in his arms and let her eyes drift blissfully shut while he tried to keep her awake. 'It's supposed to be guys who fall asleep—'

'Have a free ego trip. You're way too lively for me,' Kerry mumbled.

'I could keep going all night. This is *all* I've thought about since that first night with you, *cara mia.*'

She uttered a sleepy laugh. 'Surely not—'

'Every minute on the minute. I've been obsessed. It can only be because five years back, you're the one that got away...' Luciano admitted as the sheer seductive power of his own relaxation took over.

Kerry froze.

Appreciating too late what he had let slip, Luciano framed a soundless swear word above her head.

'It's the same for me,' Kerry whispered back sweet as saccharine and felt the big, powerful length of him tauten against her. 'I knew you had a reputation for being good at this caper, and at twenty-six years old I thought it was time I—'

'No, you didn't. Don't cheapen yourself by talking like that!' Luciano grated angrily. 'Virgins don't think that way—'

'How would you know?'

Luciano thought about that and frustration made him simmer like oil in a boiling cauldron. He just *knew* he was special to her but to say so might suggest that he was arrogant, which he knew he was not. 'I know... OK?'

Kerry was very pale. So, on his terms, she was the one who had got away, was she? The only woman he had not scored with? Could Luciano be that caveman basic? She decided he might well be. Pulling free of him in hurt rejection, she scrambled out of bed. Making for the first door her tearful gaze lit on, she found herself in a bathroom and hurtled thankfully into the shelter of the shower cubicle. She remembered the rose he had given her, the reference to the fantasy, and a rueful smile tinged her lips. He was telling her stuff that once he would never have told her. Some of it was bound to be total rubbish, wasn't it?

Luciano groaned out loud. Why was she the only female he blew it with on a regular basis? He sprang out of bed, went through one of the other two doors available and discovered that there were *two* adjoining bathrooms. That infuriated him because it would not be cool to insist on sharing a shower with her when there was no need to do so. When he returned to the bedroom, Kerry was back in bed pretending to be asleep. He decided to settle for that, for she was at least still within reach.

When he wakened at some timeless hour of the night, disorientated and in the grip of his usual nightmares, Kerry had both arms wrapped round him. 'Where do you go in those dreams of yours?' she whispered.

He breathed in deep and slowly exhaled again. 'Back to that cell eight feet wide by ten feet deep—'

'It was…*that* small?' She sounded shocked.

'I had to share it too…no big deal.' Luciano strove hard for a macho shrug of indifference even when his heart was still thumping with sick fear in his chest.

That must have been torture for a loner who had always cherished privacy, Kerry reflected painfully. In the darkness, her eyes were wet. 'If you'd phoned me or written to me just one time, just one line, even one word—'

Luciano froze and yanked himself free of her embrace. '*Per meraviglia!* Why would I have wanted to do that?'

'Are you planning to punish me forever?'

He raised himself against the pillows. 'I'm not punishing you… What do you think I am? A cross little boy?'

Sometimes his emotional responses seemed disturbingly similar. He lived in rigorous denial of his own anger and pain, she thought ruefully. That anger and pain got to leap out of his subconscious and attack him only while he slept. Silence fell. The gap between them widened. When she wakened soon after eight, she was alone.

A maid brought her fruit, fresh baked rolls and coffee while she sat at a shaded stone table out on the terrace. A glorious new day had dawned to display the colourful living tapestry of the Tuscan countryside. She could see fields of waving green grain and golden rape interspersed with silvery green olive groves and orchards. Here and there rows of fresh lime-green grape vines marched up the slopes with geometric exactitude, but the valley still rejoiced in dense tracts of natural woodland.

She was finishing her breakfast when a phone was brought to her.

'Good morning,' her sister, Misty, declared chirpily, making Kerry sit up straight with a frown of surprise.

'How did you know where I was? How did you even get this phone number?'

'Do I have to confess to being a snoop?' Misty groaned in comical apology. 'We spent years looking for you and we really would die if we lost track of you now! Will you give me some tips in advance of meeting Grandpa and Grandma? I've heard this vague rumour that our grandparents may be rather individual personalities.'

Involuntarily, Kerry smiled. 'That's not a rumour.'

Almost an hour passed while she talked to her sister. When the call ended, Kerry was amazed that they had chatted for so long without any awkwardness. But then, Luciano's name had not been mentioned once. She was convinced, however, that once he allowed her sisters to buy back the castle, their hostility towards him would vanish. Was it disloyal of her to still want to get to know her siblings even though they had threatened Luciano? Presumably, though, there would be no further threats. How loyal ought she to be to a male who had yet to utter a caring word to her? Without further hesitation she decided that she was right to pursue further contact with her sisters.

Mid-morning, Luciano strode out onto the terrace. Faded denim jeans hugged his long, powerful thighs, a casual aqua shirt accentuating his bronzed skin. He sank down in a fluid motion into the seat beside hers. Lean, handsome features taut, bright eyes veiled, he set another white rosebud down on the table-top next to her hand. She glanced at it, then ignored the offering with pointed determination. In a sudden movement, Luciano leant forward, curved one hand to the nape of her neck to entrap her and brought his sensual mouth down in hungry appeal on hers. Her body tightened and tingled, terrifingly eager to respond.

He lifted his proud dark head again. 'I went out very early. The vines are beautiful at dawn when the dew rises off the ground like a mist…tomorrow morning I'll take you out with me.'

Grapevines at dawn…how could she resist such an invitation?

The rose, the kiss, the vines, all evasion tactics to keep her from discussing more controversial topics. 'Last night—' Kerry dared unsteadily.

Before she could say any more, Luciano closed his hand over hers. 'I just want to *be* with you…'

Warmth enclosed her, squeezed out her fears and insecurity. He had said enough to soothe her. She told him about Misty's phone call. 'I expect she'll stay in touch. Do you mind?'

A stark little silence fell.

His strong jawline clenched. 'Why would I?'

Luciano had already spent a day and a half ring-fencing his companies from potential threats. After all, come hell or high water, he had *no* intention of selling Ballybawn to her sisters but he saw no reason to worry Kerry with that announcement. Her desire to communicate with her siblings and satisfy her curiosity was natural. Rationally he knew and accepted that but he was not happy about it. He was already convinced that her sisters would do everything within their power to destroy his relationship with her.

'Why do you never mention the case you're still pursuing to clear your name?' Kerry asked him then.

His keen gaze hardened. 'What's to mention? To have the case retried, I need new evidence. I have investigators working on it but it *is* five years since that money was syphoned out of the accounts. It was a neat and clever scam and the culprits have had a long time to cover their tracks. It will be difficult to find a fresh lead—'

'You think there was *more* than one person involved?'

'It's possible.' Aware that she was still very much in contact with Miles, Luciano regretted even saying that much.

'You know, Miles suspects my cousin, Steven,' Kerry confided.

Thinking about wimpy Steven, Luciano almost laughed out loud, but he didn't want to hurt her feelings. An honest, straightforward woman was a pearl beyond

price and that was Kerry, for she could not recognise
cunning in others. Without hesitation she had repeated
what Miles had undoubtedly primed her to repeat. How
could he ever have believed that Kerry could have been
involved in framing him for his prison term? Now he
could only smile at the very idea. But Miles had severely
underestimated Luciano's intelligence when he had used
Kerry as a vehicle for his misinformation campaign.

Luciano plucked yet another ripe cherry from the ne-
glected tree and crouched down to dangle the succulent
fruit just within reach of Kerry's juice-stained lips. 'I'm
sure you can manage one more, *bella mia*.'

Stretching up, Kerry swiped the cherry from his lean,
elegant fingers with her mouth. 'You tempt me...'

'Temptation is the spice of life.' Luciano flung himself back down on the rug spread in the shade and leant
over her, slumberous golden eyes pinned to her with
mockery. 'Don't you dare fall asleep on me again. I
could set a clock by your naps. At midday, off again
late afternoon, dead to the world before midnight. What
happened to the livewire who used to get by on a few
hours a night?'

'Obviously endless sunshine makes even livewires
sleepy.' Kerry blamed the summer heat for her unusual
tiredness.

For three glorious weeks, day after sun-drenched day
at the Villa Contarini had dawned fresher and brighter
than the last. The sky above would seem a more heav-
enly blue and the sun would drench the fertile earth with
ever more golden warmth. She was wonderfully, wildly
happy just to be with Luciano. That lean dark-angel face

of his made her very heart lurch with longing and as he was the first thing she saw when she opened her eyes in the morning and the last at night, how could she be anything other than blissfully content?

The Villa Contarini had shaken off all the gloom that she had once found daunting. Curtains had been thrown back to let the light flood in, windows flung wide and all the doors lay open on to the terraces. Informality ruled. Cushions were often tumbled on the floor, for lovers had no interest in sitting on antique sofas twenty feet apart, and meals were eaten at odd hours and most often in the fresh air.

By day, Luciano had shown Kerry all the places he remembered from his childhood. He had begun by taking her to see his former home and he had been disconcerted to find the old farmhouse lying in ruins. That he and his mother should have been evicted all those years ago only for the house to lie empty and unused angered him. On their return to the villa, he had had his father's portrait taken down from the wall.

'*Santo cielo.* I thought in time I might be able to look at him, at least acknowledge who he was,' Luciano had confessed in a ravaged undertone that night. 'But I can't even do that. We had so little but even that he took from us to protect his name from gossip and he got away with it because we were powerless.'

'Don't even think about him.' Kerry had curved round his lean, muscular frame in sympathy, hurting for him, wondering why she had never appreciated that anyone who felt anything as deeply as he did had to be much more vulnerable than he might seem on the surface.

Exploring the extensive Contarini estate often on foot

had been very enjoyable. She had not cared where they went or what they did as long as he was with her, and he was very energetic. The designer clothes he had bought her got laughably dirty, torn and stained while they roamed through the woods, climbed over fences and tumbledown walls and picnicked in fields. In the evening, however, they often ate out in exclusive restaurants in Siena. Then she would see other women look at his bold, bronzed profile and lithe, powerful physique with a frank appreciation and sexual avidity that scared her. For Luciano never mentioned love, the future or even the past that they had once shared, and she soon realised that without even one of those important elements insecurity was to be her lot in life with him.

Most mornings he dragged her out of bed early to tour the vineyard with him. She thought all wine tasted like nasty medicine and had never been interested in how the grapes made it from the vines into the bottles, but she was really pleased that he should want to share his interest with her. Shamefully, however, what lingered longest in Kerry's memory was the passionate excitement of making love with him in a dusty cellar below the winery, her wild cries of pleasure silenced by his marauding mouth.

Occasionally he would leave her alone for an hour or two while he caught up with business. When they were apart, Kerry spent virtually every minute on the phone. If she wasn't chatting to Miles, she was chatting to one of her sisters. That first call from Misty had soon been followed by others from Freddy and Ione. Kerry was getting acquainted with her siblings through their daily phone conversations. But she found herself trying to conceal from Luciano the sheer frequency of the calls they exchanged, for she could not help feeling that, in getting on like a house on fire with *them*, she was being disloyal to *him*.

'Will this keep you awake long enough for me to have my wicked way with you?'

Dredged from her last uncomfortable thought back to the present, Kerry blinked and muttered, 'Sorry?'

With a husky laugh, Luciano lifted her hand so that the sunlight drew a rainbow glitter from the sapphire and diamond bracelet he had clasped round her wrist while she lay drowsing by his side.

Kerry's eyes widened to their fullest extent and she sat up. 'Oh, my goodness…it's…it's amazing!' She watched the jewels flash and catch the light. 'Are they real?'

'Of course they are!' Luciano was insulted.

The gift made her feel uneasy. 'You shouldn't have bought me something so expensive—'

'Why not? I can afford it.'

Registering from the flare in his brilliant eyes that she had offended, Kerry forced a smile. 'I suppose you can now that you're rid of the responsibility of Ballybawn.'

He quirked a brow. 'But I'm not rid of it.'

That was the moment when Kerry grasped the worst drawback of avoiding the discussion of sensitive issues with both him *and* her sisters. 'But I just assumed that you would accept my sisters' bid for the castle—'

'Why would I allow them to dictate what I do?' Luciano demanded. 'You have more right to Ballybawn than they have. But for your efforts, your grandparents would have lost their home years ago.'

Kerry was taken aback by his attitude. 'That's not how I feel. If you let my sisters buy Ballybawn, it will still be in the family. That's all that matters and I just want peace. I can't believe that you're being so stubborn—'

'Believe it, *mia carina*,' Luciano urged as he pulled her close to his lean, sun-warmed length. 'I never liked being bullied. Stop worrying about me. I can look after myself.'

'You're very obstinate.' Kerry met slumberous golden eyes full of amusement. 'I gather that nobody has yet tried to put you out of business.'

'Not so far. *Dio mio*, I want you all the time.' Tasting her lush mouth, dipping his tongue into the moist, tender interior to make her shiver, Luciano slowly tugged her back down to the rug and came over her. She could feel him, hot and hard and hungrily aroused against her stomach. In answer tiny tremors of desire quivered through her and damp heat burned at the heart of her.

It was not the most timely moment for a mobile phone to start ringing from the Toyota Landcruiser parked only a few feet away.

'Don't answer it. I wish you'd switch it off,' Luciano commanded as he angled back from her. 'If I can leave mine off, so can you—'

'But it might be Freddy, and with the time difference between Europe and Quamar it's so hard for her to reach me at a reasonable hour—'

'Misty sent you a mobile that works abroad so that you could be reached twenty-four hours a day. Do you know why? Not one of your sisters can bear to wait five minutes for anything!' Luciano breathed with an amount of derision that shook her. 'You are the latest toy in your sisters' lives. Some day soon, I will smash that phone—'

'Look…the call might be something important.' Endeavouring to ignore his annoyance, Kerry got into the car to reach for the phone she had left lying there. It was Ione, ringing to ask whether or not Kerry would be attending the party Ione and Alexio were holding to celebrate their wedding anniversary the following month.

Conscious of Luciano's brooding scrutiny as he stood by the driver's door, Kerry reddened and lowered her head, her fingers plucking nervously at the pocket of her skirt. 'I'm not sure yet how I'm going to be fixed that week.'

'That's what you said the last time I asked. Can't you make a move without Luciano?' Ione groaned ruefully.

Kerry flushed. She was uneasily conscious of Luciano's proximity, for he had settled into the driver's seat beside her. 'How many moves do you make without Alexio?'

Without the smallest warning, Luciano lifted her phone from her hand and slotted it into the handset on the dashboard so that the call would be broadcast over the car speakers.

In the tense silence, Ione's voice emerged as clear as a bell. 'I'm married. You're still single and free to do as you like. If the date doesn't suit Luciano, come to the party on your own!' Her sister laughed. 'Do I have to bribe you by promising to line up some hot Greek guy for you?'

Dark colour had fired over the fierce slant of Luciano's cheekbones and shimmering outrage blazed in his incredulous golden eyes. 'Kerry is *not* free to do as she likes!' he interrupted her sister with raw emphasis, speaking so that the microphone above the driver's door would pick him up. 'Nor should I need to state the obvious…a hot Greek guy would be superfluous to your sister's needs.'

An aghast silence buzzed at Ione's end of the line before her sister exclaimed, 'Is that Luciano I'm speaking to?'

'Yes, and I can tell you right now, Kerry won't be attending your party!'

'Luciano, stop it…' Kerry hissed in embarrassment.

'Do you make a habit of listening to my sister's calls?' Ione asked worriedly.

'From here on in, I'll be listening to all of them!' Luciano ground out without any hesitation whatsoever. 'I won't let you interfere in our relationship.'

'But I wasn't trying to interfere between you,' Ione contradicted in audible dismay.

With an angry stab of one lean brown hand, Luciano cut off her sister's call.

Kerry did not know who she was most annoyed with: Luciano for eavesdropping or Ione for her provocative sense of humour. In silence, Luciano swept up the rug and the picnic hamper and pitched them into the Landcruiser with a violence that spoke louder than any words could have done.

Indeed, Luciano was so enraged that he did not trust himself to speak. His worst suspicions had been proven true. He was now convinced that all Kerry's sisters were working against him and pouring spiteful poison into her innocent ears in an effort to cause trouble.

But that was not the least of it. *Some hot Greek guy?*

Luciano seethed at that basest of all insults. How could Ione Christoulakis offer to set Kerry up with another man? That was downright immoral and disgusting! The very idea of it made Luciano feel sick to the stomach. He wanted to tell Kerry that she was never under any circumstances to accept a call from one of her sisters again. After hearing Ione in full flow, he knew he would be equally unhappy about allowing Kerry to even visit her siblings' homes. It would be like sending a little child into a den of iniquity.

'You know…Ione was only joking about lining up a Greek guy,' Kerry muttered in the smouldering silence.

Like hell had Ione been joking! Bold profile rigid, Luciano sent the four-wheel-drive raking up the dirt track towards the road. He was incredibly grateful that the revealing look of guilty embarrassment on Kerry's face had made him break in on that phone call. Forewarned was forearmed!

Evidently there were no depths to which her sisters would not sink in their determination to oust him from Kerry's life. Even if it meant tempting her into infidelity. It was not that he didn't trust Kerry…he trusted her *totally*. But she was very naive, always doubting herself, a prime target for unscrupulous manipulative tactics. Hadn't he occasionally used those same tactics on her himself? And very successfully? Suppose they got her drunk? Who could tell what lies her sisters might be prepared to tell about him? Hadn't she once listened to Rochelle's lies and swallowed them whole?

Just when had the balance of power changed in their relationship? Luciano asked himself angrily. When had the casual affair he had initially planned fallen by the wayside? Why had he made her his mistress but treated her as his lover? Just when too had he become so possessive of Kerry that even her sisters' antagonism towards him could make him feel threatened? He had always been possessive of her, he acknowledged grudgingly. But then Kerry was essentially his in a way no other woman had ever been…

On their first night in Tuscany, she had asked him when he planned to stop punishing her. But by that stage, Luciano recognised, he had already moved on beyond that need. The discovery that there had been no other man in her life or her bed while he had been in prison had gone a long way to easing his bitter sense of betrayal. Seeing what a hard, cold, *miserable* slog she had endured at Ballybawn during those same years had helped as well. He had also relished the belief that he was in control of their relationship. However, her sisters had destroyed his complacency…

Now he knew what he was up against. Misty, Freddy and Ione would be waiting to pounce on his every mistake and magnify it into a hanging offence for Kerry's benefit. Sexy, eligible guys of Greek, Sicilian and Quamari extraction would be trailed in front of her like seductive bait at every opportunity. Every time he had to go away on business or even work late, her sisters would see it as an opportunity to undermine their relationship. As long as they were plotting and scheming in the background, he would never know a moment's peace. Her siblings would not be happy until their kid sister was as respectably married as they were themselves. He could spike their guns by marrying Kerry himself…husbands were a lot harder to exclude and destroy!

Kerry stole a troubled glance at Luciano's brooding profile. Her own tension was increased by the fact that there had been a certain amount of unwelcome truth in Ione's contention that she ought to make up her own mind about the party. Kerry knew that she needed to make her own plans rather than just drift from day to day in what was essentially Luciano's world. Two days earlier, her grandparents had flown to London to stay with Misty and her husband, Leone, and were to remain there until the castle was ready for their occupation again. Within another couple of weeks at most, she would have to go home to Ballybawn...yet Luciano was already talking as though he would be making a pretty much permanent return to Italy. Where did that leave her?

As they entered the palazzo, the housekeeper hurried up to speak to Luciano.

'I believe we have visitors.' An arm lightly curving to Kerry's spine, Luciano walked her straight into the drawing room with him.

Two women, one young and exceptionally pretty, the other an older version of the first, rose to greet them. Kerry's recognition of Paola Massone was instantaneous. The sight of the Italian beauty who had talked in her magazine interview as though she was only waiting for Luciano to name the date for their wedding, made Kerry tense in surprise and dismay. Luciano introduced her to Paola and the brunette's frosty-faced mother, neither of whom paid Kerry the slightest attention. Kerry felt at a horrible disadvantage with her hair tossed, her face bare of make-up and her mouth swollen from his kisses.

Paola had chocolate-brown eyes and silky black hair and her trendy caramel suit was the last word in fashion. A determined smile on her face, Kerry endeavoured to conceal the grass stains on her skirt. Luciano tried to include Kerry in the conversation but Paola and her parent would only speak Italian. As Kerry began to appreciate the extent to which she was being ignored and treated as though her very presence was an affront, her cheeks began to burn with mortified colour.

Finally, Kerry stood up and without a word went upstairs to their bedroom. She had been made to feel about an inch high. Did Paola and her mother regard her as Luciano's mistress, just some silly little foreigner sharing his bed for a while and unworthy of any further interest? Did it matter? Their treatment had cut her to the bone.

Why had she never questioned Luciano about Paola? Well, she had not believed what she had read in Paola's magazine interview, for it had not made sense. Why would Luciano be pursuing his former fiancée if he had plans to marry some other woman? The very fact that Rochelle had drawn Paola's existence to Kerry's attention had also ensured that Kerry was even less impressed by Paola's dramatic claims. But Paola here on the spot, making a confident visit with her mother in tow, was a very different matter. It was proof that Luciano and Paola *did* have an ongoing relationship, and if that was true, what else might be true as well?

It was time for her to leave the Villa Contarini, Kerry told herself fiercely, fighting the shell-shocked feeling of loss already tearing at her. She had to take hold of her own life again. What was it about Luciano that prevented her from holding back, being sensible and protecting herself in their relationship? Love was not an excuse for her to lose her wits and make a fool of herself. Somehow just being with Luciano again had stripped her of her independent shell and strength. She was very happy with him and happiness was seductive. She could not conceive a day without him, never mind a lifetime, but she would have to learn how to do so.

From the dressing room, Kerry lifted the overnight bag with which she had originally arrived. She changed into the trouser suit in which she had flown out to Italy. It felt hot and scratchy. She almost laughed at herself. Was she being ludicrously petty? What odds would it make to him that she was leaving behind the fancy wardrobe which he had bought for her? She was removing the sapphire and diamond bracelet when Luciano appeared in the bedroom doorway.

'I apologise for my visitors' bad manners,' Luciano drawled, his keen gaze noting her rigidity and scanning the overnight bag at her feet. 'Going somewhere?'

Blue eyes hollow, Kerry gave him a jerky nod. 'It's time for me to leave.'

The cool, relaxed pose fell from Luciano as he moved deeper into the room. 'What's that supposed to mean?'

Her spine tightened. 'That I'm...*leaving*?'

'Like hell you are!' Luciano slung back at her. 'You're not using the Massones as an excuse to walk out on me!'

Her chin came up, eyes bright with bitter strain. 'I wasn't aware I needed an excuse—'

His lean, strong face clenched hard. 'You're annoyed about Paola—'

'Why would I be?' Kerry demanded.

'But all that's between Paola and me is the business proposal that she asked me to consider a few months ago—'

Kerry had meant to demonstrate no interest but that claim disconcerted her. 'Business?'

'Paola's a distant cousin of mine. Her father, Armanno, inherited my father's title but both Tessari's entire estate and his money came to me. Armanno Massone is a famous wine-maker. Aware of my ambitions for the vineyard here, Paola suggested a very practical alliance between us all.'

'Alliance?' Kerry queried.

His sensual mouth twisted. 'If I agreed to marry her, her father would take charge of the Contarini vineyard. She also believed I would benefit from her family's superior status in society. The Massones may not be wealthy but they're very classy.'

Kerry was hanging on his every word. 'And what was Paola going to get out of this arrangement?'

'A very rich husband. Being classy is a challenge on a budget.'

Kerry's lips parted, rounded and then closed again, her smooth brow still indented. 'And what was your answer to this incredible proposal?'

'*Santo cielo!* I said I'd think about it…and why not?'

As Kerry fully grasped what Luciano was telling her, furious anger lanced up through her and a shaken laugh of disbelief fell from her taut lips. 'No wonder you were so keen to let me know that marriage wouldn't be on the cards! All the time you've been with me, you've been planning to marry Paola!'

'*Dio mio!* That's *not* how it was!' Luciano was startled by that accusation. 'I don't have a relationship with Paola. What she offered me was a business deal and as such worthy of consideration. I won't apologise for that—'

'Oh, won't you?' Kerry gasped in fevered interruption.

'No, I will not. At the time that offer was made, I was still in prison. I was in the mood to consider a practical marriage that had nothing to do with sentiment,' Luciano launched back at her with hard golden eyes. 'I was very bitter... I'd lost five years of my life, five years when I had expected to be married, setting up a home and starting a family. But I'd forgotten what the outside world and freedom would feel like!'

'So you then decided to make the most of your freedom *before* you made the sacrifice of settling down with her!' Kerry condemned, brushing past him in her eagerness to reach the door.

'But I'm obviously not cut out for much in the way of freedom,' Luciano murmured with wry self-mockery. 'Within weeks of my release, I was back with the same woman I was with before I went into prison.'

Only a couple of feet past him, Kerry stopped and tried to swallow the thickness of tears in her throat. 'Yes, but—'

Lean hands closed over her slight shoulders and gently imposed pressure to turn her back to him. 'It's also several weeks since I informed Paola that I wouldn't be taking her up on her offer. But she's persistent.'

'It doesn't matter. All she's done is force me to think about stuff I should've thought about sooner than this.

When you said that what we once had was gone, I didn't really listen because I didn't want to believe that,' Kerry admitted unevenly.

His strong jawline clenched hard, golden eyes screened by his thick lashes as his wide, sensual mouth compressed. 'And *I* didn't want to believe that what we once had could still be there. Now I'm afraid that your sisters have managed to convince you that I'm bad news—'

'No, they're not like that—'

Luciano snatched in a ragged breath. 'But, bad news or not, I want to marry you, and if you say no I'm just going to lock you in here and deprive you of sleep until I wear you down into agreeing.'

Engaged in fighting back the tears stinging behind her eyelids, Kerry could not persuade herself that he had truly said those words. Slowly she tipped her head back and looked up at him with questioning intensity.

His brilliant gaze clung to her pale, taut face. 'I feel like we've never been apart, only we're closer than we used to be. I want you with me all the time, *bella mia.*'

'Are you s-serious?' Kerry stammered.

'When I reach the stage where I'm worrying that your sisters will send in a hit squad to steal you away in the middle of the night, it's time to bite the bullet like a man and head for the church...before I lose any claim to sanity that I ever had,' Luciano mocked in a roughened undertone.

'But you said you *weren't* going to marry me—'

Beautiful dark golden eyes sought and held hers. 'I was wrong. I *want* to marry you—'

Kerry was starting to tremble, almost afraid to believe,

for she could see how much her answer meant to him in the depths of his clear gaze and it was a look she had believed he might never give her again. 'I know you're saying that but—'

'As soon as possible. I'd like to get married here in Italy and I won't wait a day longer than necessary…we've already lost out on too many years.'

The gruffness in his accented drawl made her own throat ache. She pushed forward into his lithe, lean, powerful frame and he crushed her so close that she could hardly breathe.

'Yes…I think I'm going to cry,' she mumbled shakily.

Luciano looked down at her, a slashing grin curving his wide, sensual mouth. 'Over *me*? Can I watch?'

'Pervert…' Kerry laughed, for he had successfully banished all threat of tears.

Just when Luciano was in the act of backing her towards the bed, dark golden eyes smouldering, she looked up at him in sudden appeal. 'Would you mind…would you mind if I just rang Misty?'

Disconcerted by that particular request, Luciano tensed.

'I can't wait to tell her our news. I know she'll be so happy for us. I'll only be two minutes, I *swear*…'

CHAPTER NINE

FOUR tall, dark men, all remarkably handsome and wearing elegant morning suits with natty grey-striped waistcoats and white cravats, stood in the vestry of the church of St Augustine.

'Kerry told you she would only be two minutes on the phone and you *believed* her?' Misty's husband, Leone Andracchi, gave Luciano a highly amused scrutiny. 'You've a lot to learn, and now that there's four of them it will only get worse from here on in—'

'You're not kidding.' Ione's husband, Alexio Christoulakis, grimaced. 'I once threw Ione's phone in the bath to stop it ringing—'

'I bet you were popular.' Leone laughed. 'I chucked one out the window.'

Freddy's husband, Crown Prince Jaspar al-Husayn, smiled with a certain amount of oneupmanship. 'I used the excuse of health concerns and banned mobile and digital phones from our private apartments.'

'Nice one, Jaspar,' Leone murmured with frank appreciation. 'In the near future I suspect I'm about to become very much more health-scare aware.'

Engaged in wondering if the bridal limo was on the way down to the village, Luciano was too tense to be amused. It was his wedding day and he was just grateful it had finally arrived. Ten days had passed since his marriage proposal, and for *nine* of those days Luciano had got no closer to Kerry than a phone call! The very evening of the day that Kerry had agreed to marry him, two of her sisters and their husbands had flown in to make his acquaintance. While that meeting had gone off very much better than he might have expected, Misty had insisted on organising the entire wedding and Ione had whisked Kerry off to Paris to buy her bridal trousseau. What Luciano had dimly imagined would be a small, intimate occasion had turned into a three-ring circus and Kerry had not got the chance to return to Tuscany before the wedding took place.

From the imposing porch of the Villa Contarini, Kerry watched her grandmother, her three sisters and those of her nephews and nieces playing an active role in the ceremony board the waiting line of cars. When the cars had driven off, she did a slow, wondering spin in front of a glittering Venetian glass mirror: the dream that she had begun dreaming almost the very first time she laid eyes on Luciano da Valenza was at last coming true.

Her gown was a bias-cut column of white duchesse satin with a crystal-beaded neckline. The classic style contrived to make her look taller, and the exquisite diamond tiara which Freddy had loaned her only added to that flattering impression. Freddy had also given her a very pretty seed-pearl and lace garter. Misty had presented her kid sister with an eye-poppingly sexy set of lingerie and Ione had given her a truly amazing pair of designer shoes that were studded with diamonds.

'I fell for them but Alexio has got this weird hang-up about me wearing shoes with jewels on them, so I bought them for you instead,' Ione had confided. 'Trust me, you'll feel a million dollars in them!'

Emerging from that recollection with a helpless smile, for Ione was so rich that she had little concept of how other people lived, Kerry raised her gown a couple of inches to watch her shoes sparkle in the sunlight, and Ione was right, those shoes *did* make her feel fantastic. It was time for her and her grandfather to head for the church. She would be precisely three minutes late.

'I don't think you'll get the chance to read anything during the church service, Grandpa.' With a grin, Kerry removed the book that Hunt O'Brien was reaching for before he could get lost between its pages again and set it aside.

'You look very lovely, my dear,' the old man said fondly. 'At a time in life when there are usually few surprises left, your grandmother and I feel very blessed. Your late mother has left us a wonderful legacy in her daughters and their children.'

Her throat tight with tears, Kerry gave her grandfather a hug for recognising what was most important: Carrie had given Kerry and her siblings the gift of life. Only in getting to know and love her sisters had Kerry finally overcome the sad sense of aloneness which had nagged at her since she was a child.

Seated in the limousine that would take her to the church, Kerry thought about the nine incredibly busy days that had just passed. While she had very much enjoyed spending time with her sisters and their respective families, she had missed Luciano almost more than she could bear. When she had contacted her father to tell him about her marriage plans, Harold Linwood had told her that she was making a fool of herself and had turned down her wedding invitation. She had not expected much from the older man but his contemptuous dismissal had hurt.

Miles's warm and accepting response to the same announcement had been very welcome. She was really looking forward to seeing her stepbrother at the reception but was a little anxious as to how Luciano would react to the younger man's presence. Ought she to have mentioned that Miles was on the guest list beforehand?

By the time Kerry walked down the aisle of the flower-bedecked church with Freddy acting as matron of honour and her twin sisters as her bridesmaids, all such superfluous concerns had left her. Luciano broke with tradition to watch her approach, and the wondering appreciation in his steady gaze made her feel like the most beautiful bride in the world. With simple dignity and warmth, Hunt O'Brien read the Bible readings for the ceremony, first in Irish and then in English. Kerry's heart was soon full to overflowing, and afterwards she could never recall posing for the flurry of photos taken as they all emerged from the picturesque stone church.

'You've got glitter on your shoes,' Luciano told her helpfully as he assisted her into the limo that would ferry them back to the villa for the reception.

'That's not glitter. Those are genuine jewels,' Kerry confided with a helpless giggle. 'Ione's gift. I think they'll have to go in a special display box afterwards.'

'*Dio mio…*' Luciano was astonished but his proud dark head lifted and he frowned as something outside the church stole his attention from his bride's amazing footwear.

'What is it?'

Luciano tore his incredulous gaze from Miles Linwood's smug, smiling face in the crowd and focused back on his bride. 'What the hell is your stepbrother doing here?'

His harsh intonation made Kerry pale. 'I invited him—'

'You should have discussed that with me,' Luciano cut in grimly. 'No Linwood ought to be at my wedding!'

Kerry lifted her chin. 'Luciano…you just married a Linwood.'

'I don't think of you as one of them. If I did, I couldn't have married you.' Lean, strong face set in hard, uncompromising lines, Luciano surveyed her with chilling golden eyes. 'It was Linwoods who banded together, stitched me up and put me in prison for five years. Think hard about where your loyalties lie, *mia carina.*'

Shock had claimed Kerry, for she had been quite unprepared for the level of his hostility towards her stepbrother. 'It's not a matter of that—'

'It *is*—'

'I'm very fond of Miles and I have been since we were children—'

'He's not a blood relative—'

'Nevertheless, I've always thought of him as my brother. I know that you and he never got on but it meant a lot to me that he was willing to come to our wedding and leave behind all the unpleasantness of the past,' Kerry confided with conviction.

Luciano vented a harsh, unamused laugh. '*Per meraviglia*! Unpleasantness? How can you dare to call five stinking years in a prison cell…mere unpleasantness?'

Every scrap of colour drained from Kerry's complexion when she realised how much she had offended. But even while she fully recognised her own clumsy lack of tact, she was dismayed by his attitude and could not help feeling that he was blaming the wrong people for his imprisonment. It was her personal belief that the shoddy police investigation allied with possible prejudice against Luciano being a foreigner had had a greater bearing on the guilty verdict reached at his original trial.

'I'm sorry...I didn't mean to make it sound as if I was belittling what you must've suffered,' Kerry responded in an unhappy whisper.

'This is the last time you will see Miles, so make the most of the occasion,' Luciano advised, his beautiful, dark golden eyes severe.

He escorted her into the villa and stood by her side while the staff offered their good wishes. His polite social smile did not fool Kerry, who remained painfully aware that he was still furious with her. She had underestimated the extent of his bitterness and in her eagerness to bury the traumatic events that had once destroyed their relationship had badly misjudged the situation. But it shook her that Luciano should demand that she abandon her lifelong friendship with her stepbrother to prove her loyalty. How could he force her to make a cruel choice like that?

During the wedding breakfast that followed, Kerry had little opportunity for private conversation with her bridegroom. But she remained aware of his vibrant proximity with every fibre of her being. Before the dancing began, her grandfather gave a short, amusing speech and concluded by raising his glass to the bridal couple and toasting them in Irish, *'Slainte agus saol agat…* Health and life to you!'

In the ballroom, which was embellished with glorious garlands of flowers, Luciano wound her into his arms, his clear gaze full of regret. 'You're the most beautiful bride ever and I'm fighting with you. Let's not talk again about our unwanted guest,' he suggested. 'This is our day and nothing should spoil it, *cara mia.'*

Much of Kerry's unease evaporated and only the fear that Miles might approach her while she was with Luciano remained with her. Circling the floor in Luciano's arms, she discovered that even his warm, virile scent could awaken both her senses and her body to the potency of his attraction. Dry-mouthed, she pressed herself closer to his big, powerful frame and succumbed to a helpless little shiver of pleasure. She felt starved of him and shamefully eager for the forceful possession which the ache between her thighs was already making her crave.

Embarrassed by the way in which she found herself clinging to him, Kerry flushed. 'I don't know myself like this…'

'I *do*…but, as I can't drag you upstairs and give you exactly what you want right at this moment, I suggest that we part and circulate rather than torture ourselves,' Luciano groaned in acknowledgement.

Away from him, that tormenting knot of hungry desire soon began to unravel to a controllable level inside her. Delighted to find herself surrounded by so many family members, Kerry danced with Freddy's eldest adopted son, Ben, as well as Prince Kareem, her sister's alarmingly mature six-year-old. Freddy also had a daughter,

Azima, and a third son, who was still a toddler, called
Akil. She had said that her current pregnancy would be
her last but Misty had whispered, 'If you believe that,
you'll believe anything…she's nuts about kids!'

Misty and Leone had three little boys, Connor, Niall
and Evan, all very lively and full of mischief. Kerry
could only smile at the sight of the cool, sophisticated
Leone Andracchi crossing the dance floor at speed to
recapture his tiny youngest son, who was making frantic
efforts to follow his two older brothers even though he
had only just learned to walk. Ione had four-year-old
twins, Apollo and Diantha, who had immense charm,
and a second son called Christan, who was always getting into fights.

When she began feeling a little dizzy, Kerry thought
that she had expended too much energy on the dance
floor and she went out on to the terrace in the hope that
the fresh air would revive her. Approaching the shaded
loggia, she was surprised to see all three of her sisters
engaged in urgent conversation there.

'I think she has the right to be told what we found
out,' Ione was saying.

Freddy looked anxious. 'It's a very difficult situation
but Jaspar believes that it's not our place to interfere
between a man and his wife, particularly over a family
matter—'

'Leone says that that's why we should just stay out
of it too *but* I have a hideous suspicion that my husband
approves of what's being done.' Misty groaned. 'It's just
I feel guilty not telling her and I can't help thinking she's
in for a heck of a shock—'

'About what?' Kerry had halted several feet away with a troubled frown dividing her brows.

Her sisters spun round. Freddy went pink, Ione gave Kerry a calm smile and Misty looked enquiring.

'I mean…you are all talking about me…*aren't* you?' Kerry prompted, for those mysterious references to a man and his wife and a family matter had seemed to indicate a very probable close connection.

'Actually, no,' Misty asserted. 'We're discussing a mutual friend who is about to discover that her husband is not quite the pussycat he might seem.'

'It's always a *big* mistake to think that a guy is perfect…or that guys are like us,' Ione continued ruefully. 'Occasionally you come across one so ruthless that he makes King Herod look kind, and not only will he not be ashamed of it, he may also even be proud!'

After chatting to her sisters, Kerry went off in search of Miles and found him in the centre of an admiring group. He was telling a funny story with a great deal of panache. Dropping an arm round Kerry, he gave her shoulders an affectionate squeeze. When his punchline had everyone laughing, he plunged straight into another story.

As the minutes passed and Miles still made no attempt to engage her in a private conversation, Kerry was bewildered by his behaviour. Miles was talking fast and furiously but with a clarity that confirmed that too much alcohol was not the problem; her stepbrother seemed to be in an unusually excitable mood.

From across the ballroom, she saw Luciano watching her. The tension stamped in her bridegroom's proud dark features was evident. Colouring, she tugged at Miles's sleeve to gain his attention.

With decided reluctance, Miles finally walked her away from his audience. 'Thanks for the invite. I'm having a fantastic time. You'll never know how grateful I was for the excuse to escape work for a couple of days.'

'Is Linwoods still having problems?' Kerry pressed worriedly.

'No way am I going to talk business on your wedding day,' her stepbrother reproved. 'Are you happy?'

'Ecstatic,' she muttered a little shyly.

'Even though da Valenza is ripping that you've invited me?'

Kerry worried at her lower lip in discomfiture.

Miles gave her a fond appraisal. 'I'm really not worth it, you know.'

'To me you *are*—'

His bloodshot blue eyes softened. 'I'm touched.'

'For once, he was telling you the truth when he told you that he wasn't worth the effort,' Luciano derided.

The intrusion of her husband's dark, deep drawl made Kerry jerk round in dismay. Dulled coins of colour highlighting his hard cheekbones, Luciano was rigid and she was fearfully conscious of the violent tension holding his lithe, muscular frame taut. It seemed providential when another guest engaged Luciano in conversation. Kerry was weak with relief at the interruption. For an alarming instant, she had been genuinely afraid that Luciano might start a fight and she made no attempt to dissuade her stepbrother from fading back into the crush of guests.

Kerry was heading off to get changed for their departure when Luciano caught up with her in the hall. He tugged her round into the circle of his arms. 'Don't take the dress off. I want to carry you out of here just as you are, *cara mia*,' he confided huskily.

When he looked at her with those smouldering golden eyes of his, Kerry could hardly get breath into her lungs and she simply nodded like a puppet.

'No arguments even though I've been an absolute bastard all afternoon?'

Mesmerised by the sheer potency of the breathtaking smile with which he accompanied that admission, Kerry could have forgiven him for anything. 'No arguments.'

'You're an angel…'

No, she knew she wasn't. An angel would have had a deeper appreciation of the traumatic experiences Luciano had gone through over the past five years and of just how recent had been his regain of his freedom. She had expected too much too soon. Naturally, he was bitter, defensive, suspicious. Naturally, he needed to feel that she was one hundred per cent on *his* side. Didn't he deserve her full attention? After all, blame him as she might for never once letting her know that he still cared about her, she could never, ever forget that he had endured his imprisonment without any support from her.

'But I haven't had the chance to say goodbye to anyone!' Kerry gasped, for he had taken a very literal interpretation of her agreement and, having seized impatient hold of her hand, was already dragging her towards the villa's rear entrance. 'I don't even know where we're going—'

'Bridegroom's prerogative…' Luciano paused to haul

her to him and claim a passionate kiss that went on and on and on.

Emerging from what could not have been termed an ordeal, her head swimming, Kerry did not protest when he swept her off her feet and carried her out into the sunlight. A rosy blush lit her face when an unexpected crowd of guests whooped and showered them with confetti.

Luciano almost groaned out loud. Her family were waiting to exchange a last word with her and his arms tightened possessively round her slender figure. He just could not bring himself to put her down and share her again. Only giving her time to wave and exchange fleeting goodbyes, he forged a determined path for the helicopter awaiting them. He had done the wedding with the five-hundred-odd guests, the socialising, the speechmaking, the whole polite thing, and now all he cared about was having his bride all to himself.

Costanza was the last to come forward. 'Be gentle with him,' she urged Kerry with a teasing grin.

Their final destination proved to be a tiny private island off the coast of Sicily. From the air, it looked to be a lush green wooded paradise and Kerry was no less enchanted when Luciano lifted her out of the helicopter and she first saw the long, low, contemporary house that sat above the smooth golden beach washed by the waves.

'I don't think that I'll ever forget that you brought me somewhere so beautiful for our honeymoon,' Kerry confided.

'Hopefully this won't be our only visit. This place is ours—'

'*Ours?*' Kerry gasped, wide-eyed.

'It is only a small island,' Luciano pointed out.

'But it's enchanting.' Kicking off her shoes and hitching up her skirt to peel off her lace-topped stockings beneath his startled and appreciative gaze, Kerry hurried onto the beach. She curled her toes in the soft, silky sand, lifted her gown to her knees and proceeded without a shade of inhibition to paddle through the whispering surf like a small child.

With a helpless grin, Luciano bent down to hook long, lean fingers into the shoes worth a small fortune that his bride had just discarded within feet of the tide coming in and watched her enjoy herself. She was so unspoilt, for she suffered neither from vanity nor the desire to impress others. She was also very kind. In every way she was different from all the other women he had ever known and he had been very proud of her at their wedding.

Their guests had hailed from all walks of life but they had all felt comfortable with Kerry. Her abundance of natural warmth attracted people, and as she gained in confidence her special qualities became all the more obvious. Just looking at Kerry, sunlight glinting off her fiery curls, bright blue eyes sparkling with enjoyment, Luciano felt very much like a guy who had made an absolute killing on the stockmarket. He had captured her and made her his and got that ring on her finger just in the nick of time!

Why had he made such a fuss about that lying, thieving little weasel, Miles? Cunning and clever as Miles had once been, Luciano could now concede that the younger man was no longer a threat to him. As for punishment? Punishment was in hand for all the Linwoods and gathering a deadlier pace with every day that the *Salut* chain traded. But Luciano believed that Miles might well be destroying his own life even faster.

However, Luciano had no intention of distressing Kerry with his belief that her beloved stepbrother might well have been high on drugs at their wedding. Luciano had known enough addicts in prison to recognise the likely cause of Miles's excitable state. That suspicion had given Luciano an even greater aversion to the younger man and he had found it intolerable to see Kerry in Miles's company. But even though he had a security man dogging Miles's footsteps, Bailey had not been seen to do anything he shouldn't. Without concrete proof, Luciano knew better than to accuse Miles of wrongdoing.

Shedding those unpleasant thoughts, Luciano accompanied his breathless bride up to the house above the beach. Leaving wet, sandy footprints everywhere, Kerry breezed through the interior of the house, oohing and aahing with unhidden delight at all that she saw. Simple tiled floors, subtle drapes and stylish beech furniture played down the outright luxury of the comfort level on offer.

'When did you buy this place?'

'While I was still in prison. Just seeing the photos was enough to lift my spirits and give me the hope that some day I would walk across that beach—'

'Oh, *no*...I paddled through your historic moment!' Kerry cut in, her dismay palpable.

Luciano loosed a long, extravagant sigh. 'And now, even worse, you're about to get sand on my hand-stitched silk sheets...'

Her lush mouth opened on a soundless ooh of surprise.

'Brides have been dumped for lesser sins, *bella mia*.' His gorgeous golden eyes glittered with amusement.

'Are you planning to dump me?'

Luciano reached behind her and ran down the zip on her wedding gown. 'Not before I've ravished you within an inch of your life—'

'Not funny—'

'—for at least fifty years!' He tipped the gown off her shoulders and watched it fall to expose the ivory silk bra and briefs she wore underneath.

'OK…I'll go wash the sand off—'

'Too late…I can't wait that long.' Luciano laid her down on the wide, luxurious divan and began to strip off his suit with impatient hands.

Her heart was racing inside her, her mouth running dry. She lay there feeling weighted to the mattress, face burning, for she was wildly conscious of the embarrassing dampness between her thighs. It seemed almost wicked to want any man as much as she wanted him, and even more shameless to watch him undress and conceal just how magnificent she found him.

Familiarity did not make him one bit less gorgeous, and nine days of deprivation had only made her all the more aware of his potent masculinity. Her eyes lingered on his wide shoulders, the cluster of black curling hair outlining his strong pectorals and the sleek muscularity of his flat stomach. As he stepped out of his trousers, her breathing fractured. His black silk boxers moulded the impressive bulge of his aroused manhood. Then the boxers fell to the tiles and he bent down to unclip her bra and remove her panties with scant appreciation for the decorative qualities of either garment.

'When I said I couldn't wait, I wasn't joking, *cara mia.*' With molten male appreciation in his gaze, Luciano scrutinised the straining peaks crowning her small breasts and let his attention drop to the auburn curls at the apex of her thighs.

Without hesitation, he parted her legs. Unaccustomed to being fully exposed to him like this, Kerry reddened and would have attempted to cover herself had he not uttered an earthy sound of appreciation at the visible evidence of her excitement.

'Luciano...'

'I know this is a very last-moment request...but can I make love to you without using protection? I'd like to spend our honeymoon trying to make you pregnant,' Luciano confided with a ragged edge to his dark, deep drawl.

Disconcerted, she looked up at him and the hungry urgency and longing she met in his bold appraisal turned her inside out and melted her. 'Hmm...'

'Is that a...*yes?*'

Unable to find her voice, Kerry nodded vehemently. She was overwhelmed, for once it had been her who was eager to start a family. He had wanted children too but he had also been frank about his desire to wait for a few years. Now she was touched to the heart that he should want a baby with her so soon. Having a family was something that she had tried not to think about because she had assumed that it would be a long time before he was ready to even consider the possibility.

'You don't think that maybe you ought to consider the concept in a little more depth?' Luciano prompted.

'No. I've always wanted your baby,' Kerry confided a little unsteadily.

'Why is a confession that once would have struck terror into my bones now so deeply, dangerously erotic?' Luciano groaned earthily.

He plundered the sweetness of her mouth just once before he shifted his attention to the stiff pink buds of her pouting breasts. She got lost in sensation fast, because, although until that moment she had not really acknowledged it, in recent weeks her breasts had felt more than usually sensitive. Luciano had only to stroke her tender nipples with his tongue to make her spine arch and provoke her into moaning out loud.

'Don't be so shy,' he scolded gently when she gazed up at him afterwards in frank mortification. 'When you respond to me like that it's very exciting for me.'

He pulled her into his arms and with sure fingers explored the slick, responsive flesh between her slender thighs, lingering on the tiny swollen nub of her desire. With a gasp, she raised her hips off the bed in helpless, eager encouragement. In no time at all she was writhing, begging, heedless of all but her own tormented need for him.

Spreading her willing body under him, Luciano mounted her and plunged his aching shaft into her delicate sheath with forceful expertise. Jackknifing up to him in welcome, she cried out. His raw dominance just increased the splintering, explosive excitement roaring through her. His every movement gave her indescribable pleasure. She was on a wild roller-coaster of sensation that pushed her closer and closer to the height that her every skin cell yearned to reach. And then she was flying up into the sun, screaming and sobbing and coming apart beneath him in a sweet agony of fierce fulfilment.

Rolling over to release her from his weight, he held her close. He pushed her tumbled hair off her brow with a hand that wasn't quite steady. Slumberous dark golden eyes sought out hers. 'I have a confession to make…the first time I made love to you at Ballybawn I forgot to use protection—'

'*Forgot?*' Kerry gasped in astonishment.

Faint colour accentuated Luciano's blunt cheekbones. 'It had been over five years for me. I got carried away and I only realised afterwards—'

'But you didn't tell me—'

Luciano gave her a wicked grin. 'You shouldn't have needed to be told,' he teased. 'I knew you hadn't noticed and I didn't mention it because I didn't want to worry you. After all, if you got caught, you got caught—'

'Caught?'

'Pregnant,' he rephrased. 'But obviously we got away with it, *cara mia.*'

'Obviously,' Kerry repeated absently while she wondered when she had last had her period. The date seemed lost in the mists of time and the calendar on which she had kept a discreet note was back in the kitchen in Ballybawn. Strain as she did to remember how many weeks it had been since that particular event, she could not. Even so, she thought it very unlikely that she might have conceived; foreign travel, a different diet and too much excitement must have put her system out of sync.

'Obviously getting you pregnant is a project which

will require lots and lots and lots of effort from me and loads of dedicated practice,' Luciano purred, flipping her over and hauling her back against him to acquaint her with the reality of his renewed arousal.

'You're also very into this project, aren't you?' Her smile could have lit up the room and she turned back to face him and closed her arms round his neck. As she met those dark golden eyes of his, her heart lurched inside her.

'Very into *you*,' he traded, lifting her over him and anchoring her knees to either side of him.

Kerry was shocked. 'We *can't* do it like this—'

'*Dio mio*…watch me…' With deft hands and shameless expertise, Luciano angled her up and brought her down on him, penetrating her with the slow, erotic precision of a male who knew how to generate the maximum excitement.

It was a wedding night to remember. She did not dare challenge him with that word 'can't' again but was tempted more than once. He even made love to her in the shower, and in the aftermath of an orgasm which wiped her out she mumbled, 'I love you…I love you so much…'

It was his ultimate fantasy, which he had pictured so often when he lay fighting sexual frustration in his narrow prison bed: Kerry telling him how much she loved him again. He knew that exhaustion had blown away her defences and that she barely even realised what she had confessed. He lifted her off the bathroom carpet, carried her back to bed and covered her with the sheet. He stood looking down at her while she slept. Her hair was a riot of curls half wet, half dry and she was pale, faint bluish shadows showing below her lashes.

Luciano went for another shower. That fantasy had lurked at the back of his mind from the minute he walked free from that court: the instant of cruellest revenge as he ditched her when she least expected it. He had lived that vengeful moment in his imagination many times over. Dressed in designer separates and shades as only a suave Italian anti-hero could be, he would stride off into the sunset without even leaving her a note.

Only if he didn't even leave a note, she might call out the rescue services thinking that he had gone swimming while she slept and drowned, mightn't she? His handsome mouth quirked. Furthermore, a mega-smooth disappearing act would be something of a challenge to pull off on a tiny island. Was he planning to swim back to the mainland? Call for a helicopter? The landing would awaken her and the cool exit would get extremely messy and human.

From a built-in unit in the dressing room, he selected beige chinos and a black shirt. As he zipped up the chinos he watched her sleep. He knew he wasn't going anywhere and he knew why. Somewhere along the way he had lost the desire to even picture her being scared, distressed or humiliated. She was his wife and he would look after her and he would not betray her trust. He had meant every word of those vows he had spoken before the priest. He had been honest when he told her that he wanted to have a child with her. There was a whole long list of good reasons why he was staying put but only one reason that *really* counted and that was the one he was least comfortable thinking about.

Kerry woke up and focused on Luciano. Lounging in the chair by the bed in an elegant sprawl, he was barefoot. His shirt hung unbuttoned and loose, revealing a muscular, bronzed wedge of chest. Blue-black stubble roughened his stubborn jawline and slumberous gold eyes enhanced by the dense black frame of his lashes rested on her. Her heart skipped a beat in response. He looked so vibrantly sexy he took her breath away.

'How do you feel?' he enquired lazily.

She ached all over. Face flaming, she dropped her eyes.

'Why are you blushing?'

'It doesn't matter—'

'Maybe I was a little too enthusiastic...?'

Her lashes swept up because he sounded so pleased with himself.

Luciano grinned with megawatt charisma and shrugged. 'It would be much worse if I'd underperformed. I'll run you a bath, *bella mia*.'

Twenty minutes later, after a great deal of mysterious toing and froing, he ushered her into a bathroom lit solely by two dozen glowing candles. She was so taken aback she let her towel fall and stepped into the scented warm water like a woman under a spell.

Luciano surveyed her with immense satisfaction. 'I knew you'd go for this sort of thing—'

'How did you know?'

He had seen her collection of candles at Ballybawn but he didn't admit that because it was much more enjoyable to bask in her wondering admiration of his extraordinary perception. 'I'll call you when dinner's ready...'

'You're cooking *too*…?' Kerry settled back into the water and gave him a dazed smile of approbation. 'I can hardly wait.'

She soaked in the bath and contemplated her candles. Ione had said that no guy was perfect but Ione was very, very wrong. Luciano was sheer perfection in masculine form! He looked gorgeous, he *was* gorgeous. He was utterly fantastic in bed and pure sex on legs even clothed. He was clever, honest, kind, incredibly thoughtful, full of insight and caring. She had to be the luckiest bride in the world.

Two days before their departure from the island, Luciano received the call that he had long awaited and almost lost hope of ever receiving from his lawyer, Felix Carrington. Normally the most cool and calm of men, Felix could not keep the edge of excitement out of his own voice as he brought his client up to speed on recent events.

The big breakthrough that five long years of frustrating investigation had failed to turn up had finally occurred. A member of the Linwood family had made a discreet approach to Felix through his own lawyer to offer startling new facts. Steven Linwood had confessed his part in creating the false evidence that had framed Luciano for the charges of theft and false accounting and set him up for his prison term. Kerry's cousin had sworn that he was prepared to go to the police and make a formal statement to that effect and accept the consequences for the crime he had committed. Why? Five years ago, Steven Linwood had been bullied into doing a blackmailer's bidding. When his tormentor had threatened him yet again in an effort to force him into further

wrongdoing, Steven had realised that he could only protect himself by coming forward to tell the truth.

'You've been so quiet all evening,' Kerry remarked
when they went to bed that night. 'Is there anything
wrong?'

'No.' Once all the facts were out in the open, everything would be right for a change, Luciano reflected with
quiet satisfaction.

It was very wrong that he could not be honest with
his own wife but what choice had she given him? All
along, Kerry had refused to take sides. It was her own
fault that he could not trust her with confidential information about his case, and until Steven Linwood had
actually *made* his statement to the police Luciano knew
he would have to keep quiet. Kerry would need heavy
persuasion before she would even consider accepting unpleasant truths about people she cared about. In a mistaken show of loyalty, she might even rush off to phone
Miles and warn her stepbrother about the allegations
about to come his way. If Miles got the chance to flee
the country before he could be arrested, Luciano knew
he would be ready to strangle his wife.

In the darkness he smiled and tugged Kerry into his
arms, acknowledging that sometimes it was wisest to
keep his own counsel. What she didn't know wasn't
likely to hurt her in the short term…

Having enjoyed an idyllic ten days of wholly sybaritic
pleasure on the island, Kerry and Luciano flew back to
London.

Early the next morning, Luciano headed straight into
the office and Kerry called her grandparents to ask how

they had settled back into Ballybawn. During her absence, her sisters had engaged staff for the castle and had overseen the elderly couple's return to their much-improved home.

'I hope to fly home tomorrow,' Kerry told her grandfather cheerfully.

'Now, don't be hurrying back just for our benefit,' Hunt O'Brien warned. 'This afternoon we're off to Quamar to stay with Freddy. Your grandmother wants to be with your sister when the new baby arrives.'

Kerry came off the telephone feeling ever so slightly abandoned: her grandparents were turning into seasoned globetrotters. Reminding herself of the very real fears that she had once had for their well-being, she shook off that instant of regret, for their future was now very much more secure. With a caring team of well-paid employees to ensure their every comfort, her grandparents would never be so dependent on their youngest granddaughter again and she had sensed her grandfather's relief and satisfaction that that should be the case.

Mid-morning, Costanza arrived and explained that she had to find a file which Luciano believed he might have left at the townhouse. Kerry watched as her husband's PA began to leaf through the filing cabinets in the room he used as an office.

'Can I help?'

The brunette gave her a surprised look and then smiled. 'Yes, please. Luciano's expecting me back as soon as possible. I do wish he'd thought to mention what a mess he'd made of the filing system!'

For a couple of minutes the two women worked side by side.

'Why is everything in the wrong place?' Kerry grumbled.

'Because Luciano finally has the excuse he has been waiting for *all* his working life,' the brunette said in her usual acerbic style. 'He is now way too rich, important and busy to put things back where he found them!'

Kerry burst out laughing.

'Of course, his current excuse might well be exhaustion. Send him to bed early tonight,' Costanza quipped. 'Only half an hour after he came in, he fell asleep at his desk!'

Kerry blushed to the roots of her hair. 'That was jet lag.'

'But you only flew back from Sicily!' The PA checked the desk drawers and then produced keys to access the wall safe.

A couple of files spilled out from the precarious pile inside the safe and fell to the carpet. Ignoring them, Costanza pulled another file from the heap with an exclamation of satisfaction. 'Got it!' Halfway to the door again in her eagerness to get back to the office, the brunette paused to take account of the files now littering virtually every surface and winced. 'Luciano's in a massive hurry for this…can I leave you to tidy up?'

'If you promise not to tease him about falling asleep—'

'He's a man…they *love* the kind of teasing that suggests they're incredible studs!' Costanza mocked on her way out.

Still smiling, Kerry knelt down to gather up the loose papers that had spilled from one of the fallen files. The bright yellow logo on the letterhead of one of the doc-

uments stole her attention: *Salut*. Stilling in surprise at
the logo of the wine-store chain that Miles had said was
cutting Linwoods' profit margins to ribbons, Kerry began to examine the papers she had been about to slot
back into the file.

The first document she scrutinised startled her, for it
was a very detailed and businesslike report on the
strengths and weaknesses of her father's wine-store operation. The information it contained was both confidential and damaging to Linwoods, and moreover the report
was marked as being only for the eyes of the *Salut* man-
agement team. What the heck was Luciano doing with
a report like that in his personal possession? As Kerry
leafed through the rest of the file, her skin began turning
clammy and her sensitive tummy churned.

Everything she looked at fell into the category of privileged information either in relation to Linwoods or to
Salut, and naturally Luciano had kept the file locked in
his safe away from prying eyes. His wife's prying eyes?
For, unless she was very much mistaken, Luciano da
Valenza, her husband, was behind the successful *Salut*
wine stores currently engaged in hammering her father's
retail operation into the ground. Gooseflesh prickled at
the nape of her neck.

Surely Luciano could not own *Salut*? Wasn't it possible that, having noted the chain's rapid rise to prominence, he was perhaps considering investing in it? With
hands that were damp and showing a distinct tendency
to tremble, Kerry flicked back through the file. There
was no room for doubt: Luciano owned *Salut*. He had
financed the launch of the chain long before he got out

of prison. For months, *Salut* had run at a staggering loss while it was stealing Linwoods' customers.

Kerry tottered upright on wobbly legs. Clutching the file beneath her arm, she called a taxi to take her over to da Valenza Technology. No way could she wait until Luciano came home that evening to confront him. Maybe he would have some explanation, maybe she was leaping to entirely the wrong conclusion, she told herself bracingly. She was married to Luciano. She adored him. He was a wonderful man. It was not the best time for her to recall Ione having said, 'It's a *big* mistake to think a guy's perfect…occasionally you meet one who would make King Herod look kind!'

CHAPTER TEN

'YOU'RE not allowed to take Luciano home for lunch… he's needed here,' Costanza teased when she came out of one of the offices and saw Kerry approaching Luciano's door.

'I'll be sure to keep that in mind.' Kerry evaded the brunette's keen gaze.

When Kerry entered Luciano's office unannounced, he was on the phone. Brilliant golden eyes zeroed in on her and lingered to admire the flattering fit of the stretchy green safari dress that made the most of her light tan and slender, shapely curves. Obviously, Luciano thought with satisfaction and without surprise, his wife had missed him. Four hours without a glimpse of him had been more than she could stick. A smouldering smile of welcome slashed his lean, darkly handsome features. Lounging back in his chair, he scrawled three words on his desk notepad and turned it round for her to see while he continued his call.

'Lock the door.'

A burning blush heated Kerry's drawn face. Most decidedly, it was the wrong moment for her to remember that Luciano had suggested that she come into his office some day so that he could live out another fantasy by having her across his desk…or up against the wall…or the door. With a complete lack of shame, he had ad-

mitted that he didn't care *where*, he just wanted the forbidden thrill of doing it.

His smile only gaining in brilliance, for when Luciano's mind focused on sex it could not be said to
heighten his ESP, he printed something else on the pad
and exhibited it to her.

'This office is sound-proofed.'

At that mortifying reference to a most personal matter,
Kerry got so hot she was convinced she had to resemble
a beetroot and she was incensed with her own inability
to immediately slap him down and freeze him out.
Wasn't she angry enough with him? In truth, she acknowledged dimly, she was still too deep in shock to
know quite what she was feeling. But raging, rampant
disbelief and horror at the deception he had practised on
her were assailing her in stormy waves. Yet more than
anything else she was still praying that her worst suspicions would somehow be proven to be wrong. In fact
never in her life had she been more eager or more hopeful of being shot down in flames.

Crossing the room, she lifted Luciano's gold pen,
flipped over a fresh page on the pad and printed one
word on it. But she printed that single word with such
force that she ripped a tiny hole in the paper.

While Luciano would have been happy to credit that
Kerry was getting into the passionate spirit of the occasion, he was not that naive. Quirking a winged black
brow and wondering if it was possible that she could be
in a bad mood with him when she had gone to so much
trouble to look sexy for his benefit, he endeavoured to
read the page on the pad upside-down. At that point, he
froze.

'Salut.'

At speed, Luciano concluded his phone call. Kerry slapped a file which he had last seen in the townhouse safe down on his desk. Now noting the feverish strain marking her blue eyes, he suppressed a groan. He reckoned that his chances of fulfilling the office fantasy currently stood at the slim-to-non-existent rating. He just hoped she was not about to throw a three-act tragedy about the *Salut* affair, for if she did he knew he was liable to lose his temper. She was his wife and there were many areas of his life that she might reasonably comment on. However, the field of business was on the forbidden list.

'Do you own *Salut*?'

'I do.' Determined to make his attitude clear from the outset, Luciano rose to his full, commanding height. 'Where did you get that file?'

'Costanza was in your safe and it fell out and I think she forgot to lock it up again…don't you dare blame her for being careless! I'm sure it's quite understandable if she assumed that a normal husband would have no secrets from his wife!'

'Obviously I'm not normal,' Luciano dared. 'But then I'm not applying for sainthood and the decisions I make in a business capacity have nothing to do with you.'

Kerry had expected him to look at least guilty and discomfited. She had not been prepared for him to fight back on the most unacceptable of macho terms. 'Are you calling your efforts to ruin my father's livelihood a *business* decision?'

Luciano leant back against the edge of his desk with a galling air of self-assurance. 'Yes, I am. In the last two months alone, *Salut* has doubled its profit margins. It's breaking records as one of the most successful new companies *ever* and I'm proud of that. You're my wife. I don't care if it kills you…it's your job to be proud of my achievement too.'

Kerry was so shattered by the outright manipulative cunning of that retaliation that she trembled. 'I don't believe I'm hearing this—'

'And by the way…' Luciano had decided that it would be unwise to conceal any information that she would soon learn for herself '…my efforts to destroy your father's firm have been equally successful. The receivers were called in at Linwoods the day before yesterday.'

Turning pale as milk at that declaration of appalling fact, Kerry took an actual step back from him.

'It is also probable that I will buy Linwoods' more profitable outlets at a knockdown price and relaunch them under the *Salut* banner,' Luciano completed.

'Dear heaven…' Kerry whispered strickenly. 'You went out after my family and ruined them—'

'But Harold won't be in need of a homeless hostel or a soup kitchen to survive. Heathlands and a sizeable pension fund were placed in your stepmother's name a long time ago to safeguard his old age,' Luciano cut in very drily. 'Let's not dramatise the situation.'

'Dramatise it?' Kerry repeated with sick distaste at his flippancy. 'You can't conceal the wrong of what you've done just by calling it business…I *looked* in that file! You set out to systematically destroy Linwoods by stealing their customers and you spent a fortune doing it. That's not normal business, that's revenge!'

Luciano lifted and spread lean brown hands in a fluid motion. 'I'm not denying that.'

Kerry was disconcerted. 'You're...*not*?'

'What's wrong with revenge? I've done nothing illegal,' Luciano drawled.

'Something doesn't have to be illegal to be *wrong*!' Kerry condemned with angry emphasis. 'Don't you have any principles? What about what you've done to me? You should be ashamed...you're married to the daughter of a man whom you've done everything within your power to ruin!'

'Possibly I should be more ashamed of having married the daughter of the man who stood back and let me take the fall for a theft I didn't commit,' Luciano traded, his strong jawline clenching. 'I'm the one in the right here. I'm the one who was wronged. It's time that you acknowledged that instead of bleating goody-goody sentiments that have little relevance in the *real* world!'

Kerry was cut to the bone. 'I don't bleat goody-goody sentiments!'

'You're out of line. What I do in business has nothing to do with our marriage—'

'If you murder someone in business, am I supposed to turn a blind eye to that as well?' Kerry demanded in furious rebuttal. 'You're totally ignoring the true issue here! Ever since you came back into my life, you've been working against *my* family in a totally underhand and dishonest way!'

'I'm not listening to this bull. I refuse to fight with you over this. Five years ago, your precious family ensured that I was locked up—'

'I don't want to hear that again...I don't believe it!'

Splintering golden eyes raked over her angry face. *'Per meraviglia.* I told you that you were either with me or against me, and now that we're married the dividing line is even more distinct—'

'Don't threaten me, Luciano. Don't you have any conscience about what you've done?'

'What are you really upset about here? Surely even you couldn't have believed that eventually we would all shake hands and end up the best of friends?' he derided harshly.

'I am shattered that you could go ahead and bankrupt Linwoods without once stopping to think or care that that might hurt me or make a difference to our relationship.'

'Why would it hurt you?'

Kerry surveyed him with shaken incredulity. 'How can you ask me that?'

'I do feel moved to ask why you should be *this* upset. Harold Linwood wouldn't cross the road for you if you were dying, and he felt like that even before you became my wife!' Luciano countered with contemptuous clarity. 'You have no relationship with him.'

Kerry recoiled from that blunt and wounding statement but stood her ground. 'He is still my flesh and blood. Is there nothing you won't say or do to come out on top? Is winning all that matters to you?'

Fierce dark golden eyes struck sparks off hers. 'I won't be sidelined into discussing this sort of emotional stuff—'

'And do you know why? Because you couldn't defend yourself!'

'Business is business. I don't owe you an explanation

and, as I have done nothing wrong, I have *no* intention of defending myself.'

'I can't believe I'm married to a guy with no scruples whatsoever…it's terrifying!'

At that emotive assurance, Luciano groaned out loud.

'I'm not overreacting. Right now, you feel like a stranger to me,' Kerry whispered chokily, pinning her tremulous lips together.

Lean, powerful face troubled and no longer hard, Luciano strode forward as if he intended to take her into his arms.

Kerry backed away from him. 'L-leave me alone!'

Ignoring that demand, Luciano reached for her hands, closing them between his when he realised how cold her fingers were. 'Don't make this a bone of contention between us, *bella mia*.'

Perspiration had beaded her short upper lip. She looked up at him and she still loved him and that tore her apart, for somehow she had expected the love to go away when she was as furious and distressed as she was. 'It's not me who's doing that…it's *you*,' she argued with desperate vehemence.

Golden eyes very intent, he gripped her hands tightly in his. 'I want you to understand and believe in me. I need that. When people damage me, I hit back hard. That's my nature—'

'And business is business…and you don't want me bleating like some good-living prig even though you know very well that you chose to *marry* a good-living prig!' In a sudden movement of rejection that took him by surprise, Kerry hauled her hands free of his. 'Obviously I should have listened to my sisters. When I first met them, they warned me that you were out for revenge and I wouldn't listen to them—'

His beautiful eyes flashed and his wide, sensual mouth compressed. 'This matter is between us…you don't discuss it with your sisters—'

'Don't I? But this is *family* business,' Kerry said defiantly. 'And just as you don't think that the business of profit is anything to do with me, I don't think family business is anything to do with you!'

Luciano did not even look marginally amused. 'Don't be facetious,' he grated. 'We're flying back to Ireland tomorrow and we'll sort out any problems we have in private.'

'In the usual way you sort out problems?'

'No, even I don't think you're ready to fall into bed with me right at this minute,' Luciano drawled.

Her blue eyes lit with fury. 'I'm not talking about sex, I'm talking about threats—'

'When have I threatened you?' Luciano demanded rawly. 'I just don't want you running off to confide in those interfering sisters of yours!'

'Don't you dare call my sisters interfering!'

'I have no quarrel with them as long as they stay the hell out of our marriage!' Luciano launched at her with ferocious bite.

Kerry shot him a look of mingled angry, wounded frustration. 'How could you think that I would want to tell another living soul about this? I'm hurt and I'm disappointed in you and the last thing I feel right now is proud of being married to you…but *I've* got enough pride to want to keep that news to myself!'

A surge of dark colour slashed his hard cheekbones

and then slowly receded to leave him unusually pale. His dense black lashes screened his brooding gaze. He was seething but not an inch beneath that anger he was much more affected than he was prepared to admit by her attack. How dared she tell him that he had disappointed her?

Fabulous bone structure taut, Luciano surveyed Kerry with fierce, chilling cool but she was not fooled, for she knew she had finally penetrated his tough hide.

Rigid-backed, she walked back to the door before making one final comment. 'And if you're so blasted proud of what you've done, why didn't you tell me about it? Why did I have to find out only by accident?'

How could she ask him that? If he had told her that he was in the process of destroying Linwoods, she wouldn't have married him. And, given the same choices to make again, Luciano knew he would still choose to remain silent. She was his wife now. She could be angry, disappointed and hurt but she was *still* his wife and on his terms that meant that she wasn't going anywhere. He was damned if he was going to fake regret to touch her soft heart. Bringing down her father had been a source of deep satisfaction to him and not only on his own account. Even before his imprisonment, he had despised Harold Linwood for the continual wounding snubs and rejections the older man had levelled at his daughter.

In a daze, Kerry walked out of her husband's office building. She was all shaken up and the irony was that she very badly wanted to call her sisters and confide in them. Only, now Luciano's derision had formed a giant wall between her and that comforting prospect. It was at that point that the final comprehension sank in on Kerry and she fell still in the middle of the street. My goodness, where had her wits been? Her sisters were *already* aware that Luciano owned the *Salut* chain and had targeted Linwoods!

In that moment, Kerry went from feeling disappointed that she could not lean on her sisters to feeling utterly betrayed by them and foolish. How could she have forgotten that strange conversation between her sisters which she had overheard at her own wedding? All that about feeling guilty about not telling 'her' and not interfering in other people's marriages? Of course that exchange had related to her!

Furthermore, didn't she have good reason to suspect that her sisters' knowledge of events went back even further than her wedding? Hadn't Misty admitted to having had Kerry checked out by an investigator prior to their first meeting? Presumably, Luciano, the male guilty of repossessing Ballybawn, had been checked out with even greater precision. What had Ione said? 'Luciano is a very dangerous man who is already hurting your family.' Kerry had assumed that Ione meant that Luciano's existence was already causing grief between Kerry and her siblings. That was what she had believed Ione meant by 'family'. Instead, Ione had been referring to the Linwoods.

A family who had never really been her family, Kerry conceded with pained honesty. Only Miles had ever made her feel as though she belonged to the Linwood clan and, ironically, Miles was a Bailey, not a Linwood. Yet he, like his sister, Rochelle, had still been much more a part of the Linwood family than Kerry had ever contrived to be. Now Luciano had wrecked even the tiniest chance of her *ever* getting closer to her father. Her husband had deliberately destroyed her father's livelihood. She was twenty-six years old. *Was* it pathetic of her to have still cherished hopes that some day she would break through her father's detachment and win his affection?

No doubt Luciano would deem such hopes another example of her unrealistic idealism! But suddenly Kerry had not a doubt about what she ought to be doing next, for her path seemed clear. She wanted to see her father. Harold Linwood was not a young man and he had just suffered a grievous blow. Was her father even aware that Luciano was responsible for the downfall of Linwoods? She paled and then squared her shoulders with determination. Her father was in need of all the support he could get and the least she could do as his daughter was express her regret and offer to help in any way that she could.

By the time that Kerry had established that her father was not at the office but at home and she had caught the train out to Surrey, the afternoon was well advanced. A taxi dropped her at Heathlands, a big, imposing dwelling surrounded by extensive gardens. Harold Linwood was in his study.

'Have you come to express your sympathy?' Her father was slumped in the imposing leather chair behind his desk, his pale blue eyes cold behind his spectacles and his intonation withering.

Kerry flushed, her tension increasing. 'I know how much Linwoods means to you *and* how hard you've worked to build it up—'

'Only for your husband to knock it down again like a pile of toy bricks!'

Squirming guilt and dismay assailed Kerry when she realised that he knew that Luciano had masterminded his downfall. 'I didn't know that Luciano was behind the *Salut* chain!' she heard herself protest in her own defence. 'I only found out today—'

'He treated me to a personal visit.' The older man pursed his lips and awarded her a bitter look of hostility. 'I can't stomach having his wife in my home!'

Kerry flinched. 'I'm sorry…I shouldn't have come and I'll leave.'

'Why *did* you come?'

'I wanted to…I wanted to show you that I c-cared.' Kerry closed her hands very tightly round the bag she was holding.

Harold Linwood loosed a contemptuous laugh. 'I can soon cure you of that notion. Why would I want you to care? I'm *not* your father…'

For several timeless moments, Kerry could only stare at the older man with straining blue eyes and a frown lodged between her brows. 'Sorry…what did you say?'

'I should have told you years ago,' Harold Linwood continued unpleasantly, 'but I didn't really suspect the truth until you were fifteen and by then I'd accepted you as mine and it would have been bloody embarrassing to say otherwise!'

Her legs were starting to shake and with an effort she forced them still again. 'Why are you telling me this now?'

'I don't see why I should pretend any more. Your stepmother and I once hoped to have children together.

That was when I found out I was sterile and unlikely ever to father a child,' he admitted flatly. 'When you went into hospital to have your tonsils out, a blood sample was taken—'

'Was it?' Kerry frowned, unable to think straight but then recalling that a sample had been taken prior to surgery in case she later required a blood transfusion.

'Well, I had testing done on that sample. It confirmed that your slut of a mother was sleeping around even in the first year of our marriage and that there was no way that you could be my daughter!'

Kerry still could not absorb what she was being told, for she was in a stupor of disbelief. 'But if you're not my father, who is?'

'Carrie went with any man who took her fancy,' Harold Linwood sneered. 'It might have been a barman at the golf club, some tradesman who worked here, even one of our neighbours…*anybody*; she wasn't fussy!'

At that point, Kerry spun round and walked out of the room. Crossing the hall, she opened the front door for herself and kept on walking, down the drive, along the road, back in the direction of the train station. It was a long walk but she didn't care. Her mobile phone kept on ringing and she ignored it. Eventually she took it out of her bag and switched it off.

So, she wasn't a Linwood. It was not the end of the world, she tried to tell herself, but just then she felt as though the ground had fallen away beneath her feet. She reminded herself that Misty and Ione had also had to come to terms with having been fathered by one of Carrie's lovers. But then at least her sisters knew who that lover had been, whereas there was very little likelihood of Kerry ever finding out that same information. Would she even *want* to know?

It had been a day which more than any other day had made Kerry feel very alone and very foolish. First she had learned that Luciano had spent months cold-bloodedly planning and executing a devastating revenge on the Linwoods wine-store chain. Next she had been forced to accept that the sisters she trusted had kept their knowledge of Luciano's unscrupulous activities to themselves rather than interfere. And finally, she had discovered that the man she had believed to be her father was not her father. Indeed, she had had that painful revelation thrown in her face!

No doubt Luciano would believe that she had received her just deserts for rushing to offer Harold Linwood her sympathy! Indeed, he would probably see it as yet another instance of disloyalty on her part. But then, Luciano had never understood why she had persisted in trying to build a family relationship with a man who made little attempt to conceal his uninterest in her. But, having been deserted by her mother as a young child, Kerry had found it almost impossible to accept that her father should reject her as well and she had made endless excuses for the older man. Now there were no more excuses to be made, she conceded.

Too upset to face returning to the townhouse, she resolved to stay out until she had come to terms with what she had learned. Certainly, she had no intention of confiding in Luciano. At least she could conserve a little pride by staying silent about her visit to Heathlands that afternoon and her subsequent humiliation at Harold Linwood's hands…

*   *   *

Luciano's day had been no more satisfying than Kerry's.

An hour after Kerry had left the building, he had decided to go home but Kerry had not been there. Irate at that discovery, he had returned to the office, only to find it impossible to settle back into work. Prolonged self-examination of the type he most disliked had eventually led to the grudging acknowledgement that he had been unreasonable, possibly even very unreasonable. Once he had become seriously involved with Kerry again, he should have reconsidered his goal of putting Linwoods out of business.

Harold Linwood was an unpleasant man but he *was* Kerry's father and Luciano saw that he should have demonstrated some sensitivity on that score. Instead he had been guilty of wanting to have his cake and eat it too. It ought to have dawned on him that he could hardly bankrupt his father-in-law without causing his wife some distress. That that very elementary fact had not once occurred to Luciano shocked him in retrospect. He finally recognised that he had always been challenged to think of Kerry as a Linwood and had speedily consigned all recollection of her unfortunate connection to the family to the back of his mind, rather than allow that blood tie to interfere with his objectives.

Soon after he had reached those conclusions, Luciano tried to call Kerry on her mobile and he left a message. By five that afternoon, he had left four messages and he was becoming concerned. By six, he was back at the townhouse and he succumbed to the temptation of calling Misty to casually enquire if Kerry was with her.

'She must be stuck in the traffic somewhere,' he said

dismissively when her sister gave him a negative answer and sounded audibly concerned.

By seven, Luciano had phoned Ballybawn to check that Kerry had not flown back to Ireland, called Ione and contacted Freddy in Quamar. Although he had told Kerry that he did not want her confiding in her siblings, by nine that evening he would have been happy if she had. He just wanted some proof that nothing had happened to her. In fact he was fighting off panic when he finally heard the front door open.

'I hope you didn't wait dinner for me,' Kerry muttered evasively, ducking past his tall, stilled figure to head straight for the stairs.

He wanted to know where she had been for so many hours. He wanted to shout because she hadn't returned one of his calls. But she looked so fragile, her face pinched with strain, her eyes dull, that he said nothing. After making a couple of necessary discreet phone calls to soothe the worries that his concern had roused he found her in the bedroom, and he plunged straight into speech, for he was suffering from an overriding compulsion to make things right between them again.

'I want you to try and understand that I planned my revenge against Linwoods a long time ago and nothing short of a loaded gun could have turned me from that goal,' Luciano breathed fiercely. 'I didn't think about hurting you. I didn't even consider you as being involved! It may sound crazy but it's been a lot of weeks since I've been able to think of you as a Linwood.'

An odd little laugh escaped Kerry before she twisted her head away again and kicked off her shoes. She had walked miles round the shops, seeing nothing, buying nothing, and her feet were very sore.

'I didn't want to hurt you…I never *meant* to hurt you,' Luciano vowed with roughened emphasis. 'I kept *Salut* and Linwoods in one compartment and you in another. But it's over and done with now.'

'Yes…' Kerry supposed it was and he had triumphed. Whether she approved or otherwise, he had brought down Linwoods by legitimate business methods. He had been right too: on some level she had hoped that as time went on hostilities would fade and everyone would shake hands and be civil with each other.

Needing some time alone, she went into the luxurious bathroom and filled the jacuzzi bath. Lying back being buffeted by the jets, she could feel the stress seeping out of her again. She was the same person she had been when she'd woken up that morning, she reminded herself. Shouldn't she be celebrating the fact that a man who had never shown the smallest warmth towards her was *not* her real father? But a painful hole had still been torn in the fabric of her life. When the wound felt a little less raw, she would tell Luciano that he need never again offend his own sensibilities by regarding her as a Linwood.

Not that that would make much difference to him. She knew that he didn't love her. Had he *ever* loved her? Weeks ago, Luciano had assured her that he had been crazy about her when they had been engaged but it might have been very naive of her to interpret 'crazy' as being what she understood as love. 'Do you love me?' she had once asked before she broke off their engagement.

He had flinched as though she had said something

horribly embarrassing and then he had shrugged, grimaced, studied the ground and said uneasily, 'What do you think?' Well, she hadn't had the nerve to tell him what she thought. If he had loved her, he presumably would have said so. Unable to comprehend what attracted him to her, she had asked no more awkward questions.

But after living with Luciano, Kerry was no longer as innocent as she had once been. Ignorance had made her blind but she now finally understood the power of sex, the sheer, *terrifying* power of sex over a male as passionate and physical as Luciano. A male who thought nothing of making love five times or more in a day had to rate sexual desire and satisfaction as being of overwhelming importance in a relationship. When he had quipped that she was 'the one who had got away' he had come closest to hitting on the secret of her enduring attraction for him.

But it *was* no big secret to her any more, Kerry reflected apprehensively. Against all the odds, Luciano had come back to her and she knew why. While he had been in prison, he had focused his fantasies on her. Endless, wild, obsessional fantasies about her. That he could have put her in such an insanely inappropriate role even in his imagination still amazed Kerry but she knew that, unlikely as she herself found it, it *was* true. She had not been a love object but a lust object.

Even the fact that she had once dumped him had made her seem more desirable in Luciano's eyes. Still viewing her as his reward and his prize, he had lost no time in reclaiming her when he had won his release. But lust would not last forever, nor would the illusion that she was fantasy or even trophy-wife material. Eventually Luciano would appreciate that what he had wanted five years back and what he wanted in the present might well be different things. Possibly about that same time, he might begin to notice that his wife was kind of on the plain and ordinary side for a guy with his looks and wealth.

Annoyed at the confidence-zapping tenor of her own reflections, Kerry wrapped herself in a large, fleecy towel. For an instant she felt horribly light-headed and she pulled a face, for it wasn't the first time that she had felt dizzy. But then in recent days she had been rather off her food as well. Perhaps she had picked up some virus, and if she didn't regain her usually healthy appetite she would have to go to the doctor.

Easing a comb through her tangled curls while she stood at the vanity basin, she found herself worrying about how the end of the Linwood wine-store chain would affect her stepbrother. Miles had worked so hard to keep Linwoods afloat. He demanded a lot from himself and he would be devastated that all his efforts had come to nothing. She wasn't surprised that he had not been able to face phoning her to tell her that the receiver had been called in at the firm. She just hoped that he wasn't trying to drown his sorrows again.

'Kerry…'

Startled out of her troubled thoughts, Kerry saw Luciano standing in the doorway.

'I was worried when you didn't come home,' he confided tautly. 'I thought you might have had an accident, so I rang your sister.'

'Which one?'

The silence stretched.

Luciano frowned, shrugged, finally surrendered. 'All of them...'

'*All*...of them?' she gasped. 'Even Freddy?'

'Yeah.' Luciano balled his hands into fists and dug them into the pockets of his well-cut trousers. There was nothing cool about having called all three of her sisters and he knew that.

Kerry studied his reflection in the mirror and she was trying very, very hard not to laugh, but the longer she studied him the less she could recall why she had wanted to laugh. A faint blue-black shadow of stubble already emphasising his hard jawline and the mobile perfection of his wide, sensual mouth, his golden eyes gleaming below the dark fringe of his lashes, he looked gorgeous. Breathtakingly, devastatingly gorgeous. And hers, still hers, she reminded herself with relief.

'Next time you're planning to stay out for hours, phone me, *mia carina*,' he urged, stepping up behind her, closing his arms round her to ease her back into contact with his lean, powerfully aroused length. 'Where have you been?'

She rested her head back against his shoulder, suddenly boneless, suddenly weak with hunger for him. 'Nowhere important...'

He loosened the towel. As it fell, baring the jutting fullness of her breasts, he vented a husky groan of appreciation and let his hands sweep up to mould her tender flesh. When his fingers massaged the engorged tips, a river of liquid heat pooled between her thighs and she moaned out loud. Just then she wanted him quite desperately and nothing else mattered. She closed her eyes and pushed back against him in wanton encouragement.

He spun her round, clamped her to him and let his tongue probe the moist sweetness of her lush mouth. While he penetrated her mouth with erotic thoroughness he lifted her against him and carried her through to the bed. She was wild for him, tugging at his belt, wrenching at his waistband, all fingers and thumbs and maddening clumsiness.

'You've got me for the rest of my life…I'll keep another five minutes,' he teased with his wicked grin.

I'll see about that, was her last conscious thought. She slid exploring fingers beneath his boxers, found him sleek and hard and amazingly responsive. Surprise mingled with even fiercer hunger in his scorching golden eyes. She pushed him flat. She bent over him and pleasured him with her mouth and her tongue. He shuddered, groaned, laced his hands into her hair, muttered in Italian. When he could stand it no more he pulled her under him without ceremony and drove into her, hard and fast. What followed was the most exquisite fulfilment she had ever experienced.

'You're amazing, *bella mia*,' Luciano told her afterwards. 'I'm never going to let you go.'

The following morning they returned to Ballybawn.

While they had been away in Italy, most of the work on the castle had been completed. Luciano was full of plans. He thought they should spend summer weekends at the castle but autumn and the whole of the winter in Tuscany, where the climate would be kinder to her grandmother's arthritis. She knew without his even tell-

ing her that when the grapes were harvested they would
be at the Villa Contarini.

In the old kitchen, which had been abandoned for a
much smarter new one that was a lot more convenient
to the dining room, Kerry checked the calendar on which
she had kept a note of her monthly cycle. She was
shaken to realise that it had been over two months since
she had had a period. It had not seemed anything like
that long to her. But she started smiling and found that
she couldn't stop. Was it possible that she was already
pregnant? She thought of the dizzy spells and the way
her appetite had faded and her hopes rose high. It would
be a long drive to the nearest shop where she would be
able to buy a pregnancy-testing kit but Kerry was un-
daunted. She had just located her grandfather's car keys
when she was called to the phone.

She was surprised to realise that her caller was Rochelle and for once her stepsister had nothing smart to
say, but what she did have to say was shocking enough.
'Miles has been arrested…'

'You're not serious,' Kerry breathed after a staggered
pause.

'He told his solicitor that he wants to see you and that
it's urgent,' Rochelle said tautly. 'He's got out on bail
but he's in really bad trouble…it's a drugs offence—'

'Drugs?' Kerry was aghast.

'He's been using cocaine for a long time…' Rochelle
was crying now, making no attempt to hide the fact either. 'I feel so guilty that I didn't *do* anything for him!'

The first thing Kerry did after that call was book a
flight back to London late that afternoon. She was in
shock at what she had learned. Miles on drugs? Why

had she never noticed anything amiss? But she tensed when she recalled his behaviour at her wedding. His life-and-soul-of-the-party act that day had been over-the-top. He was thinner than he had once been, more moody and irritable as well, but she had put those changes down to stress and too many late nights. That he might have a problem with drugs had not once crossed her mind.

Luciano was inspecting the new plumbing arrangements in the mediaeval tower. Communicating doors had been knocked through to the once derelict wing where Kerry's great-uncle Ivor had lived, and bathrooms rejoicing in every luxury had been installed there.

'Can I interest you in a tour of my power shower, *cara*?' Luciano enquired lazily when Kerry found him there.

Kerry bit her lip and winced. 'I've got to go straight back over to London,' she told him in a rush. 'I know you're not going to be pleased about this but I just can't not go when Miles needs me.'

His dark golden eyes narrowed, grew watchful, wary. 'Why would Miles need you?'

'Rochelle called to tell me that he's been arrested...drugs,' Kerry extended shamefacedly. 'Presumably he's been caught in possession of them.'

'About time too.' A sardonic smile curved Luciano's expressive mouth.

Kerry was appalled. 'How can you smile?'

'I don't like him. I hate drugs as well. Take your pick,' Luciano advised curtly. 'I don't want you getting involved in Miles's sleazy life—'

'I'm afraid that that isn't something that I have a choice about—'

'There's always a choice—'

'He wants to see me; he's asked for me. I can't ignore that—'

Without warning, Luciano vented a derisive laugh. 'I was in prison for five years...you ignored *me*. But Miles only has to get arrested and you're ready to drop everything and run!'

Kerry was disconcerted at the comparison he was making. 'I didn't ignore you. How can you say that? I thought you didn't want me—'

Eyes that had no shade of gold and were hard as black diamonds stayed steady and cold on her pale face. 'You turned your back on me. You didn't come and ask whether or not I *wanted* to see you. You wouldn't give me five minutes of your time and yet you think I'm about to stand back and watch you race out of here to offer Miles support?' he raked at her, his temper igniting with volatile suddenness. 'No, no way will I accept that!'

'I've said I'll go and I don't go back on my word. If I had known five years ago what I know now, I would have come to see you in prison. In fact, you'd have seen so much of me that you'd have ended up sick of the sight of me!' Kerry asserted chokily, tears of painful regret convulsing her throat. 'But it didn't happen that way for us. You didn't ask for me. You were too damned proud and too strong. And I'm grateful that you're proud and strong because it meant you got through an ordeal that would have broken someone weaker—'

'Thank you for the compliment. But I still don't want you charging to Miles's rescue. That's the bottom line and, for a change, what I want is what should matter most to you. I may have buried the past, I may have forgiven you for a lot,' Luciano bit out rawly, golden eyes glittering with raw anger, 'but the forgiveness wasn't unconditional. If you go to Miles now, I'm finished with you!'

Kerry studied him in shaken reproach. 'Don't say something like that...you don't mean it.'

'You're not listening to what I'm saying yet I've been saying it ever since I came back into your life.' His strong jawline clenched. 'You can't have both Miles and me. You needn't ask me for compassion where he's concerned either, as I have none to give—'

'This is an emergency...be reasonable,' Kerry pleaded. 'I can't cope with a big fight with you at the same time!'

'*Santo cielo!* I am out of patience with you. This is not some stupid fight. Don't try to trivialise what *I* feel just because you believe that you somehow know better!' Luciano condemned with growing fury. 'Look back to our not-so-recent past when you were equally sure of your own judgement. Who was right and who was wrong then?'

Hit hard by that tough, uncompromising reminder, Kerry lost colour. 'I think that we both made mistakes but I accept that mine were the worst,' she muttered unhappily. 'But this is a very different situation—'

'No, it's not. When it comes to important issues I expect my wife to respect my feelings and wishes. I don't want you communicating in any way with Miles Bailey. I've already made that clear but you haven't listened.'

Angry rebellion stirred inside Kerry and killed her innate urge to soothe and placate for the sake of peace.

'Maybe I'm *not* going to agree with you on every important issue in life but that doesn't mean that I'm automatically in the wrong!'

'This is a non-negotiable issue. This is our marriage on the line—'

'I won't be threatened with losing you over something that has no relevance to our relationship!' Kerry argued vehemently, her temper only getting hotter at the fear that his intimidating assurances roused in her. 'You don't like Miles and you resent me giving him any attention—'

Outraged dark golden eyes rested on her. 'I hope I'm not that immature. Don't underestimate what I'm trying to spell out to you. My objections to Miles rest on much more than personal animosity. I don't want you to go anywhere near him, and if you *do* go I will see it as a betrayal of my trust—'

'When did you get so domineering that I can't disagree with you without being told that I'm disloyal?'

Dark colour accentuated his bold cheekbones. 'If you have so little respect for my intelligence that you can believe that, you shouldn't be with me.'

Kerry snatched in a sustaining breath but she was only becoming angrier with him. He was telling her what to do as if she were some little Victorian wife, content to believe that her husband was a superior being who always knew best. But she had her own opinions and a strong conviction of what was right and what was wrong, and she would not change her mind unless he could give her a good reason for doing so. That Miles's current problems should relate to drugs and his breaking of the law was very regrettable but it was unthinkable to her that she should ignore his cry for support on that basis alone.

'I'm appalled that you can say that our marriage is at risk if I don't do what you want me to to.' Kerry tilted her chin, blue eyes troubled but determined.

'If you go to him, I won't be here when you come back,' Luciano ground out in a low, lethal undertone. 'I'll return to Italy and divorce you.'

Her shaken face blenched. He was taking intimidation to new and serious limits. Had she been so tolerant and easy-going that he now expected her to do exactly as he told her? She refused to credit that he could be serious in making such a threat when they were so happy together.

'I promise that I won't be away longer than twenty-four hours.'

The terrible silence hummed.

Kerry looked at Luciano, praying that he would show some understanding of the awful position he was putting her in. Lean, strong bone structure rigid, Luciano was pale beneath his bronzed skin. When she met the savage shimmer of his golden gaze she realised that he was not pale with stress so much as pale with absolute seething, sizzling rage. Was he jealous of her affection for Miles?

Uneasy at that suspicion, she turned away to pack an overnight bag, for she needed to head for the airport almost immediately. Miles was the closest thing to a best friend that she had ever had but she felt that that admission would be even less pleasing to Luciano. Five years ago, when her own life had fallen apart almost overnight with Rochelle's revelations and Luciano's subsequent arrest, Miles had made the effort to *be* there for Kerry. Nothing could have cured her heartache but his caring interest had warmed her at a time when she had been in despair.

Luciano could never recall feeling a more violent-centred anger. He was outraged at her lack of respect for his feelings. He was frustrated by the impossibility of telling her what Steven Linwood had confessed because that confession was virtually worthless until Steven got up the courage to make an official statement to the police. Her relationship with Miles had ensured that Luciano could not trust her with Steven's revelations. But what embittered Luciano beyond belief was her unquestioning trust in Miles and her eagerness to offer the younger man support.

Deep in her own thoughts, Kerry was disconcerted when she lifted the bag she had hurriedly packed and discovered that she was alone in the bedroom. Her dismay increased when she realised that Luciano had driven off in his car, forestalling any hope of further dialogue before she left for the airport. But, although she was troubled, the belief that Luciano was being totally unreasonable stiffened her resolve...

CHAPTER ELEVEN

KERRY had just got off her flight to London when Miles rang her to tell her that he was at Rochelle's apartment and not his own.

'For goodness' sake, what have you been doing?' Kerry gasped.

'Look, we'll talk when you get here. Don't tell anyone where I am,' Miles urged tautly.

When her stepbrother answered the door of his sister's apartment, he peered out into the hallway with a furtive air and hurried Kerry inside as fast as he could. 'Thanks for coming. This may be our last chance to talk for a long time and I wanted you to hear the whole story from me and not from anyone else.'

'I can't believe you've been taking drugs. You need professional help,' Kerry began worriedly. 'What have the police charged you with?'

'Possessing and smuggling cocaine…'

'Possessing and s-smuggling…?' A look of shock stamped on her face, Kerry collapsed down on the sofa in the ultra-modern lounge. *'Smuggling?'*

'I've got a very heavy habit to feed,' Miles protested. 'I needed the money—'

Her faith in him had been badly shaken. That Miles should have become addicted to drugs was one thing, that he should have sunk to the level of smuggling them was another thing entirely.

'I first got into debt a long time ago,' Miles confided with an uneasy laugh. 'I borrowed funds from the wrong people. They threatened to break my legs if I didn't pay them back, so I had to find money from another source. There isn't any way to wrap this up nicely, Kerry. So I'll just spit it out…I was the real thief at Linwoods five years ago!'

Kerry gaped at him. 'No…don't tell me that—'

'I persuaded Steven to doctor the account books for me…our Steven is very talented with figures. Of course, he didn't initially want to frame Luciano to save my sorry skin.' Her stepbrother grimaced. 'So I informed Steven that I'd tell his homophobic parents that he was gay and that I'd expose his double life…and he couldn't do enough to help me after that!'

'You blackmailed Steven?' A semi-hysterical laugh was dredged from Kerry, for she could not credit what she was hearing. 'Are you drunk? Are you serious? You're standing there telling me you did these monstrous, appalling things and you're talking as if they were just understandable little *mistakes*?'

'I wanted you to hear my side from me so that you would understand. I'm very fond of you. I want you to know that I didn't *plan* to hurt anybody,' Miles argued with disturbing vehemence. 'I got deep in debt and everything got out of my control—'

'People get into debt but they don't all steal and blackmail to save their own skins!' Kerry felt nauseous as she continued to look at him and she could not stop staring at his familiar features. It seemed all wrong that he should look just the same as usual with his thin, good-looking face tired, his eyes full of rueful appeal and his blond hair flopping on his forehead. But though he might look the same, there was an essential difference, she grasped painfully. He was not the guy she had thought he was and he never had been.

'My mistake this time around was telling Steven that he had to tidy up a few loose ends from events five years back—'

'You tried to involve him again?' Kerry swallowed hard and looked away from him in disgust.

'I had no choice! Luciano has had private detectives snooping everywhere and I had to be sure that there was no trail to lead back to Steven and me—'

'Or did you hope that if there was a trail it would lead *only* to Steven?' Kerry recalled how, weeks earlier, Miles had suggested to her that Steven might have been the thief.

'Well, Steven was always a gutless wonder and I'm afraid he's done for the both of us now!' her stepbrother launched at her with festering resentment. 'He couldn't take the pressure and he panicked. A few days ago he came clean with his parents and then he made a full confession to the police. His stupid father just rang me to boast that now there's another warrant out for my arrest!'

Good, she might have said could she have found her voice at that point, but she could not.

'Knowing that the police will charge me with that too, I tried to leave the country. But they found the coke in my hand luggage. I only got bail by handing over my passport.'

'Luciano never got bail at all…' Her voice emerged all choked and squeezed and shaky. 'And Rochelle was telling the truth, wasn't she? You *did* get her to lie to me about Luciano so that I would break off our engagement—'

'Kerry…can't you see how I was trying to protect you from the fall-out of his being done for theft and false accounting?' Miles demanded with a troubled frown. 'It was the *only* thing I could do for you. It set you free from the whole ghastly business!'

His flawed arguments only made Kerry feel worse than ever. She saw how weak and self-serving he was, how he had a twisted view of his own actions that enabled him to kid himself that he wasn't as bad as his offences might suggest. But what shook her most of all was his total lack of remorse. He wasn't one bit sorry for anything that he had done. Not the theft, the blackmail, not even the long imprisonment of an innocent man for the crimes he had committed. No, Miles had no regrets other than that he was about to be caught. Yet he had ruined Luciano's life, her life and Steven's life. And *this* was the man she had regarded in the light of a best friend and a brother?

Miles was a thief, a liar, a blackmailer and also, it seemed, not averse to smuggling drugs. In a stumbling movement Kerry rose from the sofa and fled past her stepbrother out to the hall, where she just managed to identify the location of the bathroom before being horribly unwell. Freshening up in the aftermath of her sickness, Kerry had to breathe in deep and slow several times to ward off her dizziness.

All the time that Luciano had been telling her that her family had stitched him up, she had believed that he was being paranoid. Yet people whom she had thought of as family members *had* conspired against him. Why had she not listened to him? How on earth could she have allowed Miles to come between her and Luciano?

'Are you all right?' Miles prompted when she emerged from the bathroom.

She compressed her lips 'No…I'm not feeling too good. I'll be glad to head home again—'

'Don't be like that with me,' her stepbrother said resentfully. 'I need a friend right now. Rochelle has already taken fright because she's scared of getting involved, but I expected more from you.'

'Sorry…' Leaving the apartment and Miles to certain re-arrest, Kerry could not even bring herself to look at him.

Back at the airport, she tried and failed to get an earlier flight back to Ballybawn. Having booked herself into a hotel for the night, she attempted to call Luciano on his mobile. When there was no answer, her heart sank.

He wasn't answering her calls. He was very angry with her and he had every right to be, she told herself wretchedly. What had she been planning to say in any case? It would be easier to grovel face to face than it would be on the phone. She had got everything wrong but at least some good was about to come out of all the bad news: Steven Linwood had gone to the police to tell all and Luciano would at last be able to get his own name cleared. Wouldn't that put any male into a better mood? A more forgiving frame of mind?

After a rather sleepless night, Kerry resisted the urge to try and phone Luciano again and attempted to cheer herself up by buying a pregnancy-testing kit instead. When the little blue line formed and confirmed that she was, indeed, carrying Luciano's baby she was ecstatic, even more ecstatic than she would have been twenty-four hours earlier, for she was certain that that information would take the edge off his fury with her. And no, she wasn't too proud to use any advantage she had to achieve that objective.

When she arrived back at Ballybawn, she could not initially credit that Luciano was no longer in residence. She walked through every room before she finally spoke to the housekeeper and tried not to take fright at the information that her husband had left the castle only an hour later than she had the day before. But Luciano was still not taking her calls or answering her messages. She decided that possibly she ought to give him a few more hours to cool down with her.

Only by that stage Kerry was beginning to fall victim to panic. Not once had she believed Luciano when he had said that he was finished with her if she went to Miles' assistance. She adored Luciano. She was willing to make a big bet that Luciano also knew that she adored him. But Luciano had still walked out on her just as he had sworn he would. Presumably that also meant that he had returned to Italy.

At that point of grudging acceptance, Kerry went into shock. Had Luciano already got bored with her? Had he been looking for an excuse to dump her? Was her support of Miles so unforgivable? Slowly and painfully she came to the conclusion that it *had* been unforgivable on Luciano's terms. She was married to a guy who was never, ever going to forget or fully forgive the fact that she had not been there for him when he had been imprisoned. She had gone out on a limb over the worst possible issue.

I need you to understand and believe in me, Luciano had told her. But she had still not had sufficient faith. When Luciano had demanded that she choose between him and her stepbrother, he must already have been suspicious of Miles. It seemed that she had stayed loyal to Miles at the cost of her marriage. Miles was, after all, the rat for whom Luciano had served five years in prison. Bearing that cruel fact in mind, how could she expect Luciano to forgive her?

On the third day after her return to Ballybawn, Kerry flew out to Tuscany. It was a very warm afternoon when her taxi dropped her off at the Villa Contarini. Her blue cotton dress sticking to her damp back, she walked into the cool, shaded interior. Nobody greeted her. Either everybody was out and had forgotten to lock the doors or Luciano had read her text message forewarning him of her arrival and had sent the staff home.

'Why did you come here?'

The effect of Luciano's dark, deep drawl coming out of nowhere at her almost made Kerry leap out of her skin. She jerked round. Luciano was watching her from the sunlit drawing-room. Proud dark head high, sheathed in a light grey business suit worn with a shadow-stripe shirt and a pale blue silk tie, he had the stunning impact of a very good-looking guy. As she walked towards him her mouth ran dry and her heart hammered.

'Kerry…?' he prompted drily.

'You're here, so I've come here…it's pretty simple,' she pointed out tautly.

'Even if I don't want you here?'

Her feverish colour ebbed. 'I'm afraid you're stuck with me. I'm going to sit on your doorstep and make a nuisance of myself until you listen to me.'

Brooding dark golden eyes rested on her without any perceptible emotion. 'There is nothing left to say.'

'Are you sure about that?'

'Yes.'

'Well, I think you need to think about that some more and I'm not going any place, so you'll have plenty of time to do it in,' Kerry told him doggedly. 'Miles is the lowest of the low and I never once suspected he was. OK! So I wasn't able to see through him...but I *love* you!'

His lean, darkly handsome features clenched. 'But not enough—'

'Now, just you hold on there!' Kerry studied him with angry bright blue eyes. 'How does a guy who has never *once* told me that he loved me define ''not enough''? I'm not perfect and I make mistakes, but you do too. You can't throw away our marriage just because I went to see Miles in London!'

'Can't I?' Luciano regarded her with chilling cool. 'I can do whatever I want to do.'

She knew she could not say what she longed to say. There was a little boy inside him who had never been loved enough and she knew that, but she had underestimated just how much it meant to him that he should believe that he was more important than anybody else in her world. That was, after all, what Luciano wanted and needed from her: unconditional love.

'You can but you won't shake me off easily. I'm *staying*,' Kerry declared.

'I'll just leave—'

'And I'll follow and it'll get embarrassing…' Kerry studied him, chin at a stubborn angle. 'I mean it. Everywhere you go, I'll go, and you'll have to go to court to make me stay away from you!'

Involuntarily, Luciano almost laughed out loud. It was the threat of a fearless extrovert and exhibitionist and she was the shyest and quietest woman he had ever known. But there she was, looking at him with positive fierceness and an amount of possessiveness that warmed him like the flames of a fire on a cold day.

'I also feel I ought to warn you that if you *were* to take me to court you'd just end up looking *really* bad.' Kerry hoped that she wasn't imagining that rueful gleam lightening his beautiful gaze.

'And why would that be?'

Her gaze veiled. 'I'm not telling you that yet…'

Luciano wondered how long it would have taken him to break through the barrier of his own pride and he strode forward then without hesitation. '*Santo cielo!* You hurt me a great deal!' he said, startling himself as much as her with that frank admission.

Kerry grabbed him with both hands before he could back off again. 'I know and I swear I'll never do it again. I was so set on not being a doormat and I thought you were being unreasonable because I never once suspected that Miles might have been the real thief—'

'I know. You're not very good at reading people, *cara mia*.' Luciano framed her face with gentle fingers. 'And I'm not very good at talking about love—'

'Let's not push our luck by talking about it, then—'

'I love you so much it terrifies me,' Luciano confided gruffly.

'Truly?' Kerry blinked.

'It was always that way and I couldn't let you see it and I couldn't even admit it to myself, *bella mia*,' Luciano groaned. 'It placed a barrier between us that should never have been there. I fought needing you, and four days ago I did the exact same thing. I was very bitter that you could put Miles before me...but it was complete madness for me to walk out over that.'

'Just as well I love you to death,' Kerry soothed, tugging him in the direction of the stairs with intent.

'Next time we quarrel I'll come to you,' Luciano intoned guiltily.

'There had better not be a next time...and I don't think my nerves would stand the wait. Just as well you succumbed before I wheeled out the big guns,' she teased.

'What big guns?'

'I'm pregnant,' Kerry told him cheerfully.

Luciano looked stunned. 'And you know...already?'

Kerry linked her arms round his neck and smiled sunnily up at him, feeling like a very high achiever and in love with the mystery of her own female body. 'You remember that very first time that you *forgot*—?'

'That far back?'

She could have drowned in his blazing smile of satisfaction. But then he frowned, guilty discomfiture darkening his troubled appraisal. 'You're carrying my baby and I've put you through hell—'

'Absolute hell,' Kerry sighed with dancing eyes of

amusement. 'You will have to be *so* perfect to keep me happy the next few months—'

'Stop teasing me…I'm crazy about you and I *will* be perfect—'

'Promises…promises—'

Luciano closed both arms round her tight and kissed her breathless.

'That was…that was definitely perfect,' Kerry confided with enthusiasm. 'Do you think you could do it again?'

Luciano laughed and proved that he could. In between bouts of kissing he carried her upstairs into their bedroom, where sheer, bubbling happiness lent an extra dimension to their loving. A long time later they lay in each other's arms, and that was when she finally told him about what she had learned from Harold Linwood when she had visited his home.

'So, you're not a Linwood born and bred, after all.' His golden eyes connected with hers and he hugged her close in silent acknowledgement of the distress that that revelation about her paternity must have caused her. 'I've got to admit it, though… Even years ago, I wondered if it was possible that you weren't his daughter. You don't resemble Harold in any way but it was his vindictiveness that first made me suspicious—'

'You never said…'

'I didn't want to hurt you. Lousy as he was in the parent stakes, you valued the relationship—'

'Not as much as I once did.' Kerry pulled a rueful face. 'After the shock had worn off, I realised that I was grateful that a man who's never shown me any affection wasn't my father—'

'Did Linwood give you any idea who your real father might be?'

'I don't think he has a clue.'

'I could have enquiries made,' Luciano suggested quietly.

'I don't think I want anyone to go digging into Carrie's past. It's really not important enough to me now.' But, touched by his thoughtfulness, Kerry tightened her arms round him in appreciation.

A long time later, Luciano uncorked a dusty bottle of wine with a flourish and poured a single glass of wine. 'The day that my conviction was squashed in court and I got my freedom back I said I wanted two things...a glass of 1925 Brunello Riserva and a woman. But I knew I wouldn't drink the wine until I had got justice and my name was cleared.'

'I'd better be the woman...' Kerry told him.

'Who else?' Lean, darkly handsome face amused, Luciano savoured a mouthful of the brilliant ruby-coloured liquid and stared down at her with teasing appreciation. 'You're also a complete philistine, incapable of appreciating a superb vintage wine, but there is one way of ensuring that you share the experience, *cara mia*...'

'Is there?'

Kerry's eyes widened in surprise as he tipped his glass and let a couple of drops of wine spill down onto her breast. But as he laved the precious liquid from her creamy skin with his expert mouth his intentions became very clear, and she lay back with a wondering sigh of encouragement.

'I'm no good at resisting you,' he told her huskily.

Kerry wove happily possessive hands into his luxuriant black hair. 'You're not supposed to be,' she told him with gentle oneupmanship.

With Luciano looking on, Kerry put their baby, Pietro, down to sleep.

'Our son has a look of intelligence,' her husband commented with quiet satisfaction.

Kerry tried not to smile, for even to her fond eyes their baby looked much the same as usual. Pietro was three months old, a laid-back, cheerful baby who ate whenever he was offered sustenance and slept at the same times every day. He was also very tolerant of a father given to lifting him from his cot at odd hours and equally at ease with foreign travel.

Ten very busy and challenging months had passed since the night she had told Luciano that their first baby was on the way. She had had an easy pregnancy and Luciano had been wonderfully supportive throughout those months. For others, it had been a more testing time. Miles had stood trial twice, first for his drugs offences, the second time for theft and other charges dating back five years. Her stepbrother would be in prison for a long time. Steven Linwood had received a shorter sentence and his family were standing by their son.

The legal system had finally acknowledged that in Luciano's case a miscarriage of justice had taken place. Luciano had finally had the satisfaction of being publicly acknowledged an innocent man. From that day on, it had been as though a dark shadow had retreated from Luciano, enabling him to leave the unhappy past behind him.

On a lighter and more startling note, the first book in

her grandfather's series had been published to rave re-
views and had become a runaway best-seller. All those
years while Hunt O'Brien had hidden behind the pretence that he was writing history of the type found in
textbooks, he had in fact been engaged in creating a
work of fantasy based on Celtic myth and legend. Seven
more books were still to be issued and her grandfather's
accountant had confidently forecast that his client would
be a millionaire long before he reached his next birthday.
Autograph hunters were now occasionally to be found
loitering in the grounds but the famous author was rarely
to be found at the castle, since he and his wife had re-
discovered their love of foreign travel.

Apart from those excitements, however, life at Ballybawn and the Villa Contarini had gone on much as
usual, although since the family circle had grown there
were many more visitors.

As Luciano and Kerry dimmed the lights and left the
nursery, he pulled her close and claimed a long, lingering kiss of undeniable passion that made her quiver. 'I
have a surprise planned,' he breathed.

'I'm listening…' Kerry was also struggling to get her
breath back because her gorgeous husband had lost none
of his ability to make her go weak at the knees.

'This week we leave Pietro in the charge of his efficient nanny and head for the island…just you and me…
and the sand, *bella mia*,' he growled sexily.

Kerry leant into his lithe, muscular frame. 'I don't
know about the sand…but you and me sounds good!'

'I love you,' Luciano breathed, and she was still smiling when he kissed her again.

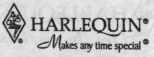

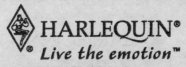

Two women in jeopardy...
Two shattering secrets...
Two dramatic stories...

VEILS OF DECEIT

USA TODAY bestselling author

JASMINE CRESSWELL

B.J. DANIELS

A riveting volume of scandalous secrets, political intrigue and
unforgettable passion that you will not want to miss!

*Look for VEILS OF DECEIT in April 2003
at your favorite retail outlet.*

HARLEQUIN®
Makes any time special®

Visit us at www.eHarlequin.com

PHVOD

These romances will entrance,
mesmerize and captivate...

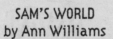

Time*twist*™

Enjoy the adventures of another time and place
with these four time-travel romances—
available in April 2003!

NOT QUITE AN ANGEL
by Bobby Hutchinson

THE DESPERADO
by Patricia Rosemoor

A TWIST IN TIME
by Lee Karr

SAM'S WORLD
by Ann Williams

Try Silhouette Timetwists...
for the ultimate escape!

*Available at your
favorite retail outlet.*

Where love comes alive™

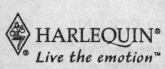

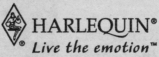